# Secrets of a Blue-Green River

*Willum Fowler*

The Fowler Companies, Inc.
ISBN 13: 978-0-9661365-3-1
wwfowlerbook@gmail.com

# Prologue

Secrets of a Blue-Green River

Joseph Bonaparte reached in his shirt pocket, pulled out the hand-held recorder and hit the record button, then START:

"It's with great reluctance that I relay this most bizarre tale in that supposedly I am a rational man…not easily taken in by hocus pocus, mystical happenings and things of that sort. Something, however, did go on that is beyond any explanation I am able to attach. Maybe it was all coincidence or some crazy mind trip that my friend and client, John Starr was on. I just don't know."

STOP

# Part One

C HAPTER 1

# Summer of '56

THE HARLEY 125 motorbike bounced along the back roads, leaving a cloud of dust and gravel in its wake. Wagging along behind swayed a gold colored canoe strapped to a rickety homemade trailer. It was the Summer of 1956.

"I think we're almost there, Bobby," yelled John Starr, his hair and shirt rippling in the wind as he steered the bike from his cramped position between the seat and gas tank.

"I sure hope so," came the reply from his passenger and best friend, Bob Savage, who, hanging on behind him, straddled the bike half on the seat and half on the rear fender, one foot resting on the exhaust pipe, and the other on the cycle's frame dangerously close to the wheel spokes. "This thing's about to vibrate my nuts off!" he shouted.

"Well, that wouldn't be any great loss to the world," John yelled back trying to raise his voice above the tinny sputter of the little engine.

The morning sun bore down, announcing another hot August day. The wind felt good on John's face as the landscape passed at thirty miles per hour. The bike lumbered by rustic farms with fields of alfalfa and corn. Cows grazed, a few looking up as the boys passed. The terrain became more rugged when they turned down into the Cahaba Valley. Except for kudzu covered banks where the road cut through and an occasional grove of mimosas, there were only vast forests of timberland along the route.

Finally, the old Helena Bridge came into view…both the destination and the point of departure. There, the wild little blue-green river flowed, offering the opportunity of a lifetime for a couple of fifteen year olds in search of high adventure. They had made it to the launch site.

"OK," said John, "Let's get the canoe off the trailer, and I'll stash the bike. If we're gonna' make it to Centerville in three days, we'd better get a move on… it's already after ten. Of all days for you to sleep late."

"Well, I wouldn't have if I hadn't been up half the night trying to convince Mom and Dad that we'd be OK."

"Yeah, I know. Mom wasn't too keen on the idea of us going either. They're probably on the phone with each other right now. We better get on the river before they come down here and queer the whole trip…you do have money to call your dad to come pick us up when we get to Centerville?"

"Yep, got five bucks."

They carried the canoe and gear down a steep path next to the bridge and placed it on the narrow rocky shore. After John hid the motorbike behind some bushes that were well out of view from the road, they were ready to launch.

Bob, knee deep in water, held the canoe steady as John took his place at the bow. Then, with a hard push, the boat slipped into the slow moving summer currents. He hopped in, and they were off.

The boys quickly adjusted from the rough ride on the motorbike to the sensation of floating, and the slight instability of their vessel.

Bob, perched on his knees, sat on the cross member at the stern, steering, while John, at the bow, leisurely paddled. The 'Goldfish', as they had dubbed the canoe, glided smoothly over the first set of shoals.

When they rounded the bend and the Helena bridge disappeared from view; so did all signs of civilization. No soul was in sight…only the river channel, more shoals and deep forest. The paddles, making a sloshing sound as they entered deeper waters, churned and accentuated the primal scent given off by the river.

"Look up…to your right," said John in a whisper.

There, on a bluff above the river, a bobcat sunned with her three kittens. She watched the boys as they passed, seemingly with little more than casual curiosity as the little ones jumped and played around her. A red-tailed hawk soared in the midday sky.

"I think this trip's gonna' be everything we dreamed it would be, John Boy."

"Yeah, Bobby, and we've got forty more miles to go."

Along the way, branches, streams and small tributaries flowed and trickled into the river where valleys and hollows met its shores.

Every few hundred yards they came upon shoals where shallow waters flowed over and around rocks and protruding boulders, sometimes forming grassy islands. In most places the boys navigated around and between the obstacles and easily slid over the rapids, but, in spots, it was too shallow. At times, in just a few inches of water, they had to get out of the canoe and drag it over slippery moss-covered rocks. Often as not, one of the two would loose their footing or stumble and take a spill.

"Looks like some good shoals up ahead," said John, 'want to ride'um at full steam?"

"Lets go for it, John Boy…by the way, how about referring to me by my Indian name from now on, OK?"

"Yeah, what's that?"

"Red Feather."

"OK, Chief Red Ass Feather, start paddlin'…hard."

"Hold on, Pale Face, I consider your defiling of my name an insult."

"Oh, I'm sorry, It's just plain Ass Feather, right? Or, is it Red Ass? I forgot."

"OK, that's it. Consider yourself challenged to a wrestling match in the rapids…to the death…or near death," said Bob with a broad grin on his face.

They pulled the Goldfish up on the rock-laden shore and went at it, laughing and chiding each other all the while.

Thinly disguised as wrestling, the boys tossed each other around with slapstick exaggeration, taking turns setting themselves up for body slams and dramatized plunges in the swift moving currents.

"I'm hungry," said Bob, water dripping from his hair and face, as he emerged from a particularly harsh dunking.

"Me too…how about those baloney sandwiches your mom made for us?"

"Good idea. I think I'm gonna' get out of these wet jeans first…damn, I forgot my swimming trunks."

"I figured you would. That's why I brought an extra pair…Red Feather."

After changing the boys settled down for a late lunch.

"These things are a little soggy," Bob commented.

"What do you expect from a paper sack, Bobby? Remember, I told you to put stuff like that in a plastic bag?"

As they rounded the bends and made their way over the shoals, time, and all sense of it seemed to slip away. The late afternoon shadows lengthened in the dense river valley. Ahead, a canopy of trees drooped over the river, looking like the pathway to some weird, forbidding, never-never land.

"We'd better start lookin' for a spot to make camp," said John, "With all these trees, it won't be long before dark."

"Yeah, you're right. How about over there?" said Bob, pointing to a wide gentle sloping shore where a grove of tall pines stood.

" Looks good to me."

They beached the canoe and began unloading camping gear.

"Why bring the tent?" asked John, "Its gonna' be a beautiful night. Let's just go with the sleeping bags."

"Well, I don't like the idea of varmints crawlin' all over me during the night."

"You don't have to worry about that, Bobby. Your usual fartin' after eating beans and wieners will keep them away."

Bob finally conceded. It would be sleeping bags only.

Upon making camp after a long day of play and few miles traveled, the boys gorged themselves on beans and wieners without much thought of rationing.

As daylight faded, the blue-green river darkened to a brackish black.

"What's that swimming across the river?" shouted Bob.

"Looks like it might be a beaver to me."

The night air was filled with the sounds of nocturnal creatures…bullfrogs, crickets, loons, owls, and the occasional howl of a lost hunting dog. The moon was almost full. Its light shimmered on the river.

"Just think," said Bob as they set around the campfire, "Indians once roamed all over these parts. I'll bet they traveled the river just like we're doin' now. Probably heard the same sounds we're hearing as they sat around the fire."

"Yeah, except we're just on a little jaunt. For them it was a way of life. They didn't have beans and wieners and baloney like we do. It was all about survival for them."

"I wonder what they used to wipe themselves with."

"Leaves, I guess…you did bring the toilet paper didn't you?"

"No, I thought you brought it."

"Crap, I guess we'll find out how well leaves work tomorrow morning."

"Oh well," said Bob as he stretched his arms out and yawned. "I'm gettin' a little sleepy, how about you?"

"Yeah, I'm pretty tired. Let's turn in, we need to get up early and make up for some lost time."

Just then, an unexpected sound came from the river, like a paddle hitting the water.

"What the hell was that?" said Bob.

"Must be that beaver we saw just before dark, hitting the water with its tail."

Then, there was a scream in the distance.

"I knew we should have pitched the tent, damn it," mouthed Bob, "We'll probably be eaten in our sleep by whatever that is."

"What would want to eat your scrawny ass? Come on, let's get some shut eye."

The boys spread their sleeping bags in close proximity to the fire, and settled in for the night. A gentle breeze rustled in the tall pines as the moon and stars in a cloudless sky peeked through their branches.

"Wouldn't you know it," said Bob, "of all places, I had to lay my sleeping bag on a rock. It's gouging me right in the small of my back."

He crawled out, rolled the sleeping bag back and started poking around the object trying to dig it out of the ground. "John Boy, it's not a rock: its something made out of metal."

John got up, put more wood on the fire and held the flashlight as Bob worked at unearthing it. As he removed the dirt around it, the object began to take shape. It appeared to be some sort of headgear with a brim that curved up to a point in front and back. A thin strip ran along its crown.

With a grunt and tug, Bob pulled it up out of the ground. As he did, something fell out of it. It wasn't clear what the object was...until John shined the flashlight on it.

"Holy crap," yelled Bob, "it's a skull!"

John looked closer. "Damn, you're right!"

"Do you think we should go get the police, Johnny?"

"There ain't no police out here. We're in the middle of nowhere, remember?"

"Well, what do you think we should do?"

"There's no telling how long it's been here. Let's just leave it where we found it."

As they sat around the campfire, John examined the iron cap in detail, trying to figure out what it might be.

"Bob, I think this is an old Spanish helmet. You know, I remember studying about de Soto, the explorer who led an expedition through these parts. I'll bet it dates back to his time."

"Now that you mention it, I remember studying a little bit about him, too," said Bob, "How far back was that?"

"I don't remember, but it was hundreds of years ago."

"So, this guy's been here a long time. 'Wonder what did him in?"

"Who knows, but I'll bet it wasn't pleasant."

They sat there for a few minutes and looked at the skull. John finally got the nerve to pick it up. Clasped in his hands, he held it close to his face and stared into the dirt-filled eye sockets.

"Who are you anyway, Buddy? How did you meet your end?"

Light from the fire cast an orangish glow on the old bone.

"I think I'll call you Buddy. Is that OK?"

"Damn, John, you sure have a weird sense of humor."

"Where's the rest of you, Buddy?" John continued, "I guess the animals took care of that a few hundred years ago, right?"

"You're really spookin' me, John."

"Well, it's not like he died yesterday. I think we should take him with us after all. We've probably made some important archeological find."

Eventually, the boys settled down from the excitement of their discovery.

"We're not gonna' be worth anything tomorrow if we don't get some sleep," said John.

They crawled back into their respective sleeping bags.

Within minutes Bob was snoring. John's mind was still racing, but it wasn't long before he, too, drifted into sleep.

Sometime, during what was left of the night, he was awakened by something crawling around on top of him. He lay there a minute, trying to deal with the adrenalin rush, then finally mustered the courage to poke his head out of the sleeping bag. There, standing on his stomach, staring him in the face at close quarters was a possum. The little marsupial didn't seem in a hurry to move.

"Get!" he shouted. Bob never missed a beat in his snoring.

The possum looked at him and hissed, showing a mouth full of jagged teeth.

"Get!" he said again, rising up. The creature scampered, but revisited all during the pre-dawn morning hours. "I sure as hell won't argue about not pitching the tent tomorrow night," he mumbled.

The next morning, at the crack of dawn, the boys made ready for day two of their journey.

John, mounted the skull, donning its helmet, on the bow of the Goldfish.

"Isn't that sort of sacrilegious?" Bob commented.

"No, of course not," he responded, "Buddy's probably enjoying every minute of it."

So, with the skull and helmet serving as its masthead, the Goldfish was launched into currents of the Cahaba.

Things were going well. They were making up for the time squandered playing the day before. Day two, thus far, was more of the same, except that the country seemed even more remote.

On this day John was at the stern while Bob, at the bow, set on a knapsack with his back resting against the cross member. He had his arm leisurely slung over the side with his hand streaming in the water.

"Man, I'm still tired from last night. Hardly slept a wink," he said.

"Well, I certainly wouldn't have known it, considering all that snoring."

Suddenly, John yelled, "Get your hand out of the water, quick!"

Bob threw his hand high above his head. His weight shifted which upset the balance of the boat. The Goldfish rolled over throwing the boys and all their gear into the water.

John quickly swam to the capsized canoe and hung on. Bob went under. In near panic John was about to dive under when Bob popped up.

"Are you OK?" yelled Bob.

"Hell, no, I'm not OK. You turned the boat over. Are you OK?"

"Hell, no, I'm not OK. You screamed and caused me to turn the boat over."

"I didn't have time to explain. There was a water moccasin, at least three feet long, swimming along just inches from your hand."

After struggling several long minutes they got the boat upright, rounded up the paddles and kicked their way towards shore.

Everything had gone to the bottom…food, tent, sleeping bags…everything except for the helmet. Somehow it had become wedged in the bow brace.

They drug the canoe onto the rocky shore and turned it on its side to drain the water. The helmet dislodged itself and a can of pork and beans came rolling out of it.

"What are we gonna' do now?" asked Bob.

Just then," cawing" sounds came from all directions. "I think those damn crows are laughing at us," said Bob.

"Well, if I were them I'd be laughing, too," John replied, "let's at least try to retrieve some of our stuff. Are you up for some free style skin diving?"

"Yeah, guess so," Bob responded.

After several failed attempts to reach bottom, John commented: "This did have to happen in what's probably the deepest part of this damn river,"

"Looks like we don't have any choice but to push on down stream and try to find a way out."

"Yep," said John, "Too bad we don't have Buddy around anymore to guide us."

They rounded bend after bend, looking along the banks for a trail leading from the river. Other than Bob's remark, "I guess we should have tied everything down," little was said between them.

As the afternoon shadows lengthened on that second day with no path yet spotted, they came upon a small sandy island in the middle of the river. On either side of it were shoals, which backed the waters up forming a shallow lake. Except for its sandy beach, only a field of slender out-of-bloom lily plants surrounded the little island.

"It's gonna' be dark soon," said John, we'd better make camp here. At least we'll be out of the way of varmints."

"OK," said Bob, "I don't think we've got much choice anyway."

They pulled the canoe up onto the gentle sloping shore to a level spot, turned it upside down and propped it up with sticks.

"This will give us a little shelter," said John, "We won't have a fire tonight; so we'd better get to work opening that can of beans."

Bob pounded on the can with a sharp rock as John gathered lily stems to pad the hard ground where they would be sleeping. Finally, the top of the can split enough to pry it open.

As the last bit of daylight shown through the trees, they hovered over the can and hurriedly took turns dipping their hands, scooping out its contents in dripping gobs until it was empty. Then, Bob began licking the inside of the can.

"I think this is gonna' be a long night," said John.

"Yeah boy, sure makes you appreciate electricity, hot water and a soft bed," Bob commented.

"And, toilet paper," John added. After a few moments passed, he said: "Some woodsmen we are. What if we had lived back in the old days? We'd be goners… you know that, don't you?"

"I hate to admit it, John Boy, but I'm afraid you're right. We're just fair weather Inguns'…do you have any earthly idea where we might be?"

"No."

"You still hungry?"

"Yeah…I'm gonna' try to go to sleep."

Within minutes from the time he crawled under the canoe, hanging half in, half out, Bob was snoring.

"Damn," muttered John to himself, "he can sleep anywhere, anytime."

He sat staring out at the full moon's reflection on the water and wondered what it really might have been like back in the old times.

The constant sound of water rushing over the shoals muffled the noises of night creatures and began to lull him. He lay down on the hastily made matt of lily stems and fell into a restless sleep.

In the grayish dawn John looked out on the river lake. A morning mist rose from it. It was mystic and inviting.

As Bob slept, he slipped out of his swimming trunks and waded into the calm warm water, splashing and washing away the dirt and grim as the mist rose around him.

Suddenly, Bob's shout broke the quiet still: "John Boy, there's a group of nuns over there on the bank!"

"So, you finally got your lazy ass up," he shouted back." Then, he stood straight up in the knee high water and shook his appendage at the opposite shore. "Come and get it girls," he yelled.

"You irreverent bastard," Bob yelled, "Come on out of there and let's find our way out of this God- forsaken place before I starve to death."

They were on the river again, searching for any path leading away from it.

In the late morning hours they rounded a bend and came upon a stone and concrete forge that stretched across the river. It was about eight feet wide and a few inches of water flowed over it. A trail led away at both ends.

"Glory Halleluiah," Bob shouted, "this is what we've been looking for…. which way?"

"The one to the right. It feels like the one we should take. Do you want to leave the canoe and come back for it later?"

"Hell no, it took me six months to save up enough to buy this thing. I sure ain't gonna' leave it out here in the middle of nowhere."

"Well, you didn't mind us leaving my motorbike stashed up there at the bridge. It took me nine months to save enough to get that."

"Well, we're not leavin' the canoe…or this," said Bob as he put the helmet on his head.

"I guess you know how ridiculous you look standin' there with nothing on but a bathing suit, tennis shoes and that helmet."

"Well, you don't look so hot yourself, John Boy…let's get goin' before I starve to death."

The boys hoisted the Goldfish on their shoulders, and having only their swimsuits on and wearing tennis shoes, they began walking.

After what seemed like being on a trail that would never end, John asked: "How are you doin'?"

"How do you think I'm doin'?" came the reply. "We've been walking at least two hours, and it looks like we're going deeper into the woods instead of getting out. Maybe we should have gone the other way."

"Maybe we should have left the damn canoe."

Finally, they came upon a dirt road.

"At least this thing looks like cars come down it," said John.

"Yeah, at least every couple of weeks, or so."

"Let's take a rest. You're gettin' a little grumpy."

"Me, grumpy…no way. It's just that not all of us mortals can be happy campers without eating once in a while, that's all…which way this time, Lone Ranger?"

"To the right, Red Ass Feather, from the direction we came."

After portaging the canoe an hour or so along the road, they heard a vehicle approaching from behind.

"Where you boys headed?" asked the man driving the old red Studebaker truck.

"Down toward Helena, to the river bridge," said John. "Are we going in the right direction?"

"Yep, load your boat up, boys," he said, "I can take you all at least to the Helena road. Then, I'll have to be headin' the other way, towards Bessemer."

John hopped in the bed of the pick-up to hold the canoe steady. Bob got in the cab.

"Hi," said John to the little girl riding in back with him, "I'm John. What's your name?"

"Anna," she replied.

"How old are you, Anna?"

"Nine."

He couldn't help but take notice of the child's natural beauty. Her dark brown hair and sunset complexion set off the bluest eyes he had ever seen.

When they reached the Helena road, instead of putting the boys out, the man turned south and took them all the way to the bridge.

"Thank you, Sir. We really appreciate it," said Bob as he and John unloaded the canoe.

"Yes, Sir, we sure do," John added.

"You boys take it easy now, and be careful," said the man as he turned the pickup around.

The little girl waved as the old Studebaker truck pulled away and headed north.

"Did you notice how blue that guy's eyes were, John? Except for that he looked like an Indian, didn't he?"

"Yeah. The little girl had those eyes, too. Must have been his daughter. You can tell she's gonna' be a knockout when she grows up.

# CHAPTER 2

# March 1977 (Twenty-One Years Later)

BOB SAVAGE TUGGED at the canoe. Waist deep in miserably cold water, he tried to dislodge it from the muddy riverbank and make for a hasty retreat. There was no doubt the pack of dogs would attack. He just hoped that they wouldn't come into the water. When he turned to see where they were, he found himself looking up at the business end of a twelve-gauge shotgun.

The old man holding it growled, "What do you want, Mister?"

"Sir," Savage responded, his body trembling, "I don't want any trouble. I'm just trying to find a Mr. Raintree."

"I'm Raintree," said the old man, showing no intention of lowering the gun.

A jumble of thoughts flashed through Savage's mind: *Please, God, Don't let him shoot…here in the middle of nowhere…nobody will know…so cold…damn, I'm peeing.*

He tried to gain composure.

"Mr. Raintree, My name is Bob Savage, and I apologize for coming here unannounced, but I didn't know any other way to get in touch with you. I just wanted to find out if you had any interest in leasing or selling your property."

"Look here, I've done told you people, this land ain't for sale! Now I think you had better git on out of here."

"Yes Sir, but…Mr. Raintree, I've come a long way to see you and would at least like to leave on friendly terms. I won't be back down here without being invited…I can promise you that. Will you at least let me leave you one of my cards?" Then, he remembered: *Hell, I don't even have any cards on me.*

By the hardest, Bob managed to conjure up a grin, hopefully the disarming one that had gotten him out of scrapes so many times before.

"You're not from Salvo Mining?" said Raintree.

"No Sir, I'm just a real-estate agent looking for property," Bob replied.

Raintree lowered the gun, and his manner somewhat softened.

"Come on up out of the water Mr. Savage…git back to the house, boys."

The dogs scampered towards an old shake roofed log cabin that stood about a hundred feet from the water's edge.

"Well, come on Mr. Savage. They won't bother you now. You can come inside for a spell to warm up and dry out if you want to."

"Yes Sir, I'd appreciate that."

Bob observed the surroundings. It was like going back in time a hundred years or more. The old man was living in virtual isolation in the backwoods, on the banks of the Cahaba River. The only giveaway that this place was even in the present century was an old rusty red pickup truck parked under a shed attached to the barn.

He followed Raintree through the rough sawn plank door and into the cabin. It was dark and rustic with lit candles scattered about. The stone fireplace blazed, giving off a warm glow and filling the room with the aroma of burning hickory.

"I'm sorry to say it, Mr. Savage, but you look like a wet dog standin' there, drippin' and shakin'. Here, try this on for size."

Raintree handed him a long fur robe that appeared to be made of Beaver skins.

"It won't take long for your duds to dry out if you put 'um up next to the fireplace."

"Thank you, Mr. Raintree, this is mighty kind of you." Bob hurriedly removed his wet clothes, placed them on the hearth, and put on the coat.

A kettle sitting on the potbellied stove across the room began to whistle.

"I was makin' myself some tea…want some?"

"Sounds good, Mr. Raintree, long as it's hot."

"Have a sit. It'll be ready in a minute."

Bob sat in a rocking chair next to the fireplace, and slowly began to regain his senses.

As his eyes adjusted to the low level of light, he began taking notice of the cabin's interior. It was much different from what he would have expected. The place was clean and neat with no clutter.

Apparently Raintree lived, slept and ate in this approximately twenty-foot by twenty-foot room. There was another room, but the door was shut with his bed pushed up against it. Across from the fireplace stood a large bookcase with at least a hundred books in it. Next to the bookcase was a desk. On the wall above it was a portrait of what looked like a country gentleman of an earlier era. Next to the painting was a collage of photographs.

"Mind if I browse your books?" he asked.

"Help yourself. Be careful though, some of them are pretty old and comin' apart."

They were very old books…everything from classic writings to instructions on how to witch for water. Many had to do with history. Of particular interest, was what appeared to be a scorched and scarred leather-bound diary. Bob carefully opened it to the first page. The writing appeared to be in Spanish.

"Do you ever read these, Mr. Raintree?" he asked.

"Most of 'um. They were passed down from my Great Granddaddy from five generations back. That's a painting of him up there on the wall."

It began to dawn on Bob that William Raintree wasn't a typical moonshining backwoods hick.

"Want a little honey in your tea, Mr. Savage?"

"Yes, sir, that would be good."

Bob walked over to the collage of photographs. Some were old and some looked fairly recent. Among the more recent ones was that of a beautiful young woman.

"It's ready," said Raintree, holding up two clay mugs.

Bob decided not to ask any more questions, at least not for the moment, and returned to the rocking chair. Raintree settled into an old easy chair across from him, and began sipping.

"Now, tell me again, Mr. Savage, just what brings you down here?"

"Well," Bob began, taking a sip from his mug, "I'm a real estate broker over in Tuscaloosa. Some clients of mine started a hunting club and asked me to find them some property along the Cahaba, because of it being one of the last Wilderness Rivers in Alabama."

"How'd you know about me and my land?"

"I went to the Bibb County courthouse down in Centerville and searched through the tax maps. It didn't take long to find out that most of the land, except for your 320 acres, was owned by large timber or mining companies." Bob took another sip.

"I knew I would be wasting my time trying to deal with them, so I decided to try and contact you. That proved to be unlikely since you don't have a phone or any neighbors; so I called the West Blocton post office. The postmaster told me that you lived so deep in the woods that your mail was held for you until you came to town…which was every month or so. I didn't want to take the time to write and wait to hear back from you…so here I am."

"Well, I'm afraid you wasted a trip, Mr. Savage. Like I said, this land ain't for sale."

"Maybe not, Mr. Raintree, but that's not the only reason I came. When I was a kid, a buddy of mine and I took a canoe trip on the Cahaba, but we didn't make it this far. We planned to go to Centerville, but a few mishaps along the way forced us to pull off the river. I've always wanted to come back, and this was a good excuse to do it…kind of like taking care of old business or finishing something you started. You know what I mean?"

"Yes, I do."

As they talked, Bob began to take note of Raintree's appearance. There was something familiar. His steel gray hair, pulled back in a ponytail, high cheekbones and skin tone gave a strong hint that he was at least partly Native American. None of his features, however, triggered recollection…except for those extraordinary blue eyes.

After finishing his cup of the concoction Raintree called tea, Bob felt a great sense of urgency coming on. He stood up and headed for the door.

"Mr. Raintree, where's the outhouse?"

"Out back, where it's always been," he answered with the trace of a smile.

As Bob sat there in the cold dank little outhouse, he couldn't help reflecting: *1977…this has been a hell of a year so far…the divorce…broke… now, I'm chasing dead-end leads like this one…thank God, there's toilet paper in here…expected corncobs…at best a Sears and Roebuck catalogue…the old man…he looks so familiar…where have I seen him before?* He looked down at his Timex calendar watch…*12:20, Mar. 15.*

As he walked back toward the cabin, Bob looked over at the old red Studebaker pickup parked under the shed. Suddenly, his mind flashed back to the summer of '56 when he and John, carrying his canoe, walked down the old dirt road, and a blue-eyed Indian looking man, with a little girl, driving a red Studebaker truck gave them a ride. A chill ran up his spine. *It's him*, his mind shouted. *No doubt about it. Raintree's the one who gave us a ride…he's much older, but I recognize him, now… and that's the truck we rode in twenty-one years ago.* "Incredible," he said out loud.

Then, the comment John made after they were dropped off at the Old Helena Bridge echoed: "That little girl's gonna' be a knockout when she grows up." *Bingo…that's Raintree's daughter in the photo.*

"Cleaned you out, did it?" said Raintree.

"Yes, Sir, it hit me all at once."

"First cup does that sometimes. Want some more?"

"No thanks. What's it got in it?"

"Holly leaves, and sassafras roots, it's an old family brew. We always called it Black Drink. Got enough caffeine in it to bring a dead man back."

Bob walked back over to the collage of photographs. "Is that your daughter, Mr. Raintree?" he asked, pointing to the beautiful young woman.

"Yes, that's Anna."

On top of the desk, beside several candles, lay a huge stone axe used as a paperweight.

"I'd hate to be hit with that thing," Bob commented, "Where did it come from?"

"Well, it's supposed to have belonged to Tuscaloosa."

"You mean like in the town, Tuscaloosa?"

"Yes…spelled a little different but it's the same man the town's named after. He was one of the great Indian chiefs back in the old days."

"That's very interesting…is your daughter married, Mr. Raintree?"

"Yes," he answered somewhat abruptly. "Now, let me ask you somethin', Mr. Savage. Do you know anything about Salvo Mining Company?"

"No Sir, nothing except that they are a big coal mining operation."

This wasn't entirely true; Bob had heard about Don Salvo. The story he got was that Salvo was a self-made multi-millionaire…making it in strip-mining coal. Bob had also heard that he was a ruthless bastard who thought nothing of rolling over anything, or anyone who got in his way.

"Are you having problems with them, Mr. Raintree?"

"No, not exactly, they've just been pesterin' me for the last several months about sellin' this land to them. I don't think they know what 'No' means."

"If you want them off your back, I know a good lawyer. One you can trust."

"I'll keep that in mind."

"Well, Mr. Raintree," I'd better get going…still a long way to Centerville. Thank you for your hospitality, and again I apologize for busting in on you like this."

Raintree walked him to the river's edge.

Bob couldn't resist asking, "Do you by any chance remember giving a ride to a couple of teenagers carrying a canoe along an old dirt road somewhere above here about twenty or so years ago?"

"Can't say as I do."

Bob shoved off…back paddling…ready to ride the currents toward Centerville.

"By the way, Mr. Savage," Raintree shouted as he headed the canoe downstream, "I wouldn't shoot an unarmed man."

"Take care, Mr. Raintree, hope to see you again sometime."

The Cahaba hadn't changed much since he and John were on it twenty–one years earlier, except this time the water was higher, swollen from heavy rains a few days before. It was almost at flood stage the day before, when Bob put in thirty miles upstream at the Old Helena Bridge.

The river had calmed down, he was making good time, and things seemed fairly normal…except for an eerie sense of being watched. Every time he turned and looked behind, he'd catch a glimpse of a large crow, sometimes perched on a limb, sometimes in flight from one tree to another.

*He's following me…no doubt about that…probably thinks I'm going to throw out some food scraps.*

C H A P T E R  3

# Raintree's Secret

IN THE FOLLOWING weeks, Bob thought a lot about his encounter with William Raintree. He figured that there must be more to the story than what had been told, and wondered…*why would Salvo want Raintree's land when he already owned enough to mine from now on?* Besides, it was so isolated…not practical to mine. He didn't know why, but there was a strong sense that his and Raintree's paths would cross again.

As the months passed, thoughts of the Cahaba and Raintree faded into just another memory of what had become a most trying year. For Bob Savage, there were matters of more immediate concern…like making a living and getting on with life the best he could. Business was bad, and the divorce still gnawed.

The call came early Monday morning, August 22nd.

"Hello, Mr. Raintree. How are you?"

"I'm not sure, Mr. Savage. I need to meet with you if that's possible…as soon as possible."

"Can we talk, now?"

"Best not. I'm at a pay phone."

"Then when and where?"

"Can you make it tomorrow in West Blocton, at a café called Huey's? It's in the middle of town, on Main Street. You can't miss it…maybe at Ten o'clock?

"OK, Mr. Raintree, I'll see you in the morning."

The next morning, promptly at Ten, Bob turned onto 'Main Street', in West Blocton.

As he drove along, looking for Huey's, his first impressions of the little town was that it was like something out of Mayberry…off to itself…miles from the main highway. *Who would come through here to go anywhere?* Then, there it was, in big red letters on the storefront window, 'Huey's'.

The old Studebaker pickup looked right at home parked out front. As Bob pulled in beside it he saw Raintree inside, sitting at a table next to the window sipping a cup of coffee.

The only other customers were two scruffy, but friendly-looking men sitting on bar stools at the counter in conversation with the slim, blond, mid-thirtyish, gum-snapping waitress. They all briefly turned as he entered.

Behind the counter, an older heavy set man in a stained T-shirt stood over the grill as a greasy column of steam rose from it. The aroma of frying hamburger patties filled the air. The tables were neatly arranged, each covered with a plastic red and white-checkered tablecloth.

"Morning, Mr. Raintree, good to see you again, but things sound kind of serious."

"They very well may be, Mr. Savage. How bout a cup of coffee?"

"Yes, Sir…sounds good."

Raintree motioned to the waitress: "Coffee for this man, please ma'am," he said.

"Comin' up," she replied.

"Is it that Salvo bunch?" asked Bob.

"Yes, and I think I might need that lawyer friend of yours. 'Say he can be trusted?"

"Yes, Sir, he can be trusted. The only problem is that he's down in Mobile. I may have spoken in haste that day. What are they up to?"

"Here, I picked this up at the post office yesterday."

Raintree handed Bob a letter dated two weeks earlier.

*Dear Mr. Raintree:*

   *This is to inform you that Salvo Mining Corporation is the legal owner of mineral rights on certain property of which you own surface rights.*

*Let me assure you that it is not our intent to disrupt you or your privacy; however we do have a vested interest and rights of which we intend to exercise. There will be a geological survey conducted on the property within sixty days. This will require access by our engineering team. Your cooperation will be appreciated.*

*Also, I want to inform you that we are prepared to increase our offer to $2,000 per acre for the purchase of your interest in the property.*

*Mr. Raintree, you must be aware that this is several times the market value of your land. I hope you will give this offer serious consideration.*

*Sincerely.*
*Richard Hardin*
*Senior Vice President*
*Salvo Mining Corporation*

"Well, "I'm no attorney, but if they own the mineral rights…"

"Mr. Savage," Raintree interrupted, "they don't own mineral rights or anything else. This land has always belonged to my people."

"Do you have proof that you own the mineral rights?"

"I have land grant deeds from back in 1830. It plainly says, three-hundred and twenty acres, the whole shootin' match, was bought and paid for in legal tender to the federal government by Eston McCloud, my ancestor from five generations back. It's been handed down in our family ever since."

"Could anybody in your family have sold the mineral rights, and you not know about it?"

"No."

"I wonder why they want your land so bad, Mr. Raintree."

"It's not the land they want…it's what's on it."

"You mean coal?"

"No, this."

He pulled an old cloth pouch out of his pocket. "Hold out your hand, Mr. Savage."

Raintree dumped the contents into Bob's palm. Lying there were three yellow nuggets, each as big as the end of his thumb.

"Is that what I think it is?"

"Yes, Mr. Savage, it is."

"And, it came from your property?"

"Yes, sir, it did…and there's plenty more where that came from. Gettin' the letter pretty much tells me that Salvo knows about it, too. I figure they were snoopin' around on the river and found traces of it. I guess they got the notion that it had washed down from my land."

"I think I'll have another cup of coffee," said Bob.

Raintree called out to the waitress: "Refills on the coffee, please." Then, he turned to Bob: "You had best close your hand, Mr. Savage. We don't need no peepin' eyes, now do we?"

"No, Sir…we definitely don't need that."

"You're in the real estate business," said Raintree. "This is about real estate. Would you be interested in helpin' me get to the bottom of this thing?"

"Why are you trusting me with this knowledge, Mr. Raintree? You don't even know me."

"Well, for good or ill, I've got to trust someone…let's just say an old black bird told me you're somebody I can trust. Take what's in your hand to cover expenses for a while…that is, if you're interested. If not, keep it anyway…for your trouble."

"Yes, I am interested. Just give me a minute to digest all this."

"Other than you, Mr. Savage, and most probably Salvo, there's only one other person who knows about this. He's a Jewish fella' up in Birmingham by the name of Harry Cohen. He deals in gold and can convert the nuggets to cash for you. I've been doin' business with him for many years. He can be trusted."

"How about you calling me Bob from now on?"

"How bout you callin' me William. By the way, I do remember pickin' you boys up back then."

"I need to know everything, William…from the beginning."

"It's a pretty long tale, Have you got time to go on out to my place?"

"Yes, Sir, I do, and just so you'll know, the boy with me that day you gave us a ride grew up to be the lawyer I was telling you about. His name is John Starr."

# Chapter 4

# The Shocking Truth

As Bob followed Raintree's truck on the back roads, he began to wonder what he was getting himself into. *Could the old man be delusional? Those rocks in his pocket… could they be fake…maybe fool's gold? Even if it all were true, why trust a stranger?*

On the other hand, there he was, alone, broke…no light at the end of the tunnel. "Hell," he blurted, "why not? I'll go along for the ride…at least for a while."

After traveling some distance, Raintree turned off on a dirt road. Bob followed, his vehicle straddling the ruts of what had become a pig trail. After going several miles through heavily wooded rolling terrain, the land opened up… relatively flat and clear except for patches of trees here and there. He passed an old abandoned cabin. On the left, behind a cornfield and about a hundred yards from the trail, rising at least twenty feet was an earthen mound…obviously man made.

Then, the cabin and river came into view. Chickens pecked around under some fruit trees, and a mule grazed next to the old log barn. The dogs came out to greet them. This time they were friendly, even playful.

"How bout us goin' out on the porch to talk," said Raintree.

"OK."

The two settled into rocking chairs facing the peaceful Cahaba. A breeze rustled through the oak tree next to the cabin.

"Most of my people were Indian folks," he began. "At one time there was a settlement on this land. The town was called 'Cahawba'. When you were comin' in and passed the cabin on the right, did you notice that mound over to your left, behind the corn field? It's no more than a couple of hundred yards from where we're sittin' right now."

"Yes, sir, I did see it."

"That's where the town was. It was here a long time before the whites came into these parts. When settlers started comin' in the early1800's, they referred to the tribe as bein' Creek, but they were really descendants of a more ancient people…the Mississippians…the ones that built the mounds down on the Warrior River below Tuscaloosa, at Moundville.

One of the dogs came up on the porch and sat next to Bob. It was an unusual looking animal, appearing to have a lot of greyhound in it. Bob began rubbing its head while being drawn into the old man's story.

"Back in those days, around 1820," Raintree continued, "a white settler by the name of Arthur Bunn set up a tradin' post about ten or so miles from here… right on the road where I picked you boys up. He traded with the Indians and settlers in the area.

Eston McCloud, my white ancestor, was a Scotsman who came through and met Iona, his bride-to-be, at that old tradin' post. She's where the Indian in me came from. Anyways, her daddy, Ishkooda, was chief of the tribe that was here. They say he didn't exactly cater to the idea of his daughter gettin' involved with a white man, but let him come on in anyway. Eston wrote in his diary that the old man gave in so that she would quit pesterin' him."

"Is that a portrait of him hanging on the wall inside?" asked Bob.

"Yep, his brother-in-law did it…made the paint from plants and berries found right around here."

"That's amazing…looks like it was done by some famous artist."

"It sure does, doesn't it. Nobody knew anything about Eston. Most figured he had a price on his head somewhere since he never talked about his past. He was a learned man, though…studied history, wrote poetry and was taken by Indian ways. They say he felt right at home with the tribe and was content to live out his days here.

"After my daddy died in '54, I found Eston's diary in an old trunk while I was cleaning out his place… that was my daddy's cabin you passed."

"Really," said Bob, wondering where Raintree was going with this tale of his.

"I read the diary through and through, and there were some mighty interestin' things in there. Remember you askin' about that old stone war-ax layin' in there on the desk?"

"Yeah, I remember thinking how I would hate to be hit with that thing."

"Well, Eston was convinced that his wife was a direct descendant of Tascalusa…or Tuscaloosa, as it might be.

"You mean like the town, Tuscaloosa?"

"Yes, he said that Tuscaloosa's wife, Na-ha-no-me, was from here…the daughter of the tribe's chief. Anyways, Tuscaloosa was a great warrior king of lands that stretched from here all the way down towards Mobile. Him and his warriors got into it with de Soto and his gang of Spanish conquistadors when they came through lookin' for gold back in 1540. It happened right after de Soto accompanied by Tuscaloosa came by here and stayed a few days. The Spaniards, about six hundred of them, were in need of provisions, and Tuscaloosa supposedly was takin' him to where he had a storehouse full of corn. Unbeknownst to de Soto, he was bein' led into a trap.

"The battle took place in an Indian town called Mabila, somewhere down below Selma…on the Alabama River. The Indians were totally whipped, but the Spaniards almost got wiped out themselves. They were out-numbered five to one, but their horses, armor and steel swords gave them the advantage. Havin' those things to fight with was their salvation.

"They say bodies piled up like cord wood, and it was so bloody the streams ran red. The Spaniards couldn't find Tuscaloosa afterwards; so they figured that he got burnt up in the battle fires. Eston said that Tuscaloosa's son, Muscoda, brought his mother and a few survivors back up here to live with her people. He said they also brought Tuscaloosa's burnt body here for burial."

"That explains something I've wondered about for years," said Bob. "My friend, John and I found an old Spanish helmet with a skull in it upstream from here when we were on our canoe trip back in '56."

"Well, that don't surprise me none," said Raintree, "cause sure as thunder those Spaniards were in these parts. Now that you mention it, I recall you wearin' an old helmet when I picked you boys up back then."

"Yeah, that was me, alright…where did Eston get all this information, William?"

"Partially from hand-me-down stories within the tribe, but he had another source, too."

"Yeah, what was that?"

"When you were here before, I noticed you lookin' at that old scorched leather-bound diary written in Spanish."

"Yes, I wondered what it was."

"Well, it was a chronicle kept by one of the monks on the deSoto expedition. That's how Eston got a lot of what he knew. He called it the 'Quiver of Truth'. It told the real story of how brutal the Spaniards were."

"That's very interesting," Bob commented.

"One of the more interestin' things Eston learned from the chronicle," continued Raintree, "was that when deSoto and his expedition came through here, they were on their way to Mobile bay where ships were waitin' to carry them back to Cuba. deSoto saw a gold medallion that Na-ha-no-me wore around her neck. When he asked her where it came from, she lied and told him it came from way over on the Mississippi river. That, they say, is why after the battle at Mabila, him and his expedition headed west instead of meetin' up with the ships."

"So," said Bob, "even in Tuscaloosa's time, the Indians living here knew about the gold on this land."

"Yep," Raintree responded.

"That's some story," said Bob, "one for the history books."

"Well, since you mentioned it," said Raintree, "Eston had a friend down in Autauga County by the name of Albert Pickett who wrote a history book about Alabama in the early days. Mr. Pickett encouraged him to write a book himself, tellin' all about it. He did just that, but a fire destroyed the print shop the day after it was printed. They say one copy survived, but if it did, nobody knows where it is."

"Did Eston know about the gold?" asked Bob.

"Oh, yeah. He briefly mentioned it in his diary, but said it had to be kept a secret, knowin' what would happen if word got out. So, the old tale about gold bein' on this land just faded away along with him. When I read the diary, I didn't think much about it...thought it was just an old wive's tale."

"When did you rediscover the gold?" asked Bob.

"Back in '56, not too long after I gave you boys a ride, my wife left and took our daughter, Anna. She said she couldn't take livin' out here anymore, and took up with a man who worked at the steel mills up in Fairfield. "

"After she left, I spent most of my time just wanderin' around in the woods tryin' to come to terms with it. It left a great scar on my mind."

"Yeah, I know that feeling well," said Bob.

"Her name was Lilly, like the Cahaba Lilly that grows in this river, and nowhere else. Have you ever seen one?"

"No...at least not in bloom."

"They grow in the shoals and shallows...fields of them. Got long green stems with a white flower on top... they bloom in May. They're beautiful...just like she was. I heard she died last year. Enough talk...do you want to go see for yourself where the gold comes from?"

"Yes, I do."

Raintree got up and went into the cabin, returning in a few minutes with two kerosene lanterns: "Let's go," he said.

Bob followed him to the riverbank.

"We've got to go over on the other side," said Raintree as he took hold of the bow of the old wooden flat-bottom boat after putting the lanterns in it: "Give her a shove and hop in."

They paddled the hundred or so feet to the opposite bank. There, the terrain was more hilly and heavily wooded. "Watch out for snakes," said Raintree

As they walked the narrow path that ran alongside the river, Raintree continued his story: "Back in Eston's day, there was a lot of trouble between Indians and whites. Squatters were settlin' on Indian lands all over Alabama. The Federal Government under Andy Jackson's orders started roundin' up the Indians and movin' them off their lands. Ever hear of 'The Trail of Tears'?"

"Yes, sir, I have. That was a sad thing."

"Yes...sad," said Raintree. "There wasn't any land grabbin' goin' on around here, though. This was a pretty isolated area. The whites, for the most part, were respectful and the Indians were pretty peaceful folks...more farmers than warriors. And, I suppose everybody was too busy tryin' to scratch out a livin' that they didn't have time for feudin'. Besides, as time went on the whites got a little redder, and the Indians got a little whiter. A lot of girls in the settlement started marryin' up with white men and movin' on out to farm plots in the Cahaba Valley where they raised their families. After a while it seemed like everybody in these parts was related in some way or another. Blood had gotten so mixed that there wasn't too much to argue about concern' who was Indian and who was white. For the most part, Indians took up the white man's ways."

After walking about ten minutes the path dipped and they came to a small stream that fed into the river.

"Let's go up this way," said Raintree.

Bob followed him on a path beside the stream that led away from the river. They walked about a hundred yards when Raintree stopped and pointed down at the streambed. "Look down there…on the bottom."

Bob looked through the twelve or so inches of crystal clear water at the sandy bottom. There, lay several small yellow nuggets.

"See 'um?" asked Raintree.

"Oh, I see them, all right."

"Look a little closer. Do you see an underwater current comin' from that crevice in the side of the streambed?"

"Yes," said Bob, "is that where the nuggets are coming from?"

"Yep, that's where they're comin' from…the source of old Eston's gold. What you see is what I first saw back in '56. The more I looked from that point down towards the river, the more I found. I started collectin' the nuggets about once a week, hopin' nobody else would come along and spot them."

Raintree pointed upstream, slightly to the left. "See that hill up there?" he asked.

"Yes, I see it."

"Let's head up there."

As they walked towards the rise, Raintree resumed recounting events that began some twenty-one years earlier: "In April of '61 some rains came through here like I'd never seen before. The river got so high I thought it was gonna' get the cabin. Anything that got into those currents was swept away, includin' my boat and two of my dogs. All I could do was wait it out.

"When the weather finally broke and things settled down, I started lookin' around to see what damage it had caused. That's when I noticed somethin' mighty peculiar about that hill."

When they reached the rise and walked around to the other side, Bob noticed nothing peculiar until Raintree began scrapping away dirt and leaves exposing a row of cedar logs. He lifted and heaved them to the side. There, uncovered, was an opening in the ground. A ladder extended down into the darkness.

"When I first saw this after the rains," said Raintree as he lit the kerosene lanterns, "it was just a small hole…hardly big enough for a man to squeeze through. I figured the ground had gotten so soaked it just caved in."

Raintree began his descent. Bob followed.

The cavern was large with at least two feet of headroom. A stream ran through it.

"Take a look around you," said Raintree.

Bob raised his lantern. A vein of yellow streaked like lightning across the cavern wall.

"My God, is that gold?"

"Yes, it's the mother lode. Look down around your feet."

Bob lowered his lantern. Nuggets scattered in and around the shallow stream. As much as he wanted to, he dared not pick one up.

"You've seen enough for now," said Raintree, "let's go on back to the house."

After making their way out of the cave and re-covering the opening, the two returned to the cabin's porch. A welcomed breeze came as they settled into the rocking chairs.

"Now, what you've seen and heard is pretty much the story. Is there any thing else you need to know?'"

"William, you said you have land grant deeds to this land…right?"

"Yes. Eston, knowin' that there could be trouble regardin' ownership got official title from the federal government. Him and his brother-in-law along with their brood of children and grandchildren were about the only ones livin' here at that time. He wanted to make sure that what was left of the tribe kept hold of it."

"What happened to the settlement?"

"Smallpox hit and pretty much wiped out the town. It got Eston's wife along with most everybody else livin' here. He made it to be an old man, but never got over his loss. Now, I'm pretty much all that's left, except for my daughter, Anna…but, she doesn't seem to have much interest."

"Your daughter…does she know about the gold?"

"No."

"Where is she now?"

"She lives in Midfield, up towards Birmingham."

"Does she ever come down here to visit you?"

"Once in a while…not very often."

"You're a very wealthy man, William…and your family can be too."

"That's not the point…"

"I know," Bob interrupted, "this thing goes way beyond gold with you, doesn't it?"

"Yes, sir…way beyond gold. From a time before anybody can remember, my people lived here on this land…they died here and were buried here. This is sacred ground, and not Salvo and his bunch, or nobody else is gonna' take any part of it as long as I'm alive. I swear to this over the graves of my ancestors. Yes, sir, it goes way beyond gold. I don't own this land; I'm just the keeper of it. On this matter, I'm Indian to the bone."

The breeze became more of a wind as high fast-moving clouds shadowed the sun. Bob felt an omniscient presence all around.

"I'll call John before the week is up, William."

# CHAPTER 5

# Bob's Call

"Hi Johnny, it's Bob."

"Hey Bob…long time, no see. How're things up there in 'Roll Tide' country?"

"Doing OK…how about down in Mobile?

"Things are fine here…good to hear from you."

"Got a few minutes to talk?"

"Sure Bob, shoot."

"Go easy with that word, 'shoot' Johnny; my legs get a little shaky just hearing it. That's part of what I want to tell you about."

"Oh, really!"

"Remember our canoe trip down the Cahaba?"

"Yeah, I remember it all right. That was some kind of adventure for a couple of wet-behind-the-ears teenagers, wasn't it?"

"Sure was…remember how we planned to make it to Centerville?"

"Yeah, we just might have made it if it weren't for us fooling around so much…and the catastrophe."

"We had a great time in spite of things, though, didn't we, Johnny?"

"Yep, loads of fun till we panicked after polishing off that surviving can of beans. Some woodsmen we were."

"Remember what a helpless feeling it was, being stuck out there in the middle of nowhere with nothing to eat and not even knowing for sure which direction to take out of there?"

"Yeah, I also remember carrying that damn canoe of yours through the woods for miles until hitting that old dirt road. Sure am glad that guy came by and gave us a ride; otherwise we'd probably still be walking…by the way, have you still got the canoe?"

"Still got the old 'Goldfish'. It's about the only thing Lori didn't want to take with her when she left…so, you do recall the man who gave us a ride?"

"I remember him all right, looked like an Indian except for those extraordinary blue eyes. The color reminded me of one of those Malamute Eskimo dogs."

"There was a little girl too, eight or nine…remember her?"

"Sure…I rode in the back of the pickup with her and the canoe. Must have been his daughter…she had those eyes too. You could tell she was going to be a looker when she grew up."

"Yeah…I think you were right about that, John. Anyway, I'm impressed. That was twenty-one years ago. Sounds like the old memory banks are still working."

"Yeah, funny how I can remember stuff like that, but draw a blank when it comes to last week."

"I know what you mean, Maybe it's because those were less complicated times."

"Probably…anyway, it was nice of him to pick up a couple of raggedy ass kids that he didn't know from Adam."

"OK, John, since your memory's on target, it'll be a lot easier to tell the rest. You know how we were always curious about what was downstream from where we pulled off the river?"

"Yeah. Seems we never got around to going back and finding out, though."

"Well, back in March I did go back."

"Really…you old son-of-a-gun. Wish you had called me. I've been needing a break…big time."

"I started to, but I know how you hot shot lawyers stay busy. It was sort of a spur-of-the moment thing, anyway."

"What was the occasion?"

"Business…some clients of mine had formed a hunting club and wanted me to find them some property they could lease or purchase on or around the river. Most of the land is owned by large timber or mining companies, though. I knew I could forget even trying to deal with them, but while I was searching tax maps I did find a 320 acre tract owned by an individual. The Cahaba flowed right through it. On the map it looked to be eight or so miles further downstream from where we pulled off. The name and address of the owner read: William Raintree, County Road 21, West Blocton, Alabama. There wasn't any phone listing, no neighbors to call, no nothing; so I decided to pull the old 'Gold Fish,' out and take a little trip down the river to find Mr. Raintree and his land. I went alone thinking it might do a little good for the old soul since I was still licking my wounds from the divorce. Anyway, a buddy of mine took 'The Goldfish' and me to the old Helena bridge where you and I put in. I strapped everything down this time."

"How was it on the old Cahaba?"

"Things haven't changed much, except that back when we went in summer, the river was at its normal level…. pretty calm and peaceful. Remember how we could throw a rock across it in most places?"

"Right."

"Well, come to find out that during rainy seasons that thing can become a holy terror in no time…rivaling any of the whitewater streams. It's really sensitive to weather conditions upstream. In fact, I've since heard that last year a couple of experienced kayakers drowned while trying to run it after a heavy rain. Anyway, when I went, the river was up. I mean really up…damn near flood level. The current was so swift all I could do was hang on for the ride. I was barely able to steer and keep the boat upright. Remember those shoal areas we played around in?"

"Yeah."

"Well, they were pure whitewater. I shot through um like a bullet. It was great, Johnny…wish you could have been there."

"Yeah, me too."

"I got to the place we made it to in less than a day. I was so bushed I decided to make camp. In fact, at that very spot we pulled out. It was cold as a witch's tit, but you know me. I was able to get a pretty good night's sleep.

"Yes," said John, "I remember you didn't have too much problem sleeping no matter what was going on around you.".

"Well, anyway, by morning the river had gone down a good bit; so I set out on a more leisurely journey. Not too far downstream I passed a big strip mining operation…coal. They had the area pretty chewed up for the next several miles…not too scenic. But, after passing all of that I was back in the wilderness. Farther down I rounded a bend. The river widened out some and up on the right bank was an old log cabin. I figured that this was the place; so I headed for shore. Unfortunately, I was greeted by a pack of dogs that wanted to tear me to pieces and an old man pointing a shotgun at my head. Things worked out OK, though. He thought I was from a big coal mining outfit that had been pressuring him to sell out to them. Ever heard of Salvo Mining Corporation?"

"No, but I do know a guy down here whose company handles the transfer of coal from barges that come down the Warrior and Tombigbee to ocean going carriers. He may know of them."

"Well, anyway, guess what."

"What?"

"The old man pointing a gun at my head was the same guy who picked us up twenty-one years ago. His name is William Raintree, and he is part Indian."

"No joke. What a coincidence."

"Hold on to your kazoo, John Boy. This is where the story begins."

"Oh, yeah."

"I got a call from Mr. Raintree Monday…this week. I don't know why, but for some reason I was expecting it…. even after five months. He wanted to meet with me immediately. I got with him Tuesday, and we ended up at his place. John, the man's property is loaded with gold. I saw it myself…in a cave."

"You've got to be kidding. Are you sure that what you saw was gold?"

"Well, he gave me three nuggets, and I walked out of a gold dealer's office up in Birmingham with fifteen hundred dollars in cash. Salvo must have found out about it because now they're sending him intimidating letters claiming owner-ship of mineral rights, and intend entering his property to do a geological survey. I told him about you. He wants our help, John. What do you think?"

"Honestly, I don't know what to think. It's one hell of a story, though…I know that."

"The pay would be good; besides we do owe the old fella something for giv-ing us a ride. Seriously, I think Mr. Raintree is in danger. I believe those bastards are determined to get their hands on his property no matter what it takes."

"Have you checked anything out?"

"Yes, I went to the court house and there is indeed a quit-claim deed recorded relinquishing all mineral rights to Salvo Mining Corporation for $3,000. It's dated August 15, 1955, signed by Thomas Raintree, William's father. I'm convinced it's a forgery."

"Why?"

"Well, in the first place, the Raintrees have always been fanatics when it comes to their land. Why would they sell out any rights to it for a few thousand bucks? Besides, Thomas Raintree,

William's father, supposedly signed the deed just a couple of weeks before his death. He had cancer and knew he was dying. William says that he was at his father's bedside taking care of him day and night a whole month before he passed away…and there weren't any visitors. Anyway, does it make sense for a man to do something like that on his deathbed? It just doesn't wash."

"Who notarized the deed?"

"A Mr. Anthony Carthorne, once an employee of Salvo Mining Corporation. I found out that he's been dead for years, but I'll bet his notary seal is still around the office somewhere."

"So, what's your take on this thing?"

"I think either somebody working at the courthouse got their palm greased to back date the stamp and slip it into the records, or someone broke in, probably during the night, and planted it. Wanna' go for it? You know there's some monkey business going on here. I'll do the legwork, and you go for their nuts once we get the evidence. Like I said, the pay should be real good."

"Let me think on it. I'll call you in a few days."

"OK, I'll listen for you. By the way, do you still have the old Spanish helmet?"

"Of course I do. My blood-brother gave it to me."

"Well, that's another part of this crazy story. I'll fill you in later. You take care, John."

"You do the same, Bob."

# Part Two

# CHAPTER 6

# Gilded Circles

"GOLD IN ALABAMA…you've got to be kidding," was the response of John's law partner, Jack Wainwright, after being told of the phone conversation earlier that day.

"I know," said John, "it's the craziest thing I've ever heard of, but Bob isn't the kind who would fabricate something like this…exaggerate things maybe, but not fabricate. He's serious about wanting me to take this thing on."

"Well, I wouldn't touch it, gold or no gold. In the first place…"

"Call for you Mr. Starr," interrupted the secretary's voice over the intercom, "It's Mrs. Starr."

"Hi, Angie."

"Hi Honey," responded the soft, silky voice at the other end, "remember we have that house warming party to go to at the Debarden's this evening. You coming home soon?"

"Oh yeah, I almost forgot. I'm wrapping it up now. 'Be home soon."

"Don't tarry now, bye bye."

"Bye, Angie.

"Damn," mumbled John as he hung up the receiver, "the last thing I want to do is go to a blasted social happening this evening. It's been a long week, and I'm bushed. Besides, I'd planned to take the kids flying tomorrow. Sure would like to hit the sack and get an early start."

"Well, John," chided Jack, "that's what you get for marrying into the blue-bloods of this town."

"Yeah, 'guess so…by the way, let's keep this thing we've been talking about confidential, OK."

"Right, have a good weekend."

"You do the same."

Mobile was an old and cliquish town…old families, old money. Through marriage, not choice, John Starr had landed in the upper crust of society. But, he knew the score before ever taking the leap.

Angie, his wife of ten years, was the only child of Carter and Fannie LeBeau, part of that closed little circle of the social elite.

Dr. LeBeau was friend and physician to much of Mobile's gentry, treating their illnesses, both real and imagined. Fannie, by birthright, was the family's connection to society. She had been born a Jeanerette, among Mobile County's oldest and most prominent families.

This particular evening, it was off to the Debarbens for the well to do…a house warming to celebrate completion of their new home, an eight-thousand-square-foot mansion that complemented twelve prime acres on Mobile bay.

It was well past eight o'clock by the time the Starrs drove up to the gate…running late as usual because of Angie's last minute primping. She paid little attention to time, and time paid little attention to her. John glanced over at her as she rummaged through her purse. She looked great as a thirty-two year old mother of two.

The distinguished looking colored gentleman stationed out front checked their invitation, then pushed the button on a box attached to the stone wall. The wrought iron gates began to slowly open, granting entry into the world of Radell and Gloria Debarden.

About three hundred feet straight ahead, lit up like a monument, stood the huge white structure. Its design was classic Greek Revival, a bigger than life version of the old plantation mansions that once scattered the landscape of the South, complete with six massive three and a half foot thick fluted columns and second story balcony.

"Wonder if they have slave quarters out back?" John remarked.

"Why, Honey, I just bet they do," replied Angie in a calm, yet sarcastic, tone. It was clear that she didn't appreciate John's subtle put-down regarding her friends and their life-style.

By most, the Debardens were held in high regard and considered to be a fine family, known for charitable works and community service. They were just like family to Angie, too. Though not related by blood, she had called them "Uncle Rad" and "Aunt Gloria" all her life.

"Not funny, John," she added.

"Just kidding Angie, just kidding."

According to what John had heard, roots of the family's fortune went back to when cotton was king and slavery was an institution in the Old South. In those days the Debardens operated as stevedores, handling the loading of cotton to ships outbound for Europe. They also brokered incoming cargo from ships that had sailed all the way from Africa. Their customers were big plantation owners like the Jeanerettes, Angie's forbears.

Trade in human chattel on the docks of Mobile was a very lucrative business at that time. Even though the importing of slaves had been legally banned in1808, who would have been crazy enough to try and enforce such a law in an isolated Dixie port like Mobile? The Debardens and Jeanerettes went back a long way in their association with one another.

Rad was the CEO of Debarden Onloading Company (DOC)…a vital link in the chain of oceanic transport. This was what the family business had evolved into. Now, it handled much of the loading and unloading of ships that docked at the Port of Mobile. A large part of DOC business came from the transferring of raw materials, such as coal, from river barges that had come all the way down from north and central Alabama on the Black Warrior and Tombigbee Rivers to huge ocean-going vessels.


Cadillacs, Mercedes and Town Cars lined the driveway that circled in front of the mansion's massive portico. John managed to squeeze the Chevy wagon between two haphazardly parked vehicles and pulled onto the newly sodded St. Augustine lawn.

Childish of me, he thought, but this little act of delinquency served as silent protest for having to give up another evening to the rich and infamous. Angie took no notice. She just seemed glad not to have to walk so far.

As they passed between the massive columns after ascending the six wide steps that lay in front of the mansion's porch, John decided that it was time to lighten up, besides, there may be a good reason to do a little hobnobbing this particular evening. Maybe Rad could shed some light on Mr. Don Salvo, whose coal was probably transferred by DOC at the Port of Mobile.

Three hits on the lion's head knocker, and the double oak doors opened.

"Why, hello Mr. John and Miss Angie. Ya'll come on in."

"Well, hello Beatrice," said Angie, as she gave a hug to the smiling, plumpish, lady of color standing in the doorway, "I just love yall's new house."

"Thank you Miss Angie. Mr. Rad worked hard to get things jus' right."

"Looks like he's even outdone himself this time, Bea," said John with a wink as he eyed the dramatic spiral staircase there in the foyer.

"Yes sir, he sure has," replied Beatrice with a little giggle, and returning wink.

She then escorted the Starrs to the huge ballroom just to the right of the foyer, where the party was in full swing.

They had barely set foot inside when an all too familiar voice pierced the air above the monotonic rumble of conversations going on among the eighty or so mixing, mingling guests.

"Angie, Dahlin', ova' here, ova' here!"

That unmistakable voice with the deep Dixie dialect belonged to Fannie, Angie's mother. And, there she was, over on the other side of the room, waving her gold cigarette holder like a baton. Angie made a beeline in that direction... John in tow.

Fannie LaBeau was a blue-blooded aristocrat...the real thing. This middle age Southern Belle may have been a little past full bloom, but she could still turn heads. Petite, blond and brown-eyed, she looked good for fifty or any other age.

"I was beginnin' to worry about ya'll, Angie. Is every thing OK? Hello, John."

"Hi, Fannie."

"Yes, everything's fine, Mama, we were just running a little bit behind, that's all. What do you think of the place? Isn't it wonderful?"

Fannie picked up the old kaleidoscope, a conversation piece lying on the table next to where they were standing, pointed it toward one of the four Strauss chandeliers that hung from the ceiling, and put it to her eye.

"Well if you ask me," she nonchalantly answered while turning the ornate tube, "it's a bit much for just two people…I do like this, though: it's so colorful, and unpredictable."

John couldn't help but think that in a way Fannie was describing herself as well as the gilded novelty she held in her hand. If, instead of glass, the fragments inside it were made of mood, emotion and impulse, the bits and pieces would, when turned, fall together in an unpredictable display of color. Depending on how turned…or in Fannie's case, flattered, provoked, or just her state of mind at the moment, she could be as charming as a magnolia blossom, or, as thorny as a briar patch…just depending. As of late, Fannie had been more of the latter… probably partly due to menopause, and partly because of a bout with melancholy.

"Where's Daddy?" asked Angie.

"Oh he's out back by the pool talkin' about whatever with Rad and that Horace the Horrid."

"Cousin Horace is here?"

"Yes, your daddy's Cousin Horace is here, all right…causin' embarrassment to our family as usual."

"What do you man, Mama."

"Well, He's shown up here with some half-breed hussy he picked up ova' there in New Orleans…runnin' around, half lit, callin' her his exotic little pussy cat. She's exotic all right…just passin' for white. I know a quadroon when I see one. Not only that, she can't be any older than you, Angie…and, him in his mid fifties and all"

"I guess Cousin Horace is trying to feel young again, Mama. It'll probably all be over with in a few days."

"That doesn't matter. It's a travesty, especially since poor Dodie has been lyin' there in her grave for less than a year."

"Maybe that's his way of grieving, Mama. You know Cousin Horace is harmless for the most part."

"Do you forget so easy, Angie? Don't you remember how he did me at Mardi Gras…humiliatin' me in front of all those people?"

"Mama, he said he was sorry."

"I don't care, I've had enough of that pot-bellied blowfish and his crude manners. I'm going to talk to your daddy about keepin' him away from me and my friends. That man's an embarrassment to our whole family, Angie."

"Now Mama, how many times have you talked to Daddy about cousin Horace? Besides, if it hadn't been for him sending Daddy to school, he wouldn't have been a doctor, and if Daddy hadn't been a doctor, you wouldn't have met him, and if you hadn't met Daddy, you wouldn't have had me...so there yourself."

"Well, I guess I better go find old Horace right now and give him a big smack on his mouth, huh Angie?"

"My, you're in an awfully prickly mood tonight, Mama...is everything all right?"

"Oh, I guess so, Honey, I'm just a little blue. You know, at this time tomorrow, it'll have been thirty-three years since poor Pa Pa's passin.'"

"I know, Mama, but every thing will be all right. 'Looks like it's going be a good get-together tonight. I'm sure Pa Pa would want you to have a good time... I see a lot of new faces."

"Well, that's another thing. It's just not like it used to be. There must be a dozen people here tonight that I don't know or haven't even heard of. Rad just keeps draggin' in this nouveau riche bunch. People like the Vanderfords don't even come to these things anymore. For all I know they might not even have been invited."

"They are in their eighties, Mama, maybe they're just slowing down a bit."

Fannie and Angie chattered on. As usual John was just a bystander. He was used to it, though. The two acted like they hadn't seen each other in a month, when, in fact, they had been together all day, shopping. That's the way it was with Angie and Fannie...not just mother and daughter, but best friends and almost constant companions.

John was well aware that he was not his mother-in-law's choice for Angie. Even so, a polite, yet restrained relation had existed between them through the years.

"See that young man over there, Angie," said Fannie, "the one Gloria's talkin' to? By the way, that new pageboy hairdo makes her look like a dike, doesn't it? I wouldn't have it on my dog, Fifi....anyway, see that man?"

"Yes, Mama, I see the man."

"Well, I heard he's a car salesman…and if that's not bad enough he's a Yankee, too. Rad bought a car from him last year; and now here he is invitin' him to his house."

"Mama, I think that's Terry Wayne. I've seen him on TV doing a commercial. If it is him, he owns one of the biggest car dealerships in South Alabama."

"Well old Rufus Jones cleaned out our septic tank last year, and he owns a fleet of honey-wagons, but I'm not gonna' have him ova' for dinner any time soon…and he's not even a damn Yankee, either. I don't guess it'll be too long before Rad'll start havin' darkies ova'. Maybe he'll even invite them all to join the 'Whale Boners' and put them on the lead Mardi Gras float…I do wish Rad would turn up the air a little bit, either that or hand out some church fans. It's gettin' awfully stuffy in here."

"Be careful with the punch Mama, you know how drinking too much of it gives you those old hot flashes. Let's go over and see Aunt Gloria. I haven't even said hello, have you?"

"Just briefly when your daddy and I first got here. You lead the way, Dear."

"Are you coming, John?" Angie asked.

"No, think I'll go to the bar. I'll catch up with you all later."

CHAPTER 7

# Cast of Characters

THERE WOULD BE no lack of entertainment, food and spirited refreshments at the Debardens this evening. Trays of oysters Rockefeller, shrimp, crab cakes, dips and sauces of all sorts, and a selection of cheeses from around the world graced the hors d'oeuvre table. In the middle sat an exquisite three tiered cut glass punch bowl the size of a number ten washtub. A waterfall of tropical delight, well spiked with rum, flowed and re-circulated over the tiers as guests filled their cups. Bea's special punch was always a hit. The open bar at the end of the ballroom was for those who wanted something stronger.

John made his way there, pasting on a smile and doing a little glad-handing along the way. Though not much of a drinker, he figured maybe a short visit with old Jack Daniels, that smooth Tennessee bourbon, might help him make it through the night.

"Crap," he whispered under his breath. Howard Bartholomew and his wife Trudy were loitering around right in the critical path between him and the bar… just the two he didn't care to see.

Howard was senior partner in the prestigious law firm of Bartholomew, Eyster and Hatch, part of the "Good old boy" network Fannie wanted John to go to work for when he and Angie married. But, instead, he chose to hook up with Jack Wainwright, a maverick lawyer from Connecticut who was twenty years his senior. Jack was an outsider too.

"Hello, John, my boy," greeted Howard, "Haven't seen you around the cou'athouse lately. You been on vacation or somethin'?"

"Hello Howard…Trudy. No," John responded, "no vacation for me. 'Guess we've just been missing each other."

Howard Bartholomew was a pompous windbag. Peering over those half-moon glasses of his while spouting oratory, or worse, giving lecture to those whose presence he graced were among his more obnoxious habits.

Trudy was the consummate socialite, and a dedicated snob…practicing the art of looking down that long nose of hers at the common folk,

How have you been, Trudy?" asked John.

"I've been doing well, thank you," she replied, barely acknowledging his presence, looking around the room with her nostrils flaring as if she smelled something.

"Howard," she said, "I must send the decorator over here to get some ideas before we do one bit of remodeling."

"That partner of yours still playin' footsy with those redbones down in Bayou La Batre?" asked Howard just as John was trying to make a graceful escape.

"Yep, Howard, I guess he's still mixin' it up with those redbones."

Howard Bartholomew despised Jack Wainwright. He never got over losing to Jack in court five years earlier. The case involved an old Creole man who had been defrauded by one of Howard's cronies.

"Well John," Howard said, looking at his watch as if he had an appointment, "it's good seein' you. If you eva' decide to practice law for real, come see me."

"Thanks, Howard, I'll keep that in mind."

As John continued his journey toward the bar, an inner voice blurted: *Thank you, God, for sparing me from getting involved with this guy.* Then he thought…*it might take two shots, maybe even three of old Jack D. to get through this evening.*

Finally, he made it. He ordered his drink and turned towards the ballroom, his elbow resting on the bar.

As he looked out over the cast of characters, his mind drifted to something he once read:

*"She may be the plain and somewhat jealous older sister of New Orleans, but Mobile has something uniquely hers…a social culture the likes of which exists nowhere else, and she is fiercely possessive of it. At the core of it all are the powerful and secretive 'Mystic Societies'. They control everything, from the great masque balls to themes of the parade floats during Mardi Gras."*

It didn't take John Starr long to learn that the 'Mystic Societies' not only ran the parties…they ran the town.

Many of the evening's guests were 'Whale Boners.' This group got its name when Otto Debarden, in 1840, happened upon the mostly skeletal remains of a whale carcass that had washed ashore out on Dauphin Island. He took thirteen vertebrae and distributed them among his closest friends and associates. Family names like Bartholomew, Vanderford, and Jeanrette were charter members. The old bones became treasured heirlooms and were passed down through the generations. Fannie used the one she inherited as an ashtray.

As John scanned the ballroom while sipping on his bourbon mixed with a little coke, his eye caught Sophie, Angie's conniving, gossip-mongering, and unmarried cousin. She was over by the punch bowl, involved in an animated gum-flapping session with a small group of fair ladies. No doubt, this flock of cackling hens was spreading the latest gossip.

Sophie was Angie's age, but it had become apparent that she would probably leave the world an old maid…*and no wonder,* thought John, swirling the ice in his drink.

And, there George was, Rad and Gloria's Son.

"Oh no," muttered John. George had spotted him and was headed his way.

"Well hello, John, You're looking good. Of course you always look good, a little tired maybe, but good."

"Hi, George, you look well yourself…how's the project going?"

John had no idea of what George had going on, but it was a safe question since he was always involved in some kind of project, all of which were doomed to failure. But at least it kept him from being idle…and totally worthless.

"Well, John," George lamented, "it would be going a lot better if everybody would do their damn job. I swear, you can't depend on anybody these days. That ass hole of a carpenter we hired to build the sets was supposed to have had them finished two weeks ago, but he's gone fishin' or something. We started off building them ourselves, but Ted cut his finger off with the skill saw on the very first board. Almost got his privates, too. After the pinkie went, the saw flew out of his hand and hit him right in the crotch. Only thing that saved him was that the saw blade guard snapped shut before it hit him. It was awful…blood all over the place. We did save the finger, though. I carried it myself in a paper towel. You know, that damn thing twitched all the way to the hospital. They were able to re-attach it…thank goodness. Well anyway, that cost us a month right there."

George never put a period at the end of his sentences. He just rattled on. This time the project was a play written by his friend Ted, to be produced by George, and financed, of course, by the Dedardens. It was to premier in Mobile to a select audience with invitations sent to some supposed New York theater hot shots…airfare and hotel accommodations included.

'Today Mobile, next stop Broadway.' This is the way it was to go…at least in George's mind.

Hard to believe, thought John, seeing how things turned out. At one time Fannie had big plans for Angie and George. She had hoped to finally forge a blood bond between the Jeanerettes and the Debardens, and put a great deal of effort into promoting a relationship between the two…that is, until George came out of the closet. On his twentieth birthday he casually announced to his parents that he was gay.

They say that Fannie was highly disappointed. But, Rad Debarden was devastated. Beyond unspeakable humiliation to the family, he had lost his only son to a world beyond his comprehension. Rad's heir apparent was no more.

It must have been tough on George too, thought John, revealing what he felt he had to…knowing that it would change everything. Maybe George's blasé attitude was just a defense mechanism to help him through it.

According to what John had heard, Gloria made a lame attempt to console her husband by saying "Better this than him being dead." Rad never replied.

Eventually things settled into some unspoken perspective, and life went on for the Debardens…like with everybody else. According to Bea, the subject was never discussed again.

As George chattered on, standing there with his hand on his hip, holding a cigarette between his thumb and index finger, palm up, John spotted Angie and Fannie out of the corner of his eye, mid-way across the ballroom, in conversation with Gloria, the evening's hostess…and the car salesman, Terry Wayne.

Adrianne, George's twenty-five-year-old sister, was conspicuously absent. From the party.

"I haven't seen Adrianne tonight, George," interrupted John, "is she OK?"

"No, sad to say. As usual Adrianne has stirred up a hornet's nest. Right now, she's over in a trailer park shacked up with one of Daddy's employees…some redneck dockhand. Daddy's furious. I don't know what he's gonna' do. That girl…I swear, she doesn't do anything but cause trouble for this family."

"Yeah, George, I know how much trouble kids can be for parents."

# CHAPTER 8

# Pull My Finger

WHILE JOHN WAS being held hostage by the likes of Howard and George, Fannie and Angie made their way toward the evening's hostess...and Mr. Terry Wayne.

"Well hello again Fannie...hi Angie," said Gloria in her usual gracious manner, "Glad you all could make it tonight."

"Gloria dear, your place is simply divine," praised Fannie, dripping with all the grace and charm of a refined Southern Lady, "I know you were glad to finally move in."

"Thank you Fannie, and yes I'm glad to finally get in here. It took six months longer to build than it was supposed to. I was beginning to wonder if it was ever going to get finished."

"It's so-o beautiful, Aunt Gloria, just like something out of a fairytale book."

"I'm glad you like it Angie. It's all pretty much Rad's doings...Ladies, this is Terry Wayne. Terry, this is Fannie LeBeau and Angie Starr. Guess who's mother and who's daughter."

"Well, Gloria, that'd be mighty hard to do," responded Terry with a Cheshire cat grin and unconvincing attempt at a southern accent.

Angie immediately extended her hand, "Hi, I'm Angie, the daughter."

"Hello Angie," he said, looking her square in the eyes as he took her hand. Fannie took notice of the lingering squeeze.

"And, you must be Fannie. It's a pleasure to meet you both."

"The pleasure's mine, I'm sure, Mr. Wayne," replied Fannie in a rather formal and cool manner. She didn't extend her hand.

"How long have you lived in Mobile, Mr. Wayne?" she asked.

"Five years. I guess you could say I'm a Mobilian now."

"One has to have been born under an azalea bush to be Mobilian, Mr. Wayne."

"Ahh, of course."

"What do you do, Mr. Wayne?"

"Oh, I'm a car salesman, Mrs. LeBeau. I sell Lincolns. Do you drive one?"

"No, we own Cadillacs. I could hardly drive an automobile named after the man who tried to destroy the South, now could I?"

"You know Mrs. LeBeau, that's exactly what my granddaddy said when he was asked to add Lincolns to his inventory…he was a car salesman too. But, old Henry Ford himself told Grandpaw that the Lincoln automobile was not named after Abe, but another Lincoln…a good old southern boy."

"Well, I neva' heard that one before," said Fannie. Then, after a brief silence she dropped her head slightly, peered up at Terry with a devilish look in those brown eyes of hers and extended her index finger: "Now that you've pulled my leg, Mr. Wayne, how bout you pullin' my finga'?"

A puzzled look came over Terry's face.

"Go ahead, pull my finga."

And, that's what Terry Wayne did…pulled Fannie's finger.

*"Phssph,"* came from her ruby red lips, making a sound like someone breaking wind.

"Mama!" Angie cried out.

Gloria just stood there with her mouth open.

As John Starr once commented…"Sometimes being in the company of Fannie was like chasing a martini with a salty dog."

"Touché, Madam," said Terry Wayne, "it seems you have the advantage…I yield. Please call me Terry: I'd like to call you Fannie, if that would be OK."

"That'll be fine Mr…Terry."

"Say, if you ladies don't have any thing planned for tomorrow, I'd love for you, and your husbands, of course, to join me aboard my new boat. I plan to take her for a spin out in the gulf. Think you all can make it?"

"Oh, I'd love to. What about it, Mama?"

"Well… I don't know…I suppose we can, if…"

"Good, she's docked at the yacht club. Just look for the Fiddle-De-Dee. How about one o'clock?"

"We'll check with the men-folk," said Fannie, "and let you know before the evening is ova'…Speakin' of which, Angie, we better go check and make sure they're stayin' outta' trouble. It was a pleasure making your acquaintance."

"Mine too," added Angie.

"The pleasure's mine, Ladies"

"By the way, Gloria, I just love your new hairdo."

"Why, thank you Fannie; George's new friend did it for me."

They were barely out of earshot when Angie lit into her mother like a fly on cow dung.

"Mama, I can't believe you…being so rude to Terry…and you have the gall to talk about Cousin Horace being crude."

"I was just havin' a little fun with that Yankee boy…besides, he started it with that tall tale of his."

"And, another thing, Mama, why did you tell Gloria that you loved her new hairdo after telling me less than half an hour ago that she looked like a dyke in it…and wouldn't have it on your dog?"

"I do love Gloria's new hairdo, Angie…as long as it's on her, and not on Fifi…now, hush up. Don't go ruinin' my evenin' just when I'm startin' to feel better. "

"Oh, Mama, you just won't do…Terry was nice though, wasn't he? Tall, tan and handsome, too. I wonder if he's married."

"Well, what I saw was tall, tan and slick as owl droppin's. You know, Angie, you've always been a bit naive. Don't you know a Chameleon when you see one?"

# CHAPTER 9

# Oil and Water

As GEORGE RATTLED on, Fannie and Angie walked up…much to John's relief.

"Hello, George, Dahlin'," how are you?"

"You don't want to know, Fannie," started George, "I was just tellin' John…"

"You can tell us another time, Dear. Right now we have to go see your father. Come along, John."

"Oh…OK, I'll talk to you all later," lisped George. "Take care, John. Hello Angie…bye bye, Angie."

The threesome walked away, leaving George casually looking over the crowd…no doubt in search of another hostage.

"I think you owe us one, John Starr…for the rescue," Fannie remarked as she led the way toward the big French doors that opened out back to the patio and pool.

It would have been hard to overlook Rad Debarden in a crowd. He stood a lean, lanky six-foot-four inches, and looked more like a stern schoolmaster than a social elitist. With quiet reserve, this fifty-eight-year-old "lord-of-the-manner" viewed his world through deep-set iron-gray eyes that gave little clue as to what he was thinking. Rad was a man of few words. He expressed himself more through action and grandiose statements…like the opulent palace he had built for himself.

This was a night of coronation. Without verbal proclamation, G. Radell Debarden crowned himself "king of the hill" among Mobile's elite.

Rad, Carter LeBeau and Horace Blair stood by the pool engaged in conversation. Appearance gave little clue that these three were among the most influential men in Mobile County.

John could not have asked for a better father-in-law. Carter LeBeau was a most pleasant man, both in appearance and character. The good doctor's bedside manners were for real. He seemed to radiate good will and compassion. At fifty-seven, he may have been a little paunchy in the mid-drift, balding and suffering from a mild heart condition, but there wasn't a wrinkle in his face. Carter not only practiced medicine, but also humility…evidently having never forgotten where he had come from. Both he and his first cousin, Horace, were sons of sharecroppers.

Horace Blair was cut from a different cloth. This frumpy, overweight one-man brass band was loud and most of the time out of tune…at least socially. Not only did he ignore the rules of etiquette so important in Mobile high society, it was debatable as to whether such things even registered with him. Horace may have looked and acted like a vacuum cleaner salesman, but inside that bumpkin head of his pulsed a razor sharp mind…one that had been put to good use. From the scorching cotton fields of South Alabama, Horace Blair rose to become chief executive officer and chairman of the board of Gulf States Savings and Loans Association. It was his baby. He was its founder, and since 1946 had been in total control. He was a country boy made good.

Many of the old guard considered, Horace, the nouveau riche self-inflating extrovert, to be vulgar and boorish. But, it would be hard to shun the man who held a mortgage on one's home.

Ashes flew from the cigarette mounted in Fannie's golden holder as she flung her left hand out to the side. With Angie and John tagging along behind, she approached the threesome:

"I sweah, what do you men folk huddle up and talk about, anyway? Rad, dahlin', your place is simply divine. I do believe I'm a little envious."

"Hello Fannie," replied Rad in his usual cool, soft spoken manner.

Horace was deaf in his left ear from an injury suffered in World War II… perhaps one of the reasons he talked so loud. After a brief delay, before realizing who had come up on his backside, he turned around to face Fannie, and it started…like so many times before.

"Well if it ain't sister Fannie, little Angie, and big bad John," he blurted, having had enough drink to be even more boisterous than usual, "I haven't seen ya'll since Mardi Gras. How's everybody doin', anyway?"

"Well," Fannie fired, "in the first place, Horace Blair, I'm not your sista'… thank God for that, and in the second place, not seein' you since Mardi Gras hasn't been long enough, thank you.…and, in the third place, I'm doin' fine. In spite of all that, how are you?"

"Not too bad for the son of a share-cropper, Fannie girl. You girls come ova' here and give ole' Horace some sugar."

Angie adored Horace. Ever since she was a little girl, he and Dodie, who were childless, would lavish her with gifts and surprises on birthdays, at Christmas and just about any other occasion. Angie immediately gave him a kiss on his ruddy-red cheek.

"How 'bout that sugar, Fannie."

"You won't be getting' any suga' from me."

"I told you I was sorry for that Mardi Gras thing, but you just won't let it go, will you?"

"Maybe you wouldn't let it go either if somebody got on a microphone and called you a hooka'."

"I didn't call you a hooker. I said you looked as good as one of them Saint Francis Street hookers. That was a compliment, Fannie girl…some of those girls look pretty good."

"Well, I guess you should know."

"Anyway, you didn't have cause to kick me in my leg. It stayed swollen for two weeks."

"Well, you betta' be glad you didn't get it in the family jewels…so there!"

John recalled the incident: it took place at a big Mardi Gras gala. As usual, after having a few drinks, Horace took over the bandstand, sang his version of "I didn't Know God Made Honky Tonk Angels," and told a couple of jokes. From the stage, he spotted Fannie coming out of the bathroom. That's when the infamous remark was made: "Boys," he said, "There goes that Fannie LaBeau. She looks as good as one of them Saint Francis Street hookers, don't she?" It blasted out all over the place, followed by a barrage of whistles and catcalls.

Though not defending Horace's heinous act, John did see more than a glimmer of truth in his remark. Fannie was flashy…from her makeup to the golden locks she wore up in a style someplace between Grecian and barmaid. Also, there were the dresses that brought a lot of attention to those shapely legs of hers. Truth was, the woman did look as good as any Saint Francis Street hooker.

"Now, I'll say it again Missy," said Horace, "I am sorry! Now, how 'bout at least a hug?"

Horace opened his arms for the embrace as Fannie approached. "Now, that's better," he said.

There was, however, no embrace…only a solid shove.

During his backward descent into the pool, Horace let out a howl that added vibrato to the Mozart Concerto playing over the patio speakers. Everyone quickly moved back to avoid being drenched by the splash.

"Now, Busta' Brown," Fannie said, "I suppose we're even."

As Horace gasped and spurted water, Carter rushed to the edge of the pool. He reached down, grabbed his hand and pulled…but Horace's weight was too much. Carter spiraled head over heels and joined his cousin in the drink.

As the two stood there, facing each other in waist-deep-water, Horace blurted, "Carter, are you ever gonna' tell that woman of yours the truth of the matter?"

Carter immediately submerged himself, acting as if he didn't hear what was said.

"The truth of what matter?" Fannie yelled.

"Ask your husband!" Horace yelled back.

Within moments, Gloria was on the scene. "Fannie, Angie," she said, obviously trying to cool things down, "let's go out back to see the art studio Rad built for me. Bea will take care of those two."

"Come on, Mama," said Angie as she ushered Fannie away…following Gloria, "time for a little walk."

John saw the window of opportunity he had been waiting for. Rad had quietly dismissed himself from the commotion and was standing alone at the edge of the patio, looking out towards the bay.

"Looks like things got a little out of hand," said John.

"Yes, its always unpredictable when those two get together. They're like oil and water."

"Rad, have you ever heard of a big time coal mining operator up in North Central Alabama by the name of Don Salvo?"

"Yes, matter of fact, DOC has a contract with Salvo Mining Company to transfer coal from their barges to ocean-going coal carriers."

"Do you know Salvo personally?"

"Yes, I know Don. Why do you ask?"

"Oh, no real reason. His name came up while I was talking to a friend of mine today…what kind of fellow is he, anyway?"

"Well, he's aggressive… and tough. It took a while to hammer out the details of our contract with him."

"I heard he's self-made."

"Yes, he is. Don was raised dirt poor in the mining camps up in Walker County. He worked in the mines, saved enough money to buy an old steam shovel and dump truck, then struck out on his own. The rest is history. He pioneered strip mining in Alabama. Are you having some dealings with him?"

"No, just curious…that's all. Sounds like an interesting man."

"Yes, he is…interesting."

John couldn't put his finger on it exactly, but definitely detected some uneasiness in Rad. He dropped the subject of Don Salvo.

"There you all are," said Angie as she approached.

" Everything OK?" John asked.

"Oh yes, Mama just got a little beside herself…that's all. She's in the laundry room with Bea, ironing out Daddy and Cousin Horace's clothes. Aunt Gloria said there was a pretty spot, with a gazebo, down by the bay. Can I borrow John long enough to walk me down there, Uncle Rad."

"Sure Angie, you all be watchful, though, the gardener killed a snake down there a few days ago."

# Chapter 10

# John and Angie

From the direction of the bay, a full moon loomed through the live oaks and Spanish moss…still low enough so as not to diminish stars that mapped the late summer sky. John and Angie made their way down the little oyster shell path, lit by frog lights on either side. Azaleas bordered the path. Ahead, stood the domed gazebo, giving off a warm white incandescence from the small floodlights that surrounded it. Climbing roses intertwined its trellised railing.

John took Angie's hand. It was up two steps and they entered. A cushioned Romanesque lounge stood out among the other furnishings.

"I do believe this is the best part of the whole spread," he remarked, breathing in deeply to catch the subtle hint of roses.

"It is nice," she responded.

The bay was just beyond a sparse grove of oaks and magnolias, and almost in full view. Lights spread along the distant opposite shore, and on the dark waters, lanterns glowed here and there from the boats of fishermen. The air was filled with the songs of crickets and frogs.

"It's nice here away from everybody, Angie. I like it when it's just you and me…like it used to be…remember? I miss those days."

Angie looked back at him. She smiled, but there were no words.

His hands settled on either side of her waist. He pulled her to him, and they began to dance, slowly, face to face in the dim glow. As he often used to, John wondered at the soft perfection that was Angie. She was just as beautiful as ever, and the moment served as a reminder of what had drawn him to her in the first place. Then came the kiss…like the one that started it all.

John and Angie met at the University of Alabama…in Tuscaloosa. It was 'sixty-four…fall semester. Angie was a freshman. John was back to complete his studies in law after serving a two-year hitch in the Army. He originally came to the university in 'fifty-nine.

John had seen Angie around campus several times during the first few months of the semester. It would have been hard not to notice this gorgeous ashen blond. She was five-foot- four inches of smooth sensuous curves with an incredible face… an extraordinary blend of the girl next door and some erotic fantasy.

One freezing December morning, a water line had burst under a walkway at the west end of the Quad…under Denny Chimes, the campus bell tower. The area was a mess from all the digging. There was mud and water all over the place. Angie was standing there, looking at the makeshift boards laid down by the workmen when John walked up.

"Need some help?"

"Oh, hi," she replied, "No, I don't guess so…but I just know I'm going to fall in that ditch if I try to go across on those rickety old boards."

"No you won't. Here, hold my books."

With that he picked her up and sloshed across to the other side.

"My, if it's not Sir Galahad," she said as he put her down.

"Well, maybe so, but I'm afraid my armor's a little rusty. I'm John Starr."

"I'm Angie LaBeau."

"Nice to meet you, Angie."

For a brief silent moment their eyes fixed, and the wispy puffs of vapor from her breath mingled with his in the frigid air.

"Well," said John, "we don't want to be late for class, I'll see you around, Angie."

"I sure hope so," she replied, "thanks for the lift…Galahad."

John had just landed a part time job at Amelia Gayle Gorgas Library, the main one on campus. It was a good job that allowed him to study some while on duty.

Two weeks had passed since his encounter with Angie, and it was just two days before the Christmas break.

At about six in the evening she came strolling into the library.

"Well, hello, Sir Galahad, I've wondered where you've been."

"Hi Angie," he said, trying not to let the adrenalin rush be obvious, "I've wondered where you've been, too. Guess our timing's been a little off."

"Well, I'll have you know that I've had to cross that old ditch by myself every day till they finally covered it up. I couldn't let just any old Tom, Dick or Harry carry me across."

"I hope you didn't fall."

"No…at least not in the ditch…OK, will you slay an old dragon for me this time?"

"Sure, if I can…what dragon?"

"It's called Algebra 101. This textbook is impossible. Do you have something around here that's a little simpler, maybe something that would make it easier for me to understand?"

"No, but I do know a little bit about the subject."

"Oh, I can't ask you to help me. I'm sure you're busy with your own things."

"Actually, I'm fixing to get off. Tell you what, if you're game, we'll grab a hamburger, and go to my place. Bet I can get you up and running in no time… you hungry?"

"Starving."

"There's a new burger joint in town. Suppose to have drive-through service. I think it's called McDonalds, or something like that…want to try it?"

"Sure, let's go for it."

They took off in John's old '57 Chevy. Angie's Mustang stayed parked at the library.

John lived in a concrete block flat over on the other side of town. The place was pretty run-down and within a hundred feet of a railroad track, but it served the purpose.

"Well, this is Galahad's castle," he jokingly remarked while getting the key out from under a rock next to the front door.

"Why do you live way out here all by yourself, John Starr?"

"Oh, I don't know…I guess being a little older and all. Besides, I concentrate better when I'm by myself."

"How old are you, anyway?"

"Twenty-three, how old are you?"

"Nineteen…you must have gotten a late start in college."

"Well, I came here in '59, but left in the summer of '60 for the army. Now I'm back to finish up."

"What's your major?"

"Law."

"Well…I'm impressed."

"Where are you from, Angie?"

"Mobile…and you?"

"Birmingham."

"Always remember," said John as they sat on the couch munching hamburgers with the algebra book open across their laps, "anything you do on one side of the equal sign, you have to do to the other side. If you add a number to one side, you have to add it to the other side. Same for subtracting or anything else you do. This keeps the equation in balance. That's what the equal sign means: one side is the same as the other side, even though it's expressed in different ways. See what I mean?"

"How did you get to be so smart?"

"A buddy of mine explained it to me back in high school. He's a math whiz and can explain things in their simplest terms.

"Who is it?"

"His name is Bob Savage."

"Is he in school here?"

"No, he's over in the enemy camp."

"What do you mean?"

"He goes to Auburn."

"Oh…Auburn, enemy camp…I get it," she giggled.

"You know, some of the girls in my sorority think you're the best looking guy on campus. They call you the mystery man, though."

"Oh yeah, why's that?"

"Well, because nobody sees you unless it's on the way to class. You're never anywhere, not even at football games."

"Well, I don't get out much. At this point all I want to do is finish school and get to work."

"You've got a girlfriend up in Birmingham…don't you?"

"No, no girlfriends. But, you've got a boyfriend…right?"

"At least a hundred," she said with a laugh, "but none of them count."

Angie's full perfect lips were like a magnet, and John Starr felt himself being drawn to them. She was so close, and he was almost there…

"You've got mustard on your chin," she said.

"Huh?" he garbled.

"Come here," she said, moistening a napkin with her tongue, and gently patting his chin like a mother would her child.

"Well, that's one way to lose control," he mumbled.

"No, you just had mustard on your chin…that's all."

Then, with his face clasped in her hands, she leaned forward and kissed him. He felt the rush as her mouth melded with his. Never, could he have imagined the softness that was Angie's lips. It was the kiss…the one that started it all.

As a child, John would now and then pick rose-petals from the bush in his backyard and put them to his lips. The sensation gave him comfort and pleasure. Angie's softness reminded him of that.

The tattered algebra book fell to the floor as he stood and took her hand. He led her across the threshold into the adjoining room.

The old space heater bathed the bedroom in a warm orange glow as shadows on the wall told the rest. John and Angie became lovers that night.

She lay there staring at the ceiling, totally unveiled, nothing left for him to imagine.

"Well, there goes my virginity," she said, "and I don't even know you."

"Any regrets?" he asked while tracing the soft, smooth curves of her body with his fingertips.

"No, but you're stuck with me now, you know."

"Damn, just when I was getting used to being a recluse."

It was almost midnight…much too late for Angie to go back to the sorority house.

"Well, John Starr, looks like I'm gonna' have to stay over. Guess I'll sleep on the couch, huh?"

"Right," he said, nibbling her ear.

The new lovers drifted in and out of sleep that night…snuggling, cuddling, kissing, touching…existing in a hazy world somewhere between dreams and reality.

As usual, in the wee hours of the morning, a train came rumbling through shaking the little cottage. John, half-awake, glanced over at the old iron helmet that sat on top of the dresser across the room. It trembled from the vibration.

"Looking for Buddy?" he mumbled.

There wasn't much of a morning after. The mid-morning train roared down the tracks and woke them both.

"What time is it?" Angie asked.

"Almost Ten."

"Oh, no! I've missed my eight o'clock algebra class"

"Yeah, I've missed my contract law class.

"What should we do?"

"Well, to hell with it," said John, "let's just play hooky today. Tomorrow's our last day before Christmas break anyway."

"Why, that's a wonderful idea, Mr. Starr."

"You drink coffee?" he asked.

"Couldn't live without it."

"I'll go make us a pot."

"Sounds great."

John was in the tiny kitchen, filling the percolator with water when he caught the earthy mixture of scents emitting from his skin…He could smell and taste them…a subtle hint of perfume, a faint taste of lipstick, and that indefinable scent of humanness that lingers afterwards…remnants from the night before.

He served coffee and toast with a kiss. They sat across the room from each other, he in the armchair, she on the sofa…he in his briefs, she in his bathrobe.

"Why do you keep smelling your hand, Honey?" she asked.

"Oh, no reason…want some more coffee?"

The morning time Angie looked great. In fact, the sleepy-eyed girl with rumpled hair and no makeup sitting across from him was even more appealing than the one he carried across the mud hole two weeks earlier.

He studied her every feature…her eyes, lips and nose, the shape of her face, the well-turned calves protruding from his robe…he drank it all in.

"I know I probably look like a hag," she said, running her fingers through her tousled hair.

"You know, Angie," he said, looking at the wall clock, "Its almost noon. Maybe you should call your house-mother and let her know that everything's OK."

"You're right. Guess I better."

"Oh, God," she said, hanging up the phone after talking to Mrs. Hatfield, the housemother. "My mother called last night…and this morning. Now they've got the police looking for me. I've got to call Mama…can I?"

"Call your mother, Angie."

It was obvious the other end picked up on the first ring.

"Hi, Mama."

"Yes, everything's OK. I just spent the night with a friend and we overslept, that's all.

"No, Mama."

"Yes, Mama."

Right in the middle of Angie's "yes's and no's," came a rapid pounding at the door.

"Yes Mama, I'll be home tomorrow. I've gotta' go, there's somebody at the door. Bye now."

"Just a minute," John called out as he jumped into his jeans. Angie shot toward the bedroom. The pounding continued.

"'Who is it?"

" Police! Open the door!"

There was two of them, one heavy set, and the other tall and lanky.

"Are you John Starr?" asked the tall one.

"Yes, sir, what can I do for you?"

"We're looking for an Angie LeBeau. Somebody said she was with you last night."

Angie walked out of the bedroom. "Are you looking for me officer?" she said, acting surprised. "I'm Angie LeBeau."

"There's been a missing persons report filed on you Miss LeBeau. May we see your driver's license?"

She rambled through her purse, finally finding it.

"Are you here of your own free will Miss LeBeau?" asked the big cop.

"Yes, I am, officer."

"Well, the next time you decide to stay out all night and half the next day, maybe you should let somebody know, OK."

"You can count on that officer."

"Good day," said the tall one. Then, they left without further discussion.

"Angie," asked John, "how did anybody know you were with me last night?"

"Well, my cousin, Sophie, said you were working at the library, and I wanted to see you…so there. And, I really was looking for a simplified algebra book."

"Come here silly girl: give me a kiss. I'm gonna' miss you over the holidays."

"I'm gonna' miss you too, John Starr."

John peeked into the bedroom and looked at the helmet that sat there in still silence on the dresser. He gave a wink. "You caused this, didn't you?" he mouthed. Then he turned to her.

"'Tell you what, Angie, let's have our own private Christmas and New Year's here tonight. We'll get a tree and some decorations, and listen to Christmas music on the radio…you never know what else might happen. 'How bout it?"

"You are one creative man, John Starr. That's two wonderful ideas in one day."

"Let's get a couple of steaks, too," he added.


They trimmed the tree and burnt the streaks, but it didn't matter. The wine and popcorn went well together. They danced to Elvis's 'I'll have a Blue Christmas without You,'

"Its true, Angie whispered in his ear, "I will have a blue Christmas without you."

"So will I, Angie…so will I."

The next day, Angie left for Mobile, and John left for Birmingham.

CHAPTER 11

# Blue Christmas

THE KISS LINGERED there in the gazebo on that hot August night of 1977. As John held Angie close, his mind continued to wander to an earlier time…when it was just the two of them.

The Christmas break of '64 seemed to last an eternity. John could hardly wait to get back to school…and Angie. The girl from Mobile had unexpectedly turned his life around…suddenly, from loneliness, to a world of possibilities.

His mother, Florence, was a war widow. John Sr., a fighter pilot serving in World War II, was shot down over the Pacific Ocean in '44 and presumed dead. John was only three at the time.

During his growing up years he didn't take notice that his mother never went out or dated. Only later did he learn that she had purposefully put her life on hold for him. Uncle Ralph, Florence's brother, told him that she had been determined to raise him without anyone's influence or interference.

Now, his mother was remarried. John came to find out that she and, Joe, her new husband, had known each other for years. Both worked at Social Security in downtown Birmingham. Joe was now head of the household where John and his mother, just the two of them, had spent so many years together.

John couldn't help but think back to the times when as a young boy he would sit on his mother's bed and study every detail of his father's photograph there on her nightstand. Then, while alone in his own bed, he would pray that his father had somehow survived, and was living on some Pacific island like Robinson Crusoe…and would one day be rescued and come home.

One day, the photograph disappeared. He was eighteen and just graduated from high school. That's when he knew it was time to move on.

Joe was a nice guy, and John was genuinely glad that his mother had a second chance at happiness. Any childish twinge that his father's memory had been betrayed would just have to be put to rest.

His mother and stepfather did everything they could to make him feel welcome and comfortable. And, he did feel welcome, but this place wasn't home anymore.

He walked the neighborhood where he and Bob Savage once roamed, and got in touch with some old memories. Bob wasn't around. He was at Auburn University with his new bride. She wasn't exactly new…Bob ended up marrying the first girl he ever dated.

There were a couple of places he wanted to visit while on Christmas break. One was a spot on the crest of the mountain called Lover's Leap. Its solid rock bluff afforded a fifteen-mile view. Sunsets were spectacular.

As a teenager, he often went there alone, just to take in the view, strum on his guitar…and think.

The other place he wanted to visit was a small woodland valley where he and Bob first met and played as boys.

The valley remained unchanged. Waters from the creek that ran through it rushed over rocks and boulders as it always had. It brought on great nostalgia.

As an adolescent, John had conjured up an imaginary wood nymph he always hoped to see when he went there. He took a lot of ribbing from Bob about it, but still, he was always hoping to at least catch a glimpse of her.

Maybe Angie was his nymph. Maybe she was what he had been looking for all along. Thoughts of her never left his mind. He truly was having a Blue Christmas.

Finally, Christmas break came to an end. John's old '57 Chevy had a 283 engine in it. That thing would fly, and he kept her on eighty most of the way down Highway 11 from Birmingham to Tuscaloosa. It took less than an hour to get there.

He pulled up to his place. Angie's Mustang was parked out front.

She met him at the door, threw her arms around him and delivered a barrage of staccato kisses.

"I hope you had as lonely and miserable a Christmas as I did," she said.

"You better believe I did, Sweetheart," he replied.

That evening, after engaging in what lovers do, they snuggled up on the couch with the photo album she brought with her.

"Now, that's my mama and daddy."

"Wow, your mom is a fox. I see where you got your looks from."

"Well, she may look like a fox, but she can be a big bad wolf when she wants to…here's Cousin Horace and his wife Dodie. They're my favorite relatives. Every Christmas and birthday, when I was a little girl, Cousin Horace brought me a sack full of brand new shiny quarters. Now he sends me a savings bond. I liked it better when he brought the quarters."

"She looks familiar," he said, pointing to the photograph of a plain unsmiling girl wearing horn-rimmed glasses.

"Oh, that's my cousin, Sophie. She goes to school here, too."

"Yeah, I think she snubbed me at the library when I was trying to help her find a book."

"She can be a little strange sometimes, but she's OK."

"Who's that gorgeous doll in the evening dress standing next to the skinny guy?"

"You know that's me, Silly."

"Well, who's the skinny guy?"

"That's Georgie, my boy friend."

"Boy friend!"

She laughed. "Not to worry, he's just a friend of the family. Besides, he's on the (She flipped her hand in an effeminate manner) side."

"What was the occasion? Oh, it was my coming out party."

"Coming out party! You mean I'm sitting here with a debutante?"

"Well, I just guess you are Mr. Starr, just like I'm sitting here with a…," she giggled and poked him in the ribs.

In the months that followed, Angie spent most her time at John's little cottage by the tracks. Cousin Sophie was to cover for her in case of emergencies or unexpected occurrences, like the one before Christmas break. The password was,

'Please page Angie LeBeau,' as if she were in the library. John had not formally met Sophie, but the rude encounter with her at the library had been enough. He didn't trust her, but it was Angie's call to make such an arrangement.

As summer break approached, Angie made the decision to enroll in summer school…to be with John.

"My parents seemed a little shocked when I told them," she said, "of course they don't know about us…yet."

Both of the 'schoolies' took light loads; so they could have more time to play…and play they did…sometimes with wreckless abandon.

As they danced to the frogs' and crickets' songs on that hot summer night in 1977, it seemed almost like old times to John, just the two of them, away from the crowd.

"Remember when," he said, "when we met…the night we first made love, and the crazy things we did back then?"

"Yes," Angie responded, " I remember…I think I was way too easy."

"No, Sweetheart. It was just us falling in love."

He led her to Romanesque lounge, and set her down.

"What do you think? Should we christen this place?"

# CHAPTER 12

# Christenings

IT WAS THE summer of 1964.

John had read that Moundville Archaeological Park, about twelve miles south of Tuscaloosa, was a good place to picnic on a Sunday afternoon. Located on the banks of the Black Warrior River, it was the site of an ancient Indian settlement. Its inhabitants, part of a culture called 'Mississippians', mysteriously disappeared centuries ago, leaving twenty-six large earthen mounds scattered about on 300 acres as the only evidence of their existence…that and their bones.

"Can you feel it, Angie…the history of this place?"

"Well, I feel that old mosquito bite I got awhile ago."

"Seriously, baby, this is hallowed ground. They shouldn't have dug into the graves of these people and put their skeletons on display for the public to gawk at."

"You're absolutely right, Honey. Let's go for a walk so you won't get so upset looking at these old bones."

John's concerns of desecration didn't stop him, however, from leading Angie to the top of the highest mound, fifty-eight feet, where they made love…in broad daylight with tourists milling around below. They called this little irreverent activity of theirs, "christening."

No place was above being "christened"…from the hallowed halls of Amelia Gayle Gorgas Library to the local cemetery.

While sitting under a picnic pavilion located on the thirty-or-so-foot-high bank above the river, they heard the distant yelping of what sounded like a puppy.

"Look, John!" Angie shouted, pointing out towards the river.

The puppy was clinging to an old wooden crate drifting on the slow moving currents about fifty feet from shore.

Half tumbling down the steep bank, John hit the water, shoes and all, and began swimming. After the rescue, he made his way back up the bank with the shaking little dog.

"Looks like we've got us a puppy," said John, as Angie, with her skirt, gingerly dried the mostly Shepherd, but definitely Heinz variety canine.

"Sure looks that way, Honey…and it's a boy! What about a name?"

"Well, how about 'Warrior,' since we found him floating in the Warrior River."

"We're not going to call this sweet little thing something like that. How about 'Moses,' since he came floating down the river."

"Naa, that's too Biblical."

"Well then, let's just call him Shep, since he looks to be mostly German shepherd."

"That's real creative, Angie," he said with a teasing hint of sarcasm.

"Then, just what do you suggest, Mr. Know It All?"

"Don't get all bent out of shape, Baby. We're just having a discussion."

"No, Sir, I think we're having an argument, John Starr."

"No, we're just having dialogue. Actually Shep is a good solid name."

"I think we should call him Sheppy," said Angie with finality in her voice.

"Sheppy it is. Now, give me a kiss, and let's don't get puffed up over little things like this any more."

Fannie and Carter's surprise visit came on a Saturday towards the end of summer semester.

Evidently the gossip train had finally made it down to Mobile.

No doubt thanks to Sophie, thought John.

Angie had made arrangements with a sorority sister to cover for her in case of such unexpected events. As far as the outside world was concerned, she spent a lot of time at the library.

The phone rang while Angie and John were taking a mid-day nap, having bathed Sheppy earlier that morning. It had been somewhat of an ordeal since the pup understandably wasn't too crazy about water.

"Please page Angie LeBeau," said the voice at the other end of the line.

"It's a page for you," John said drowsily, handing Angie the phone. She held the receiver out so he could hear.

"Hi Angie, its Pam…guess what? Your Mama and Daddy are here. I told them you were at the library…here's your mom.

"Hi, Mama. What a surprise."

"Hello Dah'lin, Your Daddy and I thought we'd drive up and see how you were doin'. I hope we didn't come when you were too busy."

"No, of course not, Mama. I'll be right on over in just a little bit…bye now."

"I know why there're here," said Angie, "Be prepared to meet my parents today."

"Surely you're not gonna' bring them here."

"No, of course not, It'll be on neutral ground. They'll want to go out to eat tonight."

Angie showered and meticulously dressed herself…like a matador before a bullfight.

"Don't worry, Sweetheart, I'll be in best behavior mode," said John.

"Just be your sweet self, and everything will be OK."

"You can count on it, Baby."

"I'll call you later, Galahad," she said, blowing him a kiss as she headed for the door, "I love you."

John had all but forgotten that Angie was from the upper crust. He wondered what he was in for.

Angie's call came around five o'clock.

"Hi John, it's Angie."

"Hi, Angie."

"My parents came up from Mobile for a visit. We're going out for dinner this evening and would love for you to join us…that is if you don't have other plans."

"Well, I don't know. Sheppy and I were thinking about going out for a few beers with the boys tonight," he chided.

"Good," she said without missing a beat, "we'll meet you at Dreamland Barbecue at seven."

"OK, sweetheart, I'll be there. Thank you for the invite."

John was there promptly at seven. Twenty minutes later, the sleek black Cadillac drove up.

"Mama, Daddy, this is John Starr. John, this is my Mama and Daddy."

" Pleased to meet you Mrs. LeBeau…Dr. LeBeau. Thank you for asking me to join you all."

"The pleasure is ours, I'm sure, John," said Fannie, extending her hand.

"Ya'll ready for some really good eatin'?" asked Angie.

It was good from John's point of view that dining on barbeque ribs is messy business. It took some of the edge off his first meeting with the LeBeaus.

"Angie tells us you're studying law, John," said Carter.

"Yes, sir. I hope to be through by '68."

"What are your future plans, deah…are you going to practice in Birmingham?" Fannie grilled.

"Well, I haven't made any definite plans, yet. Right now, I'm just concentrating on finishing school."

"I know what you mean," said Carter, "Angie may have told you…Alabama is my Alma Mata. I can remember wondering if I would ever get out of here."

"How old are you, John?" asked Fannie.

"I'm twenty three."

"My, you must have gotten' a late start in college."

"Actually, I took two years off …spent them in the Army."

"Oh really," said Carter, "where were you stationed?"

"I was sent to Vietnam…U.S. Advisory Group Command. I was an observer for Army Intelligence."

"Things sure are heating up over there," said Carter, "Looks rough…I hope we don't get into something over our heads."

"Yes, sir. It was rough when I was there…I saw some bad things."

"John has been so helpful to me," said Angie, redirecting the conversation. "I don't think I could have passed algebra without him." She looked his way and winked.

"What caused you to become interested in being a lawyer, John?" asked Fannie, "Is your fatha' a lawyer or something'?"

"No, Ma'am, we lost my dad in World War II. Mom says he wanted to become a lawyer when the war was over. I guess that's what got me interested."

"Angie's only nineteen, you know," said Fannie.

"Do you have any hobbies, John?" Carter asked.

"Well, Sir, I learned to fly light aircraft in the army. Hopefully I can take that up again someday.

"Sailing is my hobby. I imagine flying is somewhat like it…gets one's mind off of things."

"Yes, Sir…and the freedom."

Early the next morning, Angie slipped between the sheets of John's bed.

"Did I pass?" he mumbled.

"You did fine. I know Daddy really enjoyed it. You did fine with Mama too. Sorry for the third degree. I think you just got christened…Mama style."

Fall semester, '65, rolled around at the Crimson Tide, and rush week was in full swing. It was the first time since connecting with Angie that she had shown any real interest in sorority activities.

"Honey, there's going be a party for the pledges this Saturday, and I need a date. You interested in taking your girl friend someplace besides Moundville Archeological Park?"

"Well, since nobody else is gonna' ask you…" he ribbed.

"You better, John Starr…or I guess I'll have to ask one of those big old football players to escort me," she shot back.

"Since you put it that way, I guess I'd better say, Yes, Ma'am. It would be an honor to escort you to the party."

"Good. Now that that's settled, you're going to have to shed those old blue jeans of yours. I picked up a nice pair of slacks, and a shirt that I want you to try on…if you will, please, sir."

Though he wouldn't admit it, and grumbled about her makeover of him, John did relish her pampering. And, going to a party now and then seemed a reasonable trade-off for her affection.

Like a butterfly, Angie flitted through an assortment of friends and acquaintances, lighting on one group then another, laughing and making light conversation. For the first time, he saw the other side of his nymph.

Resigned to the fact that it was going to be a long evening, he decided to grin and bear it…and play the game. At Angie's side, he met and wooed them all, the pretty girls, the not so pretty girls, the jocks and even the drunks …forgetting their names within minutes after being introduced…except for one.

"John, this is my cousin, Sophie. Sophie, this is my friend, John Starr."

"So, I finally get to meet the mystery man."

"Hello, Sophie. I think we met briefly at the library last year. I work there."

"Really, I don't seem to recall."

"You were a little frustrated at the time…looking for a book we didn't have."

*Don't recall, my ass,* rolled through his mind.

"Oh, I hope I didn't offend. Sometimes I'm dreadful when under pressure."

"No, no offense taken." *Sometimes dreadful?* Came in a second wave of thought..

"You certainly were charming this evening, Mr. Starr," Angie commented as they drove home, "maybe just a little too much to Patricia Robinson, though. I think she has a crush on you."

"Was she the one with braces?"

"No, that was Charlotte Culpepper. Patricia was the one with the big boobs."

"Oh, yeah…I remember."

"I'll just bet you do…you've got to admit it, Honey, we had a good time."

"Sure, Angie, but all I really want is to be with you."

"Likewise, Galahad."

As the university years rolled by, Angie's social agenda increased. John reluctantly tagged along from one sorority event to the other, sometimes at the expense of valuable study time.

Like a smooth little pebble skipping across a pond, without a care…unconcerned about what lay beneath the surface, this was the girl he had fallen in love with.

For him, life was not so simple. Serious concerns constantly loomed…money, or lack thereof, school, job…his future with her. He often wondered what held them together.

One Saturday afternoon, John lay stretched out on the couch browsing through Angie's psychology textbook while she was putzing around in the kitchen. He came upon the subject of pheromones, a hormonal scent given off by animals, which attracts the opposite sex.

John, in one of his lighter moods called out, "Angie, do you think the reason we stay together is because of the way we smell?"

"What on earth are you talking about, Honey?"

"Well, it says right here that all animals give off a certain scent that makes them go bananas over the opposite sex. Can you come in here a minute? I want to see if its true."

"Don't be silly, John…I sure hope there's more to us than the way we smell."

John and Angie married in 1967.

# Changing Tides

"I THINK YOU best get control of yourself, John Starr; that's what I think…and no, we're not going to christen this place."

Angie's response to John's hint that they make love in the gazebo was crystal clear.

"Sometimes I think you'll never grow up regarding that sort of thing," she continued, "besides, there's something I want to talk to you about."

"Talk about what, Angie?" he asked in his miffed 'after-being-rejected' tone of voice.

"We've been invited to go for a ride on Terry Wayne's yacht tomorrow."

"Terry Wayne?"

"The car dealer Mama pointed out…remember?"

"Angie, you know I planned to take the boys flying tomorrow."

" You can go flying any old time, John. Mama and I really want to go."

"What about your Dad?"

"You know good and well Saturday is Daddy's and Uncle Rad's golf day.

"Hell, Angie, why can't I ever plan anything without you and your Mama conjuring up something to spoil it? Don't I deserve a day-off, away from all this social crap?"

He couldn't stop the acid words that spewed from his mouth.

"I'm damn sick and tired of playing second fiddle to that bunch of over-bred self-centered egocentric friends of yours. Don't you know that not a one of them would piss on you if you were on fire!"

"Well, just forget it, Mister! We'll make other arrangements!"

Angie turned and stormed back up the trail toward the house.

"Angie, come back here!"

She briefly turned.

"Go fly your kite…Asshole!"

Elvis was dead, Galahad had fallen off his horse…and John Starr knew he was in deep mud.

"How the hell did this happen?" he vented, which only served to momentarily silence the frogs and crickets.

A jumble of thoughts raced through his mind: *no way to take the words back… blew it in the blink of an eye…less than a heart beat… sugar's turned to sh…oh, screw it. At least she knows how I feel, now…ten years of holding it in… long enough.*

He made his way to the water's edge. A breeze came in off the bay, giving relief from the warmness of the evening. The dark bay waters danced and shimmered in the moonlight. Little waves lapped the shoreline every few seconds or so. The tides were changing.

Distant thunder served notice that an ever-present, all-powerful sea churned out beyond the bay.

It occurred to him: *It could wipe this whole freakin' place out if it wanted to…the gazebo, Rad's mansion…even Mobile…wash it all clean…in a heartbeat…in the blink of an eye.*

A gull sailed over the water, and crossed the moon. Like a little white ghost it flitted off to some unknown rendezvous. He would find out who this Terry Wayne was.

The subject of John's search wasn't difficult to find among the mingling guests. He knew he had his man after spotting the tall, lean mid-thirties hotshot with a head full of dark wavy hair and Hollywood tan. Terry was picking around at the hors d'oeuvres when John approached.

"Hello, I'm John Starr," he said, trying not to let the chip on his shoulder show.

"Well, hello Partner. I'm Terry Wayne. You must be Angie's other half," he responded.

"Yeah, I'm Angie's other half."

"Good looking woman you have there, Pal."

"Thanks…is your wife here tonight?"

"Nope, I shed that baggage a couple of years ago…you all gonna' make it to the yacht-party tomorrow?"

"We'll be there, thanks for the invite."

John Starr did not like what he saw of Terry Wayne.

# CHAPTER 14

# Bonaparte's Retreat

THINGS WERE WINDING down when it occurred to John that he hadn't paid his usual visit to Beatrice. They had shared a special rapport ever since he wandered into her kitchen some ten years earlier during his first Debarden function. It was shortly after he and Angie married.

Somewhat bewildered and having overindulged a little in her 'special punch,' he took an aspirin she handed him, a cup of coffee laced with chicory, and refuge from the unfamiliar world he was being ushered into. Ever since, while visiting the Debardens, he made a point to go to the kitchen for a cup of coffee and a little small talk before the evening was over. He called her kitchen Bonaparte's Retreat.

"Well, hello Mr. John. I was jus' wonderin' if you were gonna' visit with me tonight."

"Have I missed one yet, Bea?"

"No, Sir," she replied with a grin.

"I'll bet you're worn out after this shin-dig," he said, sitting down on a bar stool next to the island.

"No, sir, Mr. John, I'm jus' fine," she said while pouring him a cup of strong blended coffee.

"How do you like this fancy new kitchen, Bea?"

"It's takin' some gettin' used to, Mr. John," she chuckled.

"I'm not sure I like it as well as the one at the old house," he said.

"Me neither, Mr. John…me neither."

Like her family in the generations before, Beatrice had served the Debardens since childhood. In fact, some forty years earlier her mother, Mammy June, held the same position of housekeeper and cook as she now did. Bea took over the reins of duty when Mammy June got too old to handle the job. Now, at age sixty-four, Beatrice, herself, had the opportunity to retire, but chose to remain on as housekeeper, cook, and sometimes family confidant. She knew the good, the not-so-good, and almost all the skeletons, both in and out of the closet.

Over the years, Bea had shared much of her family history with John, and even some of the Debarben's secrets. She was six years older than Rad, and had been caregiver and companion to him since his birth. She told how it was not uncommon in the Old South for children of servants to assume the roll of playmate and steward to the children of their white patrons…always as, subordinates, of course. Black children were taught early on to understand their subservient position, but decent whites taught their youngsters not to abuse or take advantage. Each knew his or her place.

Rad and Beatrice grew close as children, and so it remained.

John could understand why many times over the years Rad leaned on her soft, but strong shoulders for consolation and advice. She possessed an instinctive wisdom.

In return for her dedication and loyalty, Beatrice would never want for anything. This lady of color was a bona fide member of the Debarden household, though relegated by birth to a position from which she could never rise.

"How in the world did you get the name, Bonaparte?" asked John early on in their friendship.

"Well, Mr. John," she began, "When the Yankees came through here and freed the slaves, there was a whole passel of folks that had no place to go. A lot headed north, but just as many wanted to hang around. Some even begged their old masters to let them stay on. When stomachs got empty, some thought that the old ways might not have been so bad after all.

Now, my side of the family descended from the Debarden's holdin's, and my husband, Hesiqui Bonaparte's side came from the old Jeanrette plantation. The story goes that Old Otis Jeanrette, Ms. Fannie's great-grand father owned a boy called Napoleon that he had won in a poker game. He wouldn't allow any of his slaves to carry the Jeanrette name with them; so he gave the boy the last name of 'Bonaparte,' before settin' him free."

All one had to do was look at Beatrice's light skin to see the obvious. There was definitely a cracker somewhere in the woodpile. There had been rumors through the years regarding Rad's father and Mammy Jane, but some secrets, even Bea didn't know.

The phone rang. Bea answered.

"Debarden residence."

"Well, hello Baby, how are you doin'?" she said…her eyes lighting up.

"Yes, I'm doin' fine. Guess who's here with me right now?"

"Sure, you can."

"Mr. John," she said, handing him the phone, "Its Joseph."

"Hey, Joseph, how's the law game up there in Birmingham?"

"Still paying my dues, John. How are you doing?" said the voice at the other end of the line.

"Still paying my dues, too…if you know what I mean. Are you still doing the court appointed attorney thing?"

"No, I quit doing that stuff. Seemed like all I did was defend petty thieves, pimps and scumbags who beat their wives. Now, I'm defending more well-to-do scumbags who do about the same thing, except they're able and willing to pay for my services."

"Sounds like progress to me, Joseph. Hang in there, Buddy."

Joseph was Beatrice's boy…her only child.

John remembered the wide-eyed fifteen-year old helping his mother when he first wandered into the kitchen back in '67…remembered it as if it were the day before.

"Looks like you've got a good helper there, Ms. Bea."

"Yes, Sir, he does real good."

"I'm John, what's your name?"

"Joseph Bonaparte," the shy boy answered.

"You play football?"

"No, sir."

"Do you make good grades in school?"

"Yes, sir."

"He makes straight 'A's," Bea piped in, "except for one 'B' last year,"

"That's great. Making good grades is the most important thing you can do for yourself, Joseph."

"Yes, Sir."

"He's a good looking boy Ms. Bea, I know you're proud of him."

"Yes, Sir, I sure am."


John liked the boy, and in time, became somewhat of a mentor to him. They had things in common, too. Joseph's father died when he was four. John's dad was lost at sea and presumed dead in World War II when he was three. Both were close with their mother. Neither had received much in the way of adult male counsel.

Many times, while the party was going on inside, they would sit out back on an old brick wall in the shade of a live oak tree or under the stars and talk about everything from race and religion to the birds and bees. John did the best he could, giving advice and answering the questions of this bright and curious boy.

"Wonder why they started calling us colored people 'Black'," he once asked, "I've never even seen a really black person."

"Well, Joseph, the only time I ever saw a really white person was when I was in the Army," John replied, "His name was Jessie Green. He was an albino colored guy. And, of all things, he had blue eyes. In other words, he was a blue-eyed, white, black man they called Green. No matter what they called him, though, he was still good old Jessie to me. I guess labels are just something all of us have to live with."

Joseph had the brains, ambition and opportunity to attend college. Rad had set up a trust fund for that purpose years before.

He wanted to become a lawyer, like John.


In 1970 Joseph readied himself to go to the University of Alabama, but not without apprehension. It had been only eight years since Governor George Wallace stood on the steps of the University of Alabama in defiance of a federal court order to allow blacks to enroll there. Joseph was nervous about the whole idea of going, thinking there may be some left over resentments…besides, he didn't want to be someplace he wasn't wanted.

"Joseph," John said, "Are you going to let what that brave little gal who walked right past old George and paved the way for the likes of you be for nothing, or are you going to stand tall and walk through those same doors with pride and dignity like she did? You'll do fine, Joseph Bonaparte," he said, "even with a name like yours, you'll do fine."

John was right; Joseph did well at the University, and the only real ribbing he got was with regards to his name.

It was approaching midnight…time to go…only, of course, after all the appropriate departing hugs and kisses.

Heading down the long driveway, leaving behind another evening with the cream of Mobile society, John glanced in the rear view mirror at Rad's statement of excess. He just shook his head, but said nothing. Angie stared out the side window…her head turned away from John. It was a long silent drive home for the Starrs.

# Chapter 15

# Fiddle-De-Dee

The sun rose as usual Saturday morning. It was a beautiful day for flying, but there were pressing issues that had to be addressed. John's first order of business was to negotiate a peace with Angie…which he did, then eat a satisfactory amount of crow as penance for his outburst the night before…which he did. Angie gave conditional pardon, which left no way to weasel out of the day's event. The boat ride was on.

"Aw, Dad," said a disappointed Johnny, their nine-year-old son, "I thought we were gonna' go up today."

"Yeah, Dad, you promised," Cart, his seven-year old brother, chimed in.

"I'm sorry fellas," said John, "I didn't know that your Mom already had something planned for today."

"She always has something 'planned for the day,' remarked Cart sarcastically, already showing signs of his Grand Ma Ma's temperament. "Who's gonna' stay with us, anyway?"

"Mrs. Johnson."

"Miz Johnson! Not Miz Johnson! Dad, she's so strict she won't even let us go in the pool," protested Johnny.

"Tell you what guys, let's all of us make it through the day, and we'll go to the movies tonight. How bout the new one everybody's talking about, 'Star Wars'?"

"Yea! All right!" shouted both boys, "Can we go flying tomorrow, Dad?" asked Cart, adding to the bargain.

"I'm counting on it, Buddy," replied John.

John and Angie picked Fannie up about 11:30 that morning for a light lunch before going to Terry Wayne's yacht party. Carter was off doing his usual Saturday morning thing…playing golf with Rad.

Fannie was unusually quiet.

The "Fiddle-De-Dee" was indeed a beauty. The sleek sixty-eight-foot luxury cruiser was pure white, trimmed in blue. Without a doubt, she was the best looking boat in the lineup.

Terry was all decked out in his whites, wearing a navy-blue captain's cap with gold scrambled eggs embroidered on its bill.

"Glad you all could make it," he said looking straight at Angie.

Boarding the yacht were only a few leftovers from the night before. Among them were Horace, accompanied by Colleen, his 'exotic' companion from New Orleans, Sophie, and, of course. the Starrs and Fannie. Most of the twenty or so guests were new-blood…a younger crowd that made it obvious they could give a hoot in hell about who was who in old Mobile society. These were Terry Wayne's friends. It would be his day to flaunt.

The big marine engines rumbled and gurgled as they powered the Fiddle-De-Dee backward and away from the pier. The helmsman on the top deck turned her and slowly headed toward the mouth of Mobile bay. Three kegs of draft, lined up in a row on the deck made it pretty clear that this little shindig was going to be a beer bust.

The lazy-dog-day summer afternoon seemed perfect for a boat ride, and the young scantily clad girls darting here and there with fleshy buttocks half hanging out of their short shorts definitely added to the scenery. The old Creole man Terry hired to do the shucking could barely keep up as dozen after dozens of oysters served on the half shell slid down the gullets of the loud and rowdy guests. Even though he wasn't particularly hungry, those plump bite-size delicacies of the sea, along with some tangy cocktail sauce, crackers and a mug of draft were just too much temptation for John. He put away at least a dozen oysters.

Colleen Boudreaux's skin was the color of light coffee milk. Her features were Anglo, but it was obvious that she truly was of some exotic blend. Maybe it was in the cut of those almond eyes, or the pouty lips…or her body language. Intentional or not, it seemed that her every move, gesture and nuance was an act of seduction.

Colleen reclined in the lounge chair beside Horace, who in spite of all the noisy goings on was intermittently nodding off…still nursing a hangover from the previous night's tomfoolery. She was sitting there, taking it all in…twisting and curling the ends of her long shiny black hair around her fingers when Sophie, and a much more mellow Fannie than the night before meandered up. Horace had drifted off into la-la land. John, still stuffing himself, was well within ear-shot.

"Looks like your friend is a little worse for wear today," said Fannie with a sly smile.

"Yeah, I'm afraid he over did it a little bit last night," responded Colleen, adding a wispy giggle.

"Everybody was junin' around so much last night, and with Horace's accident and all, we neva' got a proper introduction," said Fannie, "which is probably for the best since I was a wretched witch all evenin'…the change, you know. I'm Fannie LeBeau, and this is my niece Sophie."

"I'm Colleen Boudreaux, pleased to meet you all."

"We heard you're from New Orleans," said Sophie.

"Born and bred there."

"What do you do over in the 'Big Easy?' "

"I'm in the entertainment business. What do you do, Sophie?"

"Well, I…do volunteer work."

"That's good."

"Are you a performer?" asked Fannie.

"I do a little dancin'…and so forth."

"Oh…I see."

"Right now, I only dance for Horace, though. Do you dance for your man, Fannie?"

"Heavens, no…I wasn't born with even an ounce of rhythm."

"You should try it…does wonders for a relationship."

"Maybe you could teach me sometimes, Deah."

"Anytime, Ms. Fannie."

Sophie, probably smelling the makings for a bucket full of gossip, continued to probe.

"What does your family do, Colleen?"

"Well, my mother worked in a brothel till the day she died, and I never knew my father. In a nutshell, that's pretty much my family history."

"Goodness Gracious, you mean to say your mother was ah…," stammered Sophie.

"Yes, She was a prostitute, and a damn good one too. Had customers who stuck with her for over twenty years."

"Heavens to Betsy. What a pity she had to live that kind of life."

"Why? She made good money and was happy most of the time."

"Well, you know what I mean, being in that profession and all."

"We're all whores, in one-way or the other, Honey. Haven't you figured that out yet?"

Fannie, apparently wanting to get off the subject, leaned down to within a foot of Horace's face. He was sprawled out with his mouth wide open, inhaling and exhaling little snippets of snores.

"Boo," she yelled.

"Woah!" yelped Horace. "What the hell are you tryin' to do, Fannie, give me a heart attack?"

"Not that you don't deserve one Horace Blair, but no, I'm just tryin' to get you back into the world of the livin: so you can give some attention to this charmin' companion of yours, that's all."

Most everybody among the younger bunch were pretty loose by the time the "Fiddle-De-Dee" passed Dog River. Mon Louis came into view. Then it was through the narrow pass between Fort Morgan and Dauphin Island. They crossed the bar and the "Fiddle-De-Dee" was in open waters.

"Which way, Angie," Terry asked.

"Why, Terry Wayne, you're the captain," she said.

"You make the call. I'd like for you to."

"Well, if you insist, go that-a-way," she said, pointing her finger in a westerly direction.

"Go starboard and open her up," he shouted to the helmsman, standing at the wheel on the top deck.

John felt his mood rapidly deteriorating. As far as he was concerned, T. Wayne had stepped over the line with his overt display of attention toward Angie. To top it off, she was lapping it up.

He felt the heat rise in his body as thoughts regarding Wayne strayed from manners and civility to something else: *Best lay off, you cocky ass daddy cool.*

Just then, a gull feather landed on Angie's shoulder. Wayne plucked it off touching her in the process.

John's face was on fire. A venomous rage ripped through his mind: *I'll throw your ass overboard you son-of-a-bitch.*

He fought for control…struggling to avoid the snap.

"Keep your cool, John," said Fannie, "I'll handle it."

"Is it that obvious?"

"Well, if the look in your eyes and the hair standin' up on the back of your neck means anything, I suppose it is, John Starr."

Fannie, began walking toward the boat's forward, and motioned Angie to come with her.

Whatever exchange occurred between mother and daughter definitely caused a change in mood. When they returned to Ship's Company, Angie was no longer wearing her bubbly smile.

Wayne quickly refocused his attention to the other females in the party, and hardly paid Angie further notice.

Fannie looked at John: "Apparently, he's not totally stupid," she said.


The big boat's bow rose and fell with great pounding splashes as she cut through the choppy gulf waters. Porpoise raced and leapt off her port side.

The Fiddle-De-Dee slid past Dauphin Island, one in a chain of slender barrier islands that make up the Mississippi Sound. Except for John's lingering anger and Angie's deflated spirit, all was well at two bells aboard the Fiddle-De-Dee.

Fannie, evidently trying to ease the awkward situation, joined Terry at the side rail for a little light conversation.

"You know," Fannie commented, "I have an ancestor who used to roam these waters. He was a pirate."

"Oh yeah, and who might that be?" asked Terry.

"You folks up North probably neva' heard of him, but his name was John Lafitte…one of the most audacious, bodacious scalawags that eva' lived.

"Well, Miz Fannie, I'll have you know that I do know about Jean Lafitte. In fact, I'm a pirate myself."

"Frankly, that doesn't surprise me one little bit, Terry Wayne."

The Sun was setting in a clear western sky as the Fiddle-De-Dee made her sweep around the west end of Dauphin Island, and into the sound. In the east, however, some nasty looking clouds were taking form.

"Head her back in," Terry ordered the helmsman.

"There, ova' there," Fannie shouted, pointing toward the mainland shore, "that's where the treasure's buried!"

"What treasure?" asked Terry.

"That's where Lafitte buried his treasure. Right ova' there, on the beach at Bayou La Batre….at least that's what they say."

As Fannie slung her hand out in the direction of Bayou La Batre, her prized gold cigarette holder slipped through her fingers and spiraled into the water. It floated for no more than a second, and then sank like a rock. Her little treasure went to join all the rest that had been claimed by the sea.

"It's gone!" she cried out, "After twenty years, it's gone…just like that… Hell fire and damnation!"

Storm clouds engulfed the eastern sky, and the sea became exceedingly choppy.

"Head for port!" shouted Terry, "full speed!"

Suddenly the Fiddle-De-Dee entered a dark wall of cloud and rain. Swells, almost as high as the top deck, and horrific winds began tossing the boat around like a cork. John hustled Angie, Fannie and Sophie below along with the others. Terry's playmates huddled in a corner, screaming, crying and throwing up while the now sobered young men, with eyes betraying their own terror, tried to give comfort.

John rejoined Wayne topside. Sheets of rain made it impossible to visually navigate.

"Head into the wind," John yelled to the helmsman, "Wayne, man the port side. Look out for anything that could hit us. I'll take starboard."

They immediately took their positions.

As waves pounded and washed across the deck, John hung on the best he could. Each time the bow dipped, huge sprays drenched him, forcing in gulps of seawater. As water spewed from his mouth, he fought to keep his air passage clear. He felt the salt burn in his nose and throat, and with a blinding sting in his eyes he was barely able to see. He felt certain that at any moment he would be swept away.

. Without warning, the boat listed at least forty-five degrees starboard. The beer kegs broke loose and rolled towards him. With all that was left of his strength he grabbed a support pole just as his feet went out from under him. He dangled in mid-air above the raging water. The kegs rolled by, missing him by inches, then crashed through the railing and disappeared. He knew that he couldn't hold on much longer.

As quickly as it had listed, the boat righted. His feet were back on the deck. He turned around and looked across toward the port side. Wayne was not there. *My God, he's gone,* raced through his mind.

"What happened to him?" he yelled to the helmsman.

"He made it below just before the boat leaned!" came the reply.

John knew he would make it, now. They all would make it.

Soon, the worst was over…plenty of rain, but less wind and waves.

Finally, the Fiddle-De-Dee made it back over the bar, then through the pass, and into the calmer waters of Mobile bay.

After docking everyone hastily departed, leaving Terry Wayne there, alone, with his battered toy, and a lot of smelly unpleasant business below to take care of.

On the drive home, and after twenty minutes of ice-cold silence, John remarked:

"That was a hell of a storm, wasn't it? I almost went overboard. That would have been it, you know."

A few moments passed without response, then: "I don't appreciate being treated like a child…by either you or Mama."

"Why are you saying that, Angie? I haven't said a word to you about anything."

"No, you just got Mama riled up, and she did the talking for you."

"Look, how am I supposed to feel when I stand there and watch some cocky bastard put moves on my wife, and she's eating it up."

"Well, in the first place, he wasn't putting moves on me, and in the second place, I didn't do anything wrong. I was just being friendly, so there. By the way, I saw you giving every one of those girls the once over…and drooling all over yourself…not to mention that Colleen whore."

"Let's just drop the matter, Angie. It's obvious we can't talk anymore without getting into it."

The Starrs didn't get home until after eight o'clock. Angie headed straight to the bedroom.

"I thought y'all were gonna' be back by six," protested Johnny.

"Can we still go to the movies, Dad?" Cart pleaded.

"I'm really sorry guys," said John, "we got caught in the bad weather,"

"Angie," he called out, "I promised the boys we'd go to the movies tonight. We can make it to the late show…how about it?"

"It's late, the weather's bad, and I'm exhausted," she replied, "why not tomorrow?"

"Because I promised them that we'd go tonight…that's why."

"You go ahead and take the boys, then. I'm already in bed."

It was after midnight before they got out of the theatre.

"That was some movie, wasn't it fellas'?"

"Yes, sir," said a still excited Johnny, "I liked Luke Skywalker. He could really fly that fighter."

"I liked R2D2 best," said Cart, "it was so funny, the way he talked."

"Darth Vader was a bad dude wasn't he?" said John, recalling some of the bad dudes he had run across in his lifetime.

John woke up at six o'clock, his usual time. He couldn't sleep late if he wanted to…force of habit. Angie lay beside him. The soft, slow rhythm of her breathing told him that she was still in deep sleep.

Her slumber was serious business. He had learned a long time ago not to disturb while she was in this state. She was rarely up before nine, anyway.

It was drizzling rain outside. A dreary overcast blanketed the sky, and it didn't look like things were going to change anytime soon. There would be no flying this day.

John went though his morning rituals. He made coffee, scanned the paper while sitting on the throne, then showered and shaved.

He looked at the man in the mirror but didn't like what he saw. The guy staring back looked haggard and strained. It was showing. He could no longer hide what had been kept buried in his gut:

*Nothing's working anymore…all slipping away…even the old haunts from Nam are coming back…something's got to give.*

"What are we going to do, Shep?" he said, stroking the old dog that had been with him and Angie since their beginnings.

Angie got up about ten and started stirring around. In her robe, sipping on her first cup of coffee, she meandered into the den where John and the boys were.

"What a miserable day," she commented,

"Yeah," grumbled Johnny, "We should have gone flying yesterday when we could have."

"Did you boys like the movie?"

"Oh yeah, Mom!" said Cart, "It was great. You should have been there. They had real space ships and funny looking people, and everything."

"Yeah, Mom, you should have been there," John remarked.

"Well, I'm sorry, but I just couldn't have made it last night. I was totally exhausted. John, do you realize just how close we came to something terrible happening, being caught in that storm and all."

"Yes, Angie, I know…we were lucky."

"What are you up to today?" she asked.

"I think I'll go to the office and catch up on a little work. There won't be any flying today, that's for sure. What about you?"

"After I got my little lecture on the boat, Mama asked me to come over this afternoon. She said she wanted to talk to me about something. I can't imagine what on earth it is, but it sounded kind of serious. I sure hope it's not Daddy's heart…I'll take the boys with me."

# Chapter 16

# John and Bob

DRIVING THROUGH THE deserted streets of Mobile on a rainy Sunday afternoon wasn't much of an incentive for work. But, the office offered refuge for John during times like this. At least he didn't have to spend what was left of the weekend over at his in-laws. He made it to the office about one o'clock.

Having thought it over, he decided it would be best not to get involved with Mr. Raintree and his problems. Bob needed to know.

"Might as well get this over with," he murmured under his breath while reaching for the phone. He dialed Bob's number. As the first ring became the second, he began to look around his office. On the wall was his diploma, 'The University of Alabama School of Law'…something he had worked hard for and was proud of. On his desk stood a silver framed picture of Angie and the boys. Despite the present difficulties, this was still what it was all about.

Across the room on the credenza sat the old Spanish helmet that he and Bob had stumbled upon during their canoe trip on the Cahaba when they were kids. It sat there, by itself, just as it had for many years.

After the sixth ring with no answer, John placed the receiver back in its cradle.

He hadn't smoked a cigarette in years, but for some reason always kept a pack around. He opened the middle desk drawer and pulled out the unopened pack of Marlboros and an oyster shell ashtray. Methodically, he removed the cellophane and peeled back the foil wrapper. Leaning back in his chair, he propped his feet up on the desk and lit up. It tasted stale and was strong from age, but he kept it burning anyway, taking an occasional draw. With his eyes fixed on the helmet, his mind wandered back to a much earlier time.

John and Bob became pals in '52, shortly after the Savage family moved into the neighborhood. Shades Mountain, about seven miles south of Birmingham, was a hodge podge of neighborhoods scattered along the crest and its relatively gentle southern slopes. This region of Alabama is at the southernmost reach of the great Appalachian chain.

In the early '50's, Shades Mountain, was semi-rural with good size patches of woodlands knitted among and between communities. It was a good place for an active boy to grow up…fresh air, open spaces, and plenty of woods to explore. There were spots with folksy (and sometimes forbidding) names like Drip Rock, Pole Cat Ridge and Devil's Den.

On a chilly Saturday afternoon in mid-March, John was casually wandering down the path leading to one of his favorite places…a small wooded ravine about a half-mile from the house. It nestled between two forested ridges, each a couple of hundred feet in height. The valley was relatively narrow, maybe a thousand feet from the crest of one ridge to the other. He had his trusty Red Ryder BB gun with him, popping it off at acorns, pinecones, and other inanimate objects as he strolled along. He also had a cigarette he had swiped from his mom. John planned to smoke it under the overhanging rock in the valley. This was something he'd never done before. To the right of the path was a lazy little branch that flowed into the valley. Once there, its waters rushed over and under boulders to create cascades and gushing spouts. To him, it was a majestic place, like what Robin Hood's Sherwood forest might have been. Being there certainly wasn't a bad way to spend his eleventh birthday.

John made his way a hundred and fifty feet or so up the steep wooded valley slope to the overhanging rock, looming there among other huge outcrops. Standing under the ledge was like being in a great room with no front wall. From this vantage point, the valley floor with its tall hardwoods and creek could easily be observed.

He was about to light up when out of the corner of his eye he caught a glimpse of something down in the valley dart from behind one tree to behind another. Whatever it was, it was big. *Couldn't be a deer, or dog,* he thought. They wouldn't move in that manner. *It sure ain't a wood nymph…maybe it's a bear.*

He raised the BB gun, for whatever good that would do, and stood there, frozen, with a bead on the tree where the apparition appeared. At least a minute passed, then it happened again. Something, human in form, draped in a big piece of rag dashed from behind one tree to behind another.

"Who's down there?" he yelled, figuring that it was better to go on and have a showdown than wait for something worse to happen. There was dead silence for about twenty seconds, then a voice yelled back:

"Bob Savage! Who are you?"

"John Starr! What are you doin'?"

"I'm tryin' to get dry!"

"Why?"

"I fell in the creek! The vine broke!"

"Come on out!"

A pitiful ragged figure slowly emerged. It was a kid about his age looking like a wet dog, wrapped in a ragged piece of tarpaulin that John remembered seeing at an old abandoned whiskey still at the edge of the creek.

John, sitting there in his downtown Mobile office, took another draw on the cigarette. He felt a much-needed smile coming on as he recalled making his way down to the valley floor where the kid he had never seen before stood, braced against a tree, shivering from head to toe.

"Where's your clothes?"

"Over there, laid out over some bushes to dry. My mother's gonna' kill me."

"Why?"

"She told me not to go in the woods. I have a cold, and she's gonna' whip me for sure if she finds out I went anyway."

"Let's tak'um up there," said John pointing to the overhanging rock. "I've got some matches. We'll build a fire, and dry'um out quick."

As the wet clothes, stretched across a forked branch, began to steam over the fire John built under the rock ledge, he said:

"You must be new, I haven't seen you around."

"Yeah, we moved up from Montgomery a few months ago, just after Christmas."

"Well, I haven't seen you at school."

"I go to a Catholic school down in Homewood," Bob replied.

"Oh, guess that's why."

As they talked, John discovered that Bob lived only a couple of blocks from him, was three months older, had a Red Ryder BB gun, too, liked peanut butter and jelly sandwiches…and loved playing in the woods.

"'Ever shot a bird with your BB gun?" asked Bob.

"Naw," answered John, almost apologetically, "never been that hungry. Have you?"

"Once, but it didn't make me feel very good."

"Yeah, I can imagine. I had one right in my sights but didn't pull the trigger. I knew it would have made me feel like crap if I did it …decided right then and there I wouldn't shoot anything unless I was hungry, or it was tryin' to get me. I've been shot though."

"Wow, really?"

"Yep, 'got shot in the arm."

"Did it hurt?"

"Yeah, it hurt like crazy."

"What happened?"

"Well, Lester Goolsby…he lives up the road from me…was bad about shootin' birds and lizards just for the heck of it. I'd talked to him about it till I was blue in the face, but it didn't do any good. I finally told him that if I ever caught him killin' anything, I was gonna' make him eat it. Sure enough, I walked up to his house one day, and he had just killed a bird…and I made him eat it."

"How'd you get him to do that, whip his butt or somethin'?"

"No, actually I just told him that I knew he was the one who broke into the school over the weekend and peed all over the teacher's desk…and on the radiator. Boy, it stunk up the whole place. I didn't know for sure he was the one who did it, but figured he was. Anyway, he fell for my bluff. I wouldn't have told on him, but he didn't know that."

"Oh."

"Old Lester halfway plucked the little bird while I built a fire. We put it on a stick and roasted it for a few minutes. He didn't eat but one bite though. It almost made me sick just watchin'. Then, the little turd said it made him sick and used it as an excuse to stay out of school for two days. He told his mom that I had made him eat a bird, and she called my mom and the principal and everybody else she could think of. I almost got suspended. I should have told on him about the peein' incident."

"What does that have to do with you gettin' shot?" asked Bob.

"Well, about two weeks later he ambushed me while I was walkin' down the road."

"What'd you do?"

"I shot him…twice…in the back as he was runnin' away."

"That was noble."

"Yep, I thought so."

"Ya'll still friends?"

"Yeah, I guess so. No point in holdin' a grudge."

John pulled the cigarette out of his pocket and lit up.

"Where'd you get that?"

"I swiped it from my Mom."

"Aren't you afraid you're gonna' go to Hell?"

"No. Why?"

"Well, in the first place you stole it, and in the second place it's bad for you."

"Are you afraid you're gonna' go to Hell for fallin' in the creek?" John retorted.

"No, that was an accident."

"Well, if you hadn't disobeyed your mother in the first place you wouldn't have been out here tryin' to swing across the creek on a rotten vine. Now, you might catch pneumonia, and die. You'll probably go to Hell on top of all of that."

"You sound like my Uncle Nick. He's a lawyer."

"Want a puff?" asked John.

"I guess I might as well get hung for a goat as a sheep," said Bob. He took a deep drag.

After all the choking and gasping, and about half way through the cigarette, both boys began feeling light-headed and green around the gills. John threw it in the fire, and that was the end of that.

John snuffed his cigarette out in the oyster shell ashtray and returned the pack to the middle drawer of his desk. He continued his mind journey.

The good sisters at Bob's school; had made him a true believer. Sin was serious business. Major ones, like playing with one's self could definitely evoke fire and brimstone. Minor ones, like poaching apples from the next-door neighbor's yard would probably slide by without much ado…at worst, a stomachache might be dealt out as punishment. Things like using the "F" word could put one on shaky grounds, but saying "GD" meant a one-way ticket. Of course, there was always the safety net of confession and penance to get out of hot water with God.

As regards to the cigarette episode, Bob said he was satisfied that feeling bad enough to puke was punishment enough, and penance was served by his vowing to never do it again. As far as going in the woods against his mothers' orders, he didn't get away with that one for sure. His mom found leaves in his socks and underpants. He got it with the belt from his dad the next evening.

John looked down at the other picture on his desk. It was a photograph of his father, John Sr…the one that sat on his mother's nightstand all those years. The young man in the picture was just a kid…more than a decade younger than himself when it was taken.

"Where's your dad?" asked Bob on his first visit to John's house.

"He got shot down in the war."

"Shot down?"

"Yeah, a Jap shot him and his plane down over in the South Pacific. They never found him."

"Do you remember him?"

"No, I was just three years old when it happened, but sometimes I think I remember him…even know him. Maybe it's from lookin' at his picture all the time. Its weird, but sometimes I feel like he's around somewhere…really close."

"Guess I should quit bitchin' about my dad being hard on me, and havin' to baby-sit all the time," said Bob.

Bob was the oldest of three kids.

As usual, on Saturday morning, he had to baby-sit his younger siblings while his mom and dad went to buy groceries.

John had come by and they were all in the back yard.

Out of the blue Bob said, "Johnny, I wanna' know what it feels like to get shot. I want you to shoot me with the BB gun."

"Are you crazy, I'm not gonna' shoot you with any BB Gun."

"Come on Johnny, you got shot. It couldn't hurt that bad."

"Oh yes it can! I'm not gonna' do it, Bobby. You some kinda' martyr or somethin'?"

Deep down, John understood, but he wasn't fixing to take a chance on getting in trouble just so Bob could have his little rite of passage.

"No I'm not a martyr, I just wanna' know what it feels like."

He then turned to Shirley, his little sister.

"Shoot me right here," he ordered, bending over and patting himself on the butt. She promptly took aim and fired.

He didn't utter a sound, but turned pale upon taking the direct hit.

Big brothers and tough hombres don't cry over a little pain; so letting loose out there in the yard in front of everybody wasn't even an option.

"I gotta' go to the bathroom," he yelled. Then, in full gate, he streaked toward the house.

Upon emergence, except for the give-away redness in his eyes, stood what was probably the most cocksure kid in the state of Alabama. Bobby Savage could now say that he had been shot.

Needless to say, He and his BB gun parted company when Shirley told her parents about the episode.

The next Saturday, Mr. Savage dropped the boys off at the Empire movie theater in downtown Birmingham. One of the back-to-back matinee features was an old Errol Flynn swashbuckler; the other starred Jeff Chandler.

On the way out, Bob commented:

"How do you think a saber scar would look on my cheek, Johnny?"

"Probably not too good."

# Bob in Love

J OHN SAT AT his desk, staring at the ancient Spanish helmet that rested on the credenza across the room. Still lost in old memories, he recalled how it came into his possession.

Bob turned sixteen in January of '57, and became a licensed driver after two failed tries…one of which the examiner tried to jump out of the vehicle when he turned the wrong way on a one-way street. It didn't take long for his dad to realize that (Bob + Car = High Risk). So, the family sedan was declared off limits. Within two weeks, however, thanks to his part time job as a soda jerk at Coppedge's Drug store, young Mr. Savage made down payment on a red '53 mercury convertible. He promptly peed on the tires christening it, "Diablo."

Not that Bob was purposely wreckless, it's just that he would get distracted and tend to drift toward the shoulder of the road.

"You're fixing to go in the ditch, Bobby! Damnit! Please watch the road, and pay attention to what you're doing!"

"Don't worry John Boy; I'm in complete control of this vehicle. Besides, if we do hit the ditch, fortunately the only fatality will occur on the passenger side. I'm confident that your limp body will cushion the blow for me."

"You're all heart, Bobby. Just watch the road, will ya!"

"Nothing like a back seat driver in the front seat," came the comment with that little grin of his.

"Why do we have the top down, anyway?" grumbled John, "It's cold as a well digger's ass."

"Because it's cool to have the top down…besides I couldn't get it up this morning. Must be hung up on something."

It was a crisp Friday evening, close to eight o'clock. The boys were on their way to 'Salem's Drive-in', a popular teenage hangout in downtown Birmingham. Bob had heard that it was a good place to meet girls.

When they got there, it was packed. Cars circled the parking lot like horses on a merry-go-round…from the street, through the parking lot, to the street, then, back through again.

"I think we've hit the jackpot, John Boy. All the girls are looking our way."

"Bobby, they're looking to see what kind of fools would have the top down in thirty-degree weather."

After circling three times, a parking space became available. They zipped into it.

"What'll you guys have?" asked the sniffling red-nosed carhop, clad in her fake rabbit's fur coat and short-shorts.

"Two burgers all the way…no, wait, hold the onions…two fries and two cokes," said Bob.

About that time a car full of giggly girls pulled in next to Diablo…on Bob's side. The girl in the front passenger seat next to him rolled down her window.

"Aren't y'all cold?" she asked, as the other girls chattered among themselves.

"No," stammered Bob, "we just like fresh air…it's invigorating."

The bubbly little flirt turned to the other girls and said, "He's cute."

Then, she turned back: "I'm Lori…what's your name?"

"I'm Bob."

"Who's your friend over there," she asked, "he's awfully quiet."

"Oh, that's John. He's a deaf mute. Can't hear a thing, but he can read lips."

"Poor thing…and he's so cute."

"Hi, Lori, don't pay any attention to him," said John, "I can hear just fine."

"It's a miracle!" Bob shouted. "He's healed! Johnny, why are you just now talking after all these years?"

"Well, I haven't had anything to say up until now…besides, you know I'm not deaf…I'm blind. John reached into the glove compartment and pulled out a pair of sunglasses, put them on, and started feeling around on top of Bob's head.

"Bob, you sure do have a lot of bumps up there. I think you might have a little mental problem. Of course, that's just the observations of a blind man."

"They say boys who play with themselves go blind," said Lori, "Is that what happened to you?"

There was momentary dead silence…then,

"Will you go to the movies with me?" Bob blurted with a quiver in his voice?

"I don't know…you're not crazy, are you?"

"No…we're just cutting up. Maybe tomorrow night?"

"Well…I guess so."

"Wait a minute, Lori," said John, "I don't know if we can let him out of his cage long enough to go on a real date."

"Shut up, Johnny! Can't you see I'm being serious, now?"

It was after Ten…time to leave the hallowed grounds known as 'Salem's Drive-in'.

"I think we impressed them" said Bob, as Diablo loped down 20th Street.

"Yeah, about like Laurel and Hardy would."

"Well, at least I got a date. You didn't even try."

"I didn't think any of them were that hot, except for Lori."

"Guess you like'um fat and ugly…like Agnes, huh, John Boy."

John felt the blood drain to his feet as he slumped down in the seat. *Damn her hide*, ricocheted in his mind, *She must have shot her mouth off.*

Agnes was Lester Goolsby's younger sister. John had a chance encounter with her in the woods the summer before, and they experimented. He never told Bob, mainly out of embarrassment. She looked like a female version of Lester.

"Looks like you found your wood nymph," chided Bob, "and didn't even tell your old buddy."

Bob's call came about three in the afternoon the next day…just a few hours before he was supposed to pick Lori up.

John listened to the panicked voice at the other end of the line. "Calm down," he said.

"Why don't you just take her out, John? Tell her I got sick, or something."

"Don't be ridiculous. This is no time to get cold feet. Now, go on and get prettied up and stop by my house on the way to pick her up. I'll play 'Bolero' for you."

"OK, Johnny, maybe that'll help. I'll be up in a little bit."

John's record of Revel's 'Bolero' served well at times like this. It could inspire, conjure up great soul stirring passion and instill unflinching confidence, all at the same time. It was powerful stuff.

As Bob listened to the haunting melody repetitiously build on itself as the snare drum pounded away, John could see the metamorphosis taking place. Then, came the masterwork's final fury which mowed down any leftover traces of insecurities and self-doubt. Bobby Savage had been transformed, at least for the moment, from a lily-livered 'first time dater' to warrior-knight. He departed inspired and brimming with confidence. John felt an inner chuckle as he watched the taillights of Diablo disappear over the hill.

About midnight, John was awakened by a pecking on his bedroom window. It was Bob, grinning from ear to ear.

"How'd it go?" he asked, as Bob crawled in.

"Great! Johnny, I think I'm in love."

"Wait a minute, this was your first date, ever, and you're in love? What happened, anyway?"

"Well, after the movie was over I took her to Lover's Leap. She said she hadn't been there before. I was telling her about our Cahaba adventure when she scooted over and started kissing me. I didn't even get to finish the story. The next thing I knew my hands were on her breasts, and she was breathin' like a panther."

There was a pause.

"Well, what happened next?"

"That's it. She had to be home by eleven…said her daddy was really strict."

"So, now you're in love?"

"I know what you're thinking, but she said I was the first one to ever touch her like that, and that I was really special. I believe her, OK?"

"OK," said John, raising an eyebrow.

The next day John and his Mom returned home late in the afternoon after a Sunday visit with Uncle Ralph and his family. In his room., on the dresser lay the old Spanish helmet found on the Cahaba.

The note beside it read:

*John Boy,*
> *Thank you for being there when I needed you.*
> *I know you always liked this thing; so here it is.*

*Bob*

As the summer of '57 drew to a close and the school year began, Lori dumped Bob for a Woodlawn High football player. He was devastated.

The spell was broken by the ringing phone there in John's office.

"Hello, this is John Starr."

"Hi, it's me. You coming home soon?"

"Yes, Angie, I'm wrapping it up now. I'll be home in a little bit."

"Well, come on in soon. I have something really important to tell you."

" I'm on my way…bye."

Still holding the receiver, he punched in the numbers he had been hesitating to for the past two hours.

"Hello," said the voice at the other end of the line.

"Hi, Bob, it's John. How's it going?"

"Hi, John. Everything's OK."

"Listen, how's your schedule look for tomorrow?"

"I'm clear. You able to come up?"

"Yeah, thought I'd fly up and take a closer look-see at the situation, that is if the weather breaks. Can you pick me up at the airport about 5:30?"

"Sure, that would be great."

"You do have an extra cot up there, don't you?"

"Yes indeedy, you can have the honeymoon suite all to yourself. I haven't slept there since Lori left."

"Now, listen, Bob...no commitments regarding the situation with Mr. Raintree. Just a closer look, OK?"

"Understood, I don't want to go on a wild goose chase either. We'll just talk it out."

"See you tomorrow, then."

"OK John, have a good flight."

John turned out the lights and locked the door behind him.

# Off to Bob's

John got home about six. He barely made it through the door before Angie started in.

"You're not going to believe this," she said. "Do you remember Cousin Horace saying to Daddy, 'Are you ever going to tell that woman of yours the truth of the matter?' after Mama pushed him in the pool Friday night?"

"Yeah, I remember. Your Daddy looked like he swallowed a frog afterwards."

"Well, when Mama and Daddy got home she browbeat him till he broke down and told her."

"Told her what?"

"That Horace is her half-brother!"

"Well, I'll be damned. So, her beloved Pa Pa was dipping his wick where he oughtn't have, and Horace was the result. How is she taking it?"

"There was a lot of emotion, but I think she's going to be fine…you know Mama…she'll be fine.

"I noticed that she was unusually subdued at the yacht fiasco yesterday. Guess it was sinking in. What about your Daddy? He must have known about it all along."

"I felt sorry for poor Daddy. Yes, he did know, and Mama came down on him pretty hard for not telling her before now, but I'm sure they'll work it out."

"Does Horace know she knows?"

"No, but I'll bet he will before the sun sets tomorrow."

"That should be interesting. How about you? How do you feel about it?"

"I'm fine with it. You know how crazy I am about cousin Horace. I just hate it that he felt like he had to keep everything to himself all those years…and Daddy too."

"By the way, Angie, If the weather's clears, I'm going to fly up to Tuscaloosa tomorrow afternoon and check out a possible case."

"Oh, really, how long are you planning to stay?"

"I'll be back Tuesday afternoon. I just want to check out a referral from Bob. I'll be staying with him."

"Bob Savage?"

"Yes, Bob Savage."

"Don't you have enough to do right here in Mobile without taking on something up in Tuscaloosa?"

"Well, I'm about to finish up on the Gulf Shores Project, and…Angie, are you trying to tell me how to run my business, now?"

"No, Mr. Attorney, I just don't understand why you've got to go up there when you have plenty to do around here."

"Look, I'm well aware that you're not particularly fond of Bob, but…"

"Why, I've always been polite to him."

"You're polite to everybody."

"I just wonder why it is that every time he calls and says frog, you leap."

"For God's sake, Angie, get off my back."

John got to the airport about three-thirty Monday afternoon. Oscar Rasberry, his mechanic, had the little bird fueled and ready to go.

"See you tomorrow afternoon, Oscar," he said as he revved the engine and began taxiing towards the runway.

"Roger, John, see you tomorrow afternoon."

It felt good, really good, to roll down the runway at full throttle, ease back on the wheel and feel the sensation of lift as the craft became airborne. *Birdman has escaped his gilded cage*, he mused…*and all the crap in the bottom of it*. He headed north, leaving, at least for a while, all concerns of Mobile, Alabama below and behind.

The Piper purred like a contented kitten as he watched the landscape a mile below slowly change from coastal plains to the delta with large squares and rectangles of cultivated fields…then change again to the more forested terrain of the Appalachian foothills.

He was struck by the thought that in a time before planes, trains and automobiles, it would have taken over ten days to cover the two hundred miles between Mobile and Tuscaloosa. He and his airplane would make it in less than two hours.

In the hypnotic hum of the engine, he thought about the land below being so casually traversed by him and his little flying machine.

What stories the land could tell, came to mind, and the secrets it must hold… knowing the joys and sorrows of all those who passed through, and of the ones who stayed and sowed their seeds. Now, Mother Earth holds it all…the blood, sweat, tears…and bones.

John's thoughts were interrupted by the sight of a big Red Tail Hawk off to the right and below him…about four o'clock. Its wings spread full as it rode the thermals.

*Freedom,* he silently remarked as he throttled the engine back and put the Piper into a glide path that placed it right beside the bird. Only a few dozen feet separated them.

He peered through the side window for a close look. The hawk cocked its head and looked him square in the eyes.

Suddenly, out of nowhere a huge eagle appeared. It swooped; its talons outstretched and struck the hawk. The two birds, entangled, spiraled downward for about a hundred feet or more. Then, the eagle let go and flew away. The Hawk continued in free-fall.

"What the Hell?" John blurted as he opened the throttle and peeled away from the scene.

The sun was setting blood red as the Piper Tri Pacer touched down at the Tuscaloosa airport. Bob was there to meet him with the usual grin on his face.

"Hey old man, how was the flight?"

"Fine Bob, a little strange at one point, but fine. Have you ever heard of an eagle attacking a hawk?"

"No, can't say that I have."

"Well, that's what happened. The hawk got the short end of the stick."

"Must have been a territorial thing. How about us going and getting some BBQ…remember Dream Land?"

"Do I ever…that's where I first met my in-laws."

As the two engaged in the messy business of devouring barbeque ribs while washing ithem down with draft beer, they began devising a game plan for the next day.

"I thought we'd do a fly-over in the morning," said John, "scope things from the air before driving way over there."

"Not a bad Idea. If we get an early start we can bring the plane back and still have plenty of time to make the drive. We might even be able to put it down in Raintree's cornfield if its plowed under."

"We better not risk that."

"I think you're going to find William to be an interesting character, John. He's calm and cool as a cucumber, but you can tell he's not the kind of man to mess with. He moves like a cat."

After their fill of BBQ they headed for Bob's place. It had been a long time since the old comrades had spent time together; so there was a lot of catch up talk to do.

The infamous "Goldfish" lay on its side next to the front door. The grass needed cutting and the house looked in need of general repairs, but it wasn't too bad on the inside…considering.

"How's bachelor life suiting you, Bobby?"

"Great…I can do what I want to, when I want to and don't have to listen to a bunch of bitching…it's great. How're things with the upper crust down there in Mobile?"

"Bob, some of those people are so out of touch with the real world, you wouldn't believe it."

"How are Angie and the boys?"

"They're doing fine."

"That's good."

"How are you really doing, Bob? Remember, its old John you're talking to."

"Not worth a damn if you really want to know the truth, John Boy."

"Still have feelings for her?"

"Yeah, I miss her. But, it really doesn't matter how I feel. There's no back-tracking under any circumstances, now, even if both of us wanted to.

"Pride?"

"It's more than that. The line's been crossed. Can't unscramble eggs or un-ring a bell, John. You know that. Betrayal is something I just can't handle.

"Bad, huh?"

"Yep, I should have known something was up when she insisted on us moving to Tuscaloosa. That doctor friend of hers said he had a head nurse position waiting on her down here. He had a position for her all right."

"That's rough."

"Well, I should have known better when I ran into her seven years after she dumped me the first time. She seemed so different than before, though…grown up…going to nursing school. And, she looked beautiful. I never did get over her the first time…you know that, though.

"Yeah, I know."

"Well, anyway, we made it thirteen years. Now, here I am right back where I started from. At least you found the right one the first time."

John made no reply. He looked at his watch.

"You know, John, "I really do miss the old days…before Lori and all the other complications of this idiotic rat race. I miss places like the valley and Lovers' Leap…and things like our canoe trip on the Cahaba. You've got to admit, we did have a good childhood."

"Yeah, we definitely had a good childhood. The Valley's gone now, you know. They put I-65 right through it."

"Yeah, I know. Remember, we were going to buy the land when we grew up, and you were going to build your house on one side and me build mine on the other…and you were going to live there with your wood nymph, and me with my perfect girl?"

"So much for wood nymphs and perfect girls, Bobby. By the way, they built a filling station up on the crest right next to Lover's Leap."

"You've got to be kidding…I guess they're going to end up making a parking lot out of the whole damn mountain before it's over with. You know, John

Boy, I think I'm gonna' dedicate the rest of my life to the pursuit of beauty and pleasure."

"What's new?"

"Well, This time around I may just do it in style…if things work out. There's a cave full of gold out there, you know."

"Better be careful, Bob. Old Raintree's gold just may have a curse on it."

John looked at his watch again and yawned. "It's been a long day, and I've about had it. Where do you want me to crash?"

John quickly drifted into sleep.

Sometime during the night, out of the mist of a dream, a young man, younger than John, appeared at the foot of his bed.

"Who are you?" John asked, feeling a trilling shiver throughout his torso.

"I'm John Starr."

"You can't be John Starr. I'm John Starr."

"You know who I am, John."

"Is it you, Dad?"

"Yes, it's me, Son," said the apparition.

"Where have you been? I've waited all my life just to see you…to talk to you. Where have you been?"

"Places you could never dream of."

"Why are you just now coming to me?"

"I've always been with you…and your mother."

"I'm sorry Mom married Joe, Dad. I know she betrayed us, but she was so lonely."

"No, she didn't betray us. I came to her, just like I've come to you, and told her that it was what I wanted her to do. Life is for the living, John. Never forget that. Now, I've come to you…to give you warning."

"Warning of what?"

"Of things that are soon destined to come your way."

"What things?"

"All I can say is that you have been chosen for a task. You'll know when it begins. Just beware of those things that seem to be real, but are not, and of those things that don't seem to be real, but are."

"I don't understand…you're talking in riddles."

"A familiar voice will guide you through…if you will listen. I've got to go now, Son, take care."

"Wait! What happened to you during the war? They said you got shot down. What really happened?"

"I was on patrol over open water when Hoshimoto came out of the clouds. Neither of us had a choice. As we both struggled to get into firing position, our planes collided. We went down together."

"That Jap took you away from Mom and me. I hope you sent him to Hell, Dad."

"No, war was the cause of it, not Hoshimoto. Now, we're brothers in spirit winds. He had a boy too, John…about your age."

The apparition began to fade.

"There's no more time left for me here, Son. I've got to go."

"WAIT, DAD!" Cried John, "WAIT!"

"What's wrong, John?" shouted Bob as he burst into the room. "Are you OK?"

"I'm OK. I was just having a crazy dream…that's all."

C H A P T E R  19

# Broken Wings

JOHN WOKE AT daybreak and stepped outside. It looked like a good day for flying…clear skies except for a few friendly cumulus clouds. Bob was still in the sack. He put on a pot of coffee and turned on the radio to catch the weather report…a fair day predicted. While going through his usual morning grooming ritual he reflected on the dream.

*Wonder what that was all about,* he pondered, *maybe the hawk and eagle thing triggered it.*

He quickly dismissed the whole thing as being nothing more than a crazy dream; just another thing in the scrambled mix of what had become his life as of late.

"Rise and shine," he called out, knocking on Bob's bedroom door, "its time to get going."

John looked at his watch. It was 9:27 when he let the breaks off and they began rolling down the runway. The heading was east, towards Bibb County. "Want to fly on up to the Helena Bridge and retrace our old canoe route?" he asked, "It's not that far out of the way."

"Yeah, let's do it…just for old times' sake," Bob replied.

John adjusted the heading a little more northerly, and they were off to the place where the adventure began.

The old Helena Bridge came into view. Moments later they were above it and making a turn towards the southwest.

The Piper cast its shadow as the fair weather aeronauts skimmed the treetops and followed the winding river valley toward Raintree's place. Birds scrambled in flocks.

"I want to come back as a bird, Bobby. How about you?"

"I don't wanna' leave in the first place, John Boy, at least not any time soon. Think you could get this thing a little higher so I won't have to make a decision today?"

"Sure buddy, hold on to your drawers."

John pulled back on the wheel, and up they went, making a giant loop in the pristine sky.

"We're free, Bobby…like the birds."

"We're not gonna' be anything but suet for the birds if you don't cut the acrobatics!"

"That's a nasty looking cloud over there in the southwest," said John, "looks like it's coming this way."

"Yeah, that thing is angry."

"We should be able to beat it. Lets make a quick run over Raintree's place, then bee-line it back to the airport."

"Better hurry, then, looks like it's moving at a pretty good clip."

The engine squalled as John pushed it to full throttle.

It was a matter of minutes before they approached the old railroad trestle that crossed the river, then Booth's Ford, then the scarred landscape left by Salvo Mining Company. Finally, William Raintree's cabin came into view.

"Lets go upstairs for a better look," said John as leaders of the swell began to move in.

He took the airplane up and banked left to begin the circle. Then, suddenly…"Oh crap, Bobby!"

A dark churning mass was directly above them.

"Let's get the hell out from under this thing," he shouted, banking the Piper even steeper, and going into a dive.

"Something's happening, Johnny!"

Without warning, a funnel dropped out of the boiling cloud center and came directly at them. The little craft was caught in the whirlwind.

"You got control, John!"

"No!"

Helplessly, the plane spun in the great spiral winds…upright, then vertical, then upside down. There was a terrifying snap as the left wing strut ripped.

Then, the whole left wing section tore completely away from the fuselage and went flying off on its own. No way to get off a "May Day"…no time to fear, pray…or curse…no slow motion or flashbacks…just vertigo.

The roar was deafening as the spinning went on and on. It seemed endless until the crackling of tree branches put a blunt end to the ordeal. There was a dead silence on the forest floor.

The awesome wind left as quickly as it had come, leaving behind only the crumpled wreckage of the small aircraft and broken twisted trees as evidence that it had ever been there. All was calm.

From above, John looked down at a battered body on the forest floor as it tried to raise its head…desperately struggling to get to its feet. Time and again it tried, only to collapse and fall back to the ground…like a wounded animal, holding on, with only primal instinct to survive. This animal, however, was human.

Finally, it rolled over on its back. He looked at the face. It was his face. The poor wretched creature writhing on the ground was him.

*Oh, my God!*

He shuddered, feeling the full blunt of horror.

Suddenly, John was back in his body, looking up through the forest canopy, at the sky. Dead or alive, he was aware of his existence.

"Hang on, hang on," he kept repeating. "Where's Bob? 'Got to find Bob!"

He was losing his battle for consciousness, and felt himself slipping into darkness…being pulled toward some abyss.

"Don't let go! 'Got to find Bob!"

Something was there…watching. He felt its presence. With blurred blood-soaked vision he scanned the woodland around him. There was nothing. Then, in a glance upward he connected with sharp piercing eyes looking down from a broken branch…a lone crow.

He let go and fell into darkness.

John woke abruptly. He was lying on his back, viewing a clear blue sky. The jarring bounces, the dust and sensation of forward motion made it obvious that he was in the back of a pickup truck. He lay on a blanket, his head toward the tailgate. His body was numb, but his face itched and stung in the baking sun.

He turned his head to the left. Bob lay beside him. He was looking up to-ward the sky, locked in a stare. He had no nose. His right arm was upright, rest-ing on the elbow. With his left arm crossed over his chest, he grasped a handless wrist. There was only a bloody rag covering the stump and makeshift tourniquet on his forearm.

"Bobby," rasped John, "We gotta' make it through this one."

"I don't think so," came the reply. Bob coughed as blood trickled from the side of his mouth."

"We've got to."

After a few silent moments, Bob turned his head to John.

"I've gotta' go, Johnny," he whispered…then, turned away.

John knew that this would be the last time he would see his old friend in the world of the living. He slipped back into darkness.

# CHAPTER 20

# Where's John?

"IT APPEARS THAT he has a brain stem concussion, Dr. LeBeau," said the chief neurologist at Bessemer Memorial Hospital, "which explains the coma, but what I don't understand is the beta waves. Look at the EEG. The brain is incredibly active, like an individual who is conscious. Frankly, I don't know what's going on. Comas are very unpredictable, as I'm sure you know."

"Do you think we could move him, Dr. Boggs…back to Mobile?"

"I'm afraid that would be too risky. With head trauma like this and possible internal injuries, I'd say no. In addition to the flesh wounds, there's a nasty break of the collarbone, too. It would be best to leave him here. We'll keep you well posted."

"By the way, Dr. Boggs, I understand the crash happened in a remote area. Do you know how my son-in-law got here?"

"An older gentleman, a Mr. Raintree, brought him and another man in a pickup truck. It happened on his property. Unfortunately, the other gentleman was DOA. We've identified him as a Robert Savage. Do you know him, or how we can contact his family?"

"Yes, we'll take care of it."

Angie knelt over her husband.

"Honey, if you can hear me, squeeze my hand." There was no response.

"John, where are you?"

"Angie," said Carter, "We need to go. There's nothing we can do for John."

"Daddy, We can't just leave him here!"

"We need to get back to Mobile. The boys need you. John's being well cared for, and they'll call us immediately if there's any change. Come on, dear, we need to go, now."

# Part Three

# CHAPTER 21

# This Ain't Real

JOHN STARR WAS lost in a strange world. Whether it was of his own making or not, he didn't know, but one thing was for sure, it wasn't particularly to his liking.

He found himself back in the wilderness, on a woodland path. The colors around him were dark and drab, like an old oil painting dulled by age. Confused and disoriented, he called out for Bob, but there was no reply. Something was there though…watching. He could feel it. He looked up, and just as he suspected, there was the crow, perched on a shadowy branch.

"Crow!" He shouted, "Who are you? What are you?"

"I am the eyes of the spirits," the creature somehow, someway communicated, "I am the watcher, the messenger."

"Why are you watching me?"

"Because, you are the one…the keeper."

"What the hell are you talking about?"

"You will know."

"When will I know, what?"

"When you have the quivers."

"What quivers?"

"The quivers of truth. They hold arrows that fly from the page, and sting with truth."

"Where are these things?"

"You possess one, Raintree the other." The crow then flew away.

John began walking down the path when a stranger approached from the opposite direction. He wore a robe of burlap-like material and carried a staff with a silver cross mounted on it. The stubbled crown of his head had obviously been shaved at one time. By all appearance, the man was a medieval monk.

John quickly concluded that he was in some bizarre dream, yet it seemed so real. He could even smell the musty scent emitting from the strange man's clothing.

*I can end this little drama anytime I want to,* went through his mind, *but I'll let it play on…at least for a while.*

"Excuse me, sir, I'm looking for my friend. He's about 5' 10", medium build, and he's seriously injured. Have you seen him?"

"Lo siento, Señor. I speak only a little Inglés."

"What is your language, sir?"

"Español, Señor."

"I've only had high school Spanish. No hablo Español muy bien, but I'll try:

"Mi amigo es Savage. I've got to find him!"

"There are many savages in this land, Señor."

"No, you don't understand! His name is Savage, Bob Savage!"

"Señor, with respect I ask, why do you not wear clothes?"

John looked down and saw that he was naked.

"I don't know. I lost them," he replied.

"I did not know there were English in this land."

"I'm not English. I'm American."

"How can this be? You do not look or speak like a savage."

"I don't know anything right now. I'm lost. Can you help me?"

"I do not think the governor-general will take kindly to a naked Englishman in our midst, but I will help. Here, take my robe. Perhaps we can find your friend among the savages and make a plea for his release."

Amazingly, between John's high school Spanish and the stranger's broken English, the two managed to communicate…at least to some degree.

As they made their way down the path, John in the robe and the Spaniard in his wool undergarments, he asked, "Are you a man of the clergy?"

"Si, Señor, I am Padre Alvaro de la Torre."

"I'm John Starr, pleased to meet you, Padre. Where are we going?"

"To the town of Cahawba. It is less than a half league away."

"What's there?"

"The expedition."

"What expedition?"

"The La Florida expedition, of course. Have you been asleep for the past year, Señor?"

"I'm not sure of anything, Padre. Who's your leader?"

"The governor-general, his Excellency, Hernando de Soto."

"What time period is this, Padre?"

"The Sun is over head, around noon I suppose."

"No, I mean what date, what year."

"It is October the second, in the Year of Our Lord, one thousand five hundred and forty, of course."

"I'll be damned,"

"I certainly hope not, señor."

*This ain't real. It's just a dream…I can wake myself any time I want to.*


The path merged with what appeared to be a well-traveled trail at least fifteen feet in width.

They had only been on the road a few minutes when the pounding, galloping sound of hooves could be heard approaching from the opposite direction.

"Quickly! Off the road with us, Señor John! Raise your hood!"

Within moments, a pack of six greyhounds followed by at least ten horsemen fitted in sixteenth century Spanish armor and fully armed with lance and sword were upon them. Their steeds were covered in plates of armor as well. One of the dogs looked squarely at John with a hellish glare as the awesome force thundered by.

John had been around modern machinery of war, but nothing he had seen before was more intimidating than this band of dogs and armor-clad horsemen.

"What was that all about?" he asked, feeling the chill go through his body.

"It was a patrol sent out to search for townspeople and escaped servants, Señor. Fortunately, it was not your scent that the dogs were seeking."

*Spanish Conquistadors…ridiculous… time to wake up.*

He strained from his head to his gut, reaching for consciousness…but, it wouldn't come.

*Holy crap, maybe I'm dead…but, where's God and Jesus and all them.*

He strained again, but couldn't escape.

*Got to get a grip.*

In silence, the man from the present and the man from the past continued their journey toward the town of Cahawba.

# Chapter 22

# Cahawba

The forest began opening to gentle rolling fields of corn with cane-roofed huts scattered about. In plain view, about a quarter mile away was the town.

An encampment of a hundred tents, more or less, sprawled in the foreground outside the town. A large congregation of men and horses were in and around the encampment.

"That is Cahawba," said the priest.

"Wait here at the edge of the woods while I fetch clothes for you. Stay out of sight, señor; It could be dangerous…I need my robe, please."

As John whiled away the time hidden in the foliage beside the road, waiting for Alvaro's return, he began replaying the events that brought him to this place. His thoughts drifted to Bob.

*Where is he, now?* he wondered. Then, he began to wonder if the padre would return.

At least an hour had passed. Gnats and mosquitoes were making the situation most uncomfortable.

*What I'd give right now for that old piece of tarpaulin Bob was using to cover himself when we first met.*

His thoughts were interrupted by distant human wailings and harsh voices issuing commands. He hunkered down in the dense vegetation alongside the road as the sounds grew louder.

From his vantage point, he saw about forty men and women walking in single file, shackled in chains…some with children alongside them. Several women were carrying infants. They were obviously Indian folk. Some were crying and wailing…some just stared ahead in silence. Behind, driving them like cattle were the armored horseman and dogs that had come by earlier. They were headed in the direction of Cahawba.

One of the dogs left the road and came in his direction.

"Bruno, aquí!" shouted one of the soldiers. The dog obeyed his master's command and rejoined the pack, much to John's relief.

Horror turned to anger as he watched the entourage pass, but it didn't take a genius to know the consequences of any rash act of heroics.

Alvaro finally showed up. He handed John a robe and a pair of sandals.

"You are now my assistant," he said, "You are to be called Fray Juan Estrella. You are a Christian, are you not, Señor, John?"

"Yes, I'm Methodist."

"What is Methodist?"

"Don't worry, Padre, we believe in the same God…I think."

Alvaro pulled out scissors and a razor from his handbag.

"One more thing, Amigo. Please sit."

He then proceeded to shave the crown of John's head.

"There, Señor. You make a fine looking man of God. Now, please do me the same service. It has been a week since I have attended this chore."

John obliged, nicking the good padre only twice.

"Now, we shall go and find your savage," said the padre. "You must, however, stay silent and away from those familiar with the clergy. There will be danger enough of discovery without the further tempting of fate. Since you do not know Español well, I shall say that you have lost your ability to speak due to some strange fever."

"Right."

"Also, you do know that I cannot protect you if you are discovered?"

"Yes, Padre, I understand."

The scenic landscape looked deceptively peaceful as they walked down the gentle rolling slopes toward the town. In many ways it was like a typical country road in the south. John would have considered it to be a pleasant stroll, except for knowing that things were terribly amiss here. He became increasingly concerned for his safety.

As they continued their walk toward Cahawba, John recalled the high school textbook version of the de Soto expedition. It was his recollection that the conquistador was presented as a noble explorer who blazed a trail into the then unknown territories of the southeast, and brought Christianity to the uncivilized Indians. The books failed to mention, however, the violation of those whose lands he invaded…and the devices of terror used, like chains and war dogs. He decided to play dumb, ask questions…get to the truth.

"What is the purpose of the expedition, Padre?"

"My fellow clergymen and I are here to bring Christendom and salvation to the savages. The other gentlemen and soldiers of the entrada are here seeking wealth and fame…for themselves, for the crown, and to bring power and glory to España.

"What kind of riches are the gentlemen and soldiers searching for, Padre?"

"Gold, Señor…cities of gold…like the Governor saw in Peru. He claims it is here, hiding in this land…somewhere."

"Have you found any gold…or saved any souls?"

"Sadly, none of this has come to pass thus far. We of the clergy have been given no opportunity to administer to the savages, nor have the gentlemen and soldiers of fortune found riches. We have traveled many leagues and known only hardship…and left only misery behind us."

"Why are towns occupied by the expedition if there's no gold…why are the Indians taken prisoner?"

"It is a matter of survival. We must secure maize and other foodstuffs from the town stores, and conscribe natives to porter equipment and provisions…and to become servants to the gentlemen and soldiers. The Governor tries always to keep at least five hundred for such purposes. There is also the matter of providing women for the gentlemen and soldiers," said the padre, looking up and making the sign of the cross, as if apologizing to God for their unholy activity. "There must be constant replenishment to maintain this number, for many become sick and die…and many escape."

"Is that what will happen to those poor devils I saw in chains on the road? There were even children among them. Will they become slaves, porters and concubines?"

"Si," lamented the priest as he made the sign of the cross again. "Those were townspeople who ran to the woods upon learning of our approach. They had received word of the Governor's tactics before our arrival. When they run away, he has them rounded up and selects the ones who will serve the expedition."

"What are the Governor's tactics, Padre…when you all enter a town or village?"

"When we arrive, the Governor attempts first to establish friendly terms with the leader. Most of the time, friendly or not, the leader will be held hostage as he bargains for maize, servants and women. If the king or chieftain complies with all demands, we take what is needed and go in peace. If he does not comply, then provisions, porters, servants and women are taken by force, and all are treated with great severity.

Some of the savages along our route have been friendly…others have been defiant and made war on us. Those who have not acted in the Governor's favor have been dealt with in a most brutal fashion. In the end, all have succumbed to the will of de Soto. Hardship and lack of reward has hardened the souls of our comrades."

"How many are there in the expedition?"

"We began with six hundred and two, not including the savage porters and servants. Now, there are five hundred and ninety six."

"It seems like the natives could overwhelm the expedition by sheer numbers, Padre. How is it possible for so small a force to control such large numbers of warriors?"

"As you have already seen, Señor John, the savage's crude weapons are no match for Spanish steel. There is also the matter of horses, war dogs, armor, and the arquebus."

A moment of silence passed as John tried to absorb all that was being told to him.

"I can see, Señor John, that what you saw on this road disturbs you greatly. It does me also. I have had to bear witness to much worse."

"As a representative of the church, can't you do something about the treatment of these people?"

"I am just as much a prisoner as those poor, unsaved souls. No, Señor, there is nothing I, nor you, can do. It is in God's hands."

John and Alvaro arrived at the edge of town...at the encampment where several hundred men milled about or lounged. Many were playing cards...jabbering in Spanish, laughing and carrying on as they placed their bets. Others were cooking, cleaning weapons, or fondling the native women. Most had beards or mustaches and goatees.

There were many Indians among them. Some wore iron collars around their neck and were on leashes of chain as they served their masters.

Hygiene apparently was not a priority. A nauseous odor drifted throughout the encampment...a combination of human sweat, stews simmering in cooking pots and animal dung. None of the men looked or smelled as if they had bathed recently.

As he and Alvaro moved through the camp, John noted that these Spaniards didn't particularly look like fierce conquistadors. Most were rather small and appeared to be fairly benign. He figured he could take any of them out with one good punch.

John spotted a small river not far from the edge of town. There, a makeshift corral contained at least a hundred horses.

Then, it caught his eye. Also corralled was a large group of natives, in chains and under guard. Pigs and piglets scampered about the area.

John said nothing, but pointed in that direction.

"Those are the defiant ones," said Alvaro, "and the captured townspeople who ran away upon hearing of our arrival into the territory."

Again, saying nothing, John shook his head.

They entered the town. Centered in the cluster of well over a hundred log buildings of varying sizes stood a large earthen mound. On its crown was a lodge-looking structure.

There was a large plaza at ground level in front of the mound.

The buildings appeared to be sound and crafted in a good and workmanlike manner. Some were plastered with clay, and troweled as smooth as any master mason could have done.

*This place was not built by primitive savages,* John contemplated.

A good number of Spaniards loitered about in the plaza…conversing in small groups, putting their native servants to task, and gambling. It appeared that they were of a more noble class than those in the encampment. Though looking worse for wear, many wore fancy hats with plumes, capes, satin-trimmed shirts, breeches, hose and boots.

"They must be the officers and gentlemen."

"Si, señor, John…the officers and gentlemen."

*This has got to be a joke… these dandies… invincible conquerors?*

Then, he recalled the incident out on the road.

*Don't underestimate, Starr. There are hard, ruthless bastards under all those adornments.*

"That is the Governor's quarters," said Alvaro, pointing to a large house decorated with ornate carvings. "He has evicted the chieftain, and now occupies his dwelling."

"Where is the Chief?"

"He is quarantined and under guard."

"In other words, he's a prisoner."

"Yes, friendly or not, the Governor always holds the leader hostage until we get from him what is needed and are ready to move on. It insures our safety."

The man emerging from the house was rather small…probably no more than five and a half feet tall. His dark eyes penetrated the air and those around him, leaving no doubt as to who was in charge. With a graying beard, he looked to be about forty years old.

"I assume that's de Soto."

"Si, Señor John, that is the Governor."

So, that's the great Hernando de Soto thought John, just a swarthy little banty rooster.

The creases in his face told of a man who had lived hard.

Then, another man emerged, a native, ducking his head as he came through the opening.

"My God, he's damn near a giant," said John.

The man was at least a head taller than any of the others around him. He was large limbed but lean and wore a bright-red turban-like headdress and a feathered robe. Though handsome, his face was somber and stern.

"That is the great Tuscaloosa," said Alvaro, "king of the vast regions south of here. He accompanies us to the city of Mabila where he has said he will furnish us with food and supplies."

As John observed the huge well-proportioned warrior chief, he remarked: "He'd make one hell of a linebacker."

"What is linebacker," asked Alvaro.

"Its somebody you don't want to mess with, Padre...surely he's not a prisoner of this bunch of little marauders."

"In a way he is. As you have already seen, Spanish steel and horses can be very convincing. The Governor keeps Tuscaloosa as a guest isolated from his entourage. There is an uneasy peace between the two."

As darkness fell upon the town and campfires glowed in the cool October night, John and the padre ate their fill of corncakes along with some roasted pumpkin laced with honey, and drank sassafras tea. There was also a meat provided by the Indians that the padre called 'little dog.' John figured that it was probably possum. He passed on it.

Shortly after dinner, his eyelids became heavy, and he drifted into sleep under the ancient southern skies.

Bob quickly appeared in John's dreams, as if he had been anxiously waiting to communicate in the only way allowed him.

"Bob, is that you?"

"Yes, it's me, Johnny."

"Are you OK?"

"I'm OK, but I've definitely departed the physical world. Felt myself leave the old bod in the bed of Raintree's pickup truck. I even watched you all from up above.

"Yeah, That happened to me, too, right after the crash, but I came back...I think.""

"I know."

"So, you're dead, Bob…am I dead, too?"

"No, you've been chosen for the task."

"What task?"

"It has to do with the land…Raintree's land. You're on it right now, you know."

"I'm on Raintree's land?"

"Yeah, but in a different time. That's what I've come to warn you about; so listen carefully. No matter what, don't do something stupid or heroic…and get the hell out of there as soon as you can. Let the past take care of itself. There's nothing you can do about what goes on there anyway. It's already happened. Get back to your time. That's where the task you've been chosen for is."

"Tell me about the task."

"I was the one chosen at first, but got too personal with the gold…wanted to become rich and enjoy all the trimmings that came with it. That was a no, no. Got kicked to the curb…deserved it, too. Now, it's up to you, John.

"Bobby, What the hell is the task?"

"It will have to reveal itself to you in its own way. You'll know when the time comes, John. I'm sure it'll be different for you than it would have been for me… see that light over there?"

"Yes, I see it."

"I'm going to it now, Amigo. Take care."

"Wait a minute, Bobby. Will I see you again?"

"I don't know. I'll come back…if I can."

CHAPTER 23

# Awakening

THE SUN ROSE…a fiery disc in the eastern sky. A chill was in the early autumn air as John awakened…still in the world of Padre Alvaro de la Torre, conquistadors and hapless Indians. Colors were now clear and vivid. This world had become all too real. John tried to leave the crazy dream again, but couldn't. Alvaro was sitting on a straw mat, reclined against the wall of a log house. He was writing in a leather bound journal that rested on his lap…dipping the quill in an inkpot on the ground beside him

"Good morning, Padre."

"Oh, Buenos días, Señor John. I tried to wake you when you fell asleep last night, to come inside, but your sleep was too deep; so I covered you and left you to your dreams."

"Yeah…my dreams. What are you doing, Padre?"

"I am keeping a chronicle of the expedition."

"That's a good idea. Are you telling it like it is?"

"I do not understand, Señor John. What means 'telling it like it is?' "

"Are you being accurate…truthful?"

"Sí, that is why I reveal it to no one. Only history will know…if my writings survive."

"I've got to go, Padre. Where's the john."

"Are you not here señor, John, and where are you going?"

"The latrine, Padre, Where is the latrine?"

"Oh, it is at the back side of the houses."


"So, that's what they used," muttered John when he noticed the stack of corncobs next to the open ditch with crude seating arrangements made from poles and spars lashed together. "Bad time not to have something to read," he mumbled.

Upon John's return from taking care of nature's call, Alvaro announced jokingly, "I think I shall also retire to the 'john', John."

In his absence, John picked up the padre's journal, just to have something in writing to look at. He could only make out a few words. Then, on impulse, he inked the quill and scribbled across the top of the page, *'This is crazy!'*

"Shall we go and search for your friend among the savages?" asked Alvaro, having returned from taking care of his business.

"I don't think he's here, Padre, but I would like for you to show me around some more."

"Sí, John. Raise your hood."

As they walked among the Spaniards in the town square, John's eyes met with those of a native manservant. He wore an iron collar…presumably the poor fellow was chained when not performing tasks for his master. There was something all too familiar about him…something deep within the eyes. The two stared at each other, as if both were trying to recall a connection. John didn't say anything…not even to Alvaro. The man's master, a brutish looking Spaniard, obviously of high rank, was within earshot.

There was a buzz of conversation in the air…as if some important event was about to take place.

"What's all the talk about, Padre?" asked John.

"The governor has put the word out that we will be departing this place in two days. After replenishing supplies in Mabila, the expedition will head for the coast…to the bay of Mobile where ships await to take us back to Cuba."

"Padre, Mobile is exactly where I need to go! Can I stay with the expedition until we get there?"

"Sí, señor John, if that is your desire, but surely the English do not have a settlement there…do they?"

"Not exactly…I'll explain everything later."

"Sí, John, I hope you do…in the meantime there will be a feast and celebration this evening…to honor Tuscaloosa."

In the afternoon, shortly after mass, the celebration got underway. Tuscaloosa sat on cushions at the foot of the mound, facing the plaza. Among the native attendants around him, one held a round, color-striped umbrella-like deerskin shield above his head. de Soto sat beside him in a large chair.

Dialogue commenced with the assistance of four bilingual interpreters. Each tongue, beginning with Spanish, cascaded to the other until it finally reached the ears of Tuscaloosa. Padre de la Torre did his best to serve as translator for John.

"Mighty Chief," de Soto began, "Your greatness and power is known throughout the land. We have come in peace and friendship, and wish only to pass through on our way to the great waters where we will board our vessels and take leave. We are in debt to you for your hospitality and the provisions you are willing to furnish us…" He went on for some time talking about brotherly love and Christian virtue.

Tuscaloosa neither smiled nor responded.

*Wonder why no smiley face from the big guy after all the praise?* John snidely remarked within. *Could it be because he's virtually a prisoner of the little bastard?*

After the speeches came a display of force thinly disguised as ceremony. Spanish mounts charged their armored beast as if in battle. Mock swordplay among the soldiers, jousting with lances and the firing of an arquebus seemed adequate to accomplish the purpose. de Soto, himself, mounted his Andalusian stallion and charged the warrior king, halting it only a few feet in front of him.

Tuscaloosa remained cool and un-rattled, and offered only a contemptuous smile to the unwanted guests in his lands.

Then, came the gifts. de Soto presented him with a crimson cap and cape, a chest full of colored glass, and five pigs.

John got it. The Spaniard's display of force was to discourage any bright idea by Tuscaloosa to challenge them. The flattery and gifts just rounded out their version of the old carrot and stick routine.

As afternoon shadows lengthened, the aroma of roasting pig filled the air. John took in the familiar smell: *Damned if the place doesn't smell like Dreamland Barbeque.*

He was tempted, but it would not have been safe to participate in the feast; so again, John and the Padre ate corncakes. For want of variety, they dipped them in a buttery bear's grease flavored with mulberries. This time John tried some of Alvaro's "little dog." It was a little greasy, but didn't taste too bad.

It was well into the night before things quieted in the town of Cahawba. John went into one of the deserted houses and lay down on a soft bed of straw covered with deerskin. Soon, he fell into a deep sleep.

From a vantage point forty feet above the forest floor, John found himself looking at the world through eyes other than his own. Images were much clearer and sharper than his vision could ever allow. He felt a tingling sensation as if low voltage electricity ran through him…as if he were in some plasmatic state.

He looked around. Pine branches surrounded him. He looked down. There was a path alongside a small river. Moments later he heard running footsteps on the path. He looked. The native manservant he had seen the day before passed below running full speed. Shortly thereafter came the sound of galloping hoofs. A horseman clad in full armor, his lance extended, passed below.

John felt lift. He was in flight, following the scene being played out below. He caught a glimpse of powerful black feathered wings flapping on either side of whatever it was that held his essence. The host then landed on a branch high above. John observed the action taking place beneath.

The native suddenly stopped, turned and faced his adversary. The horseman lowered his lance and charged. The native dodged just in the nick of time and managed to grab the lance. He pulled, dismounting the horseman. The horseman hit the ground with a clanging thud. The native quickly took the lance, and standing over the stunned Spaniard raised it above his head and thrust it down, piercing the armor and heart of the downed warrior.

*The skull…the helmet…Buddy.* It all shot through John's mind like an arrow. *Could it be?* Could it be that it was the remains of this man that he and Bob found on the canoe trip so many years ago…or in the future? John woke up.

The Sun had risen high enough to kill off the morning chill when the trumpet blared. Everyone, including the soldiers bivouacked outside the town had slept late because of the previous night's celebration.

"What's going on, Padre?" John asked.

"It is a call to muster. There has been an escape by some of the servants. They have taken two swine and other provisions."

"Are the soldiers going after them?"

"Si, the Governor will not rest until they are found and punished. He has no tolerance for acts such as this."

John and the padre watched as the mounted squadron led by war dogs departed.

The rest of the morning hours passed in preparation for the march to Mabila.

It was mid-afternoon when the squadron returned with four badly beaten natives in chains, one of which was the man who was in John's dream the night before…the one so hauntingly familiar.

The prisoners were taken to the corral near the river where other shackled natives were being held. Then, it hit…this 'somebody' was Bob, yet it wasn't him at all. It couldn't be. The man was obviously an Indian. But, much of his features and body language belonged to Bob. John had seen that stubborn, determined look many times before.

"Is this the ring leader?" shouted a furious de Soto.

"Si, Excellency," answered Captain Baltasar de Gallegos, the native's master, "also, Lazaro, one of our finest cavalrymen is missing."

"Remove his nose…and his right hand! Let it be a reminder to him the next time he smells pork and thinks of stealing it. Throw the rest of them to the dogs."

"No!" shouted John.

There was a dead silence. de Soto walked over, grabbed the hood and threw it back, exposing John's face. "What did you say, Señor?"

Alvaro broke in, "Excellency, this man suffers a fever and babbles in some unknown tongue."

"Quiet, Padre, I do not recognize this man, but I do recognize his words as Ingles. Speak your native tongue, Señor!"

John remained silent.

de Soto unsheathed his saber and put its point to John's right cheek.

"I said speak!"

"Kiss my ass, you sawed off son of a bitch!"

A brief moment passed. The cold black eyes stared into John's. Then, de Soto raked the sword down John's face, from cheek to jaw. He felt a sharp pain as the sword scraped passed his jawbone. He felt the blood flow through his fingers as he clasped the wound.

In that instant, the condemned native jumped up and landed a blow to de Soto's mouth, bringing the taste of blood home to him.

"Seize him and carry out my orders!" shouted de Soto. "Restrain the imposter."

It took three men to hold John as he was forced to watch in speechless horror as Baltasar put his knife under the native's nose and with a quick flick of the wrist upward, cut it completely off. Then, with soldiers holding the poor soul writhing in anguish, he took an axe and chopped off his right hand.

The dogs were then released on the other three men.

"Damn you all," John cried out, tears streaming from his eyes as he witnessed the devil dogs ravage and tear apart fellow humans while the Spanish officers and gentlemen watched as if it were sport.

Suddenly, Bob's words rang in his ear: *"Don't try to change things; they've already happened. Don't do something stupid. Get the hell out of there!"*

With all the strength he had left, he managed to tear himself away from the smaller, lighter Spaniards who were holding him. Swinging wildly with his arms and fists, he sent them tumbling like bowling pens. The river, less than a hundred and fifty feet away, was his only hope for escape. He made a break for it, running harder than he had ever run before. But, everything went to slow motion. He couldn't seem to get enough traction, and his legs were heavy and wouldn't move fast enough. Finally, though, he made it to the riverbank, with several Spaniards in pursuit.

He was waist deep in water when he heard the explosive sound of gunfire. A micro second later he felt a sharp pain creasing the top of his skull.

He dove deep down into the blue-green waters.

John's eyes popped open. He was lying on a narrow bed with white sheets. There were rails on either side. He sat straight up.

*Am I alive, asleep, awake… out of the dream, in a dream…what?*

He looked down at the tubes in his arm.

*Not dead…must be in a hospital.*

He pulled the tubes out, threw back the covers and struggled to his feet. Weak, and barely able to walk, he made it to the window. Outside, three floors below were cars, pavement, and people.

*"I'm back. Thank God I'm back."*

His thirst was overwhelming. He made it to the bathroom where he cupped his hands under the lavatory faucet and drank the cool sweet water until he had his fill. He stood there, facing the man in the mirror. What he saw was gaunt and pathetic. The crown of the head was shaved with a bandage running front to back, and another bandage on the right cheek.

The cemetery where Bob was buried was within a few miles of the hospital. Upon his release, John insisted that Angie take him there before departing for Mobile.

She waited in the car while he limped to the gravesite. He looked down at the simple marker at the foot of Bob's grave:

Robert Arnold Savage

January 2, 1941 – August 30, !1977

"I never knew that your middle name was Arnold," said John.

He felt himself well. His eyes began to water.

"I don't know if I really saw you from wherever I was during that crazy dream, or if you can hear me now, but I want you to know that I'll miss you, old buddy.

By the way, I got that saber scar you wanted back when we were kids. You probably know that though…I'm so sorry, Bobby."

John let go and allowed himself to cry.

# Chapter 24

# "This is crazy"

John's injuries were healing well. His hair had grown out; he had put on a few pounds, and except for a nasty scar running from his right cheek down to his jaw, was looking pretty much like his old self. Things were getting back to normal.

The insurance company replaced the plane; he was putting in a three-day work week, and home life seemed to have improved. The boys were being especially helpful around the house, and Angie was more attentive than she had been in years…still not in a romantic sense, but in attitude. She and her mother had somewhat curtailed their shopping excursions since the 'Horace revelation.' Fannie was focusing a great deal of attention on Ms. Hope, Horace's elderly mother, as if she were her own…looking in on her at least once a week. She and Horace were still picking at each other and carrying on as usual, but somehow it was different…more of a concerning nag on Fannie's part with regards to his health…his self-abusive and excessive lifestyle, especially when it came to drinking and overeating. To make matters worse, at least from Horace's point of view, she even began invading sacred ground, Gulf States S & L, on a regular basis.

"Hell, I'm sorry she knows," he said, "The woman is motherin' me to death."

John was having a hard time with the loss of Bob. Not only had he lost his best friend, but there was that constant gnaw…that feeling of guilt. Even though the FAA acknowledged the probability that a freak airborne tornado caused the crash on that damnable day two and a half months earlier, John was at the controls…Bob's safety was in his hands. Also haunting, was the dream while in the coma. It seemed as real as the world he had come back to, and then there was the coincidence of injuries…what looked like a gunshot wound creasing a shaved head, and the scar on his cheek.

He decided to pass it all off as the subconscious mind's way of rationalizing what had happened. He told no one of his weird dream while in the coma, not even Jack Wainwright.

It was a mild November in Mobile…warm enough for him to kick back in his favorite lounge chair out by the pool and do a little reading.

"John," Angie called out, "supper's ready…by the way, a package came for you in the mail. It's in the den."

Before the accident, sharing evening meals as a family was a rare event. John usually sat in front of the TV, feeding his face while watching the evening news. The boys ate early, and Angie just picked at whatever she had been cooking. Now, dining together had become more the rule than the exception.

"After we're finished eating, would you guys like to go out back and build a fire? I've got a story to tell you about Uncle Bob and me when we were kids, not much older than you two."

"Dad," said Johnny, "you know you've already told us all the stories about when you and Uncle Bob were kids."

"OK, then let's roast some marshmallows."

"Dad," asked Cart, "was Uncle Bob really our uncle?"

"No, son, he was kind of like Uncle Rad is to your mother."

John really enjoyed his boys. Sometimes he felt a little sad for Angie, in that she didn't have a girl to pamper, dress up and do girl stuff with, like Fannie did her. Of course, it wasn't too late to have another child, but that just didn't seem to be in the cards.

Coming to terms with her lack of interest in physical intimacy was difficult, but he did his best to cope, putting all the emphasis he could muster on the fact that he was alive and his family was still intact. Still, it was tough sharing a bed with someone he had great desire for, knowing the feeling was not mutual.

After helping clear the dishes, John and the boys went to the back yard. With charcoal lighter, he set ablaze the small stack of wood lying in the circular fire pit that was built into the patio, and then ripped open the bag of marshmallows.

Cart, always full of questions and possessing the tenacity of his grandmother, asked,

"Dad, do we have any Indian blood in us?"

Interestingly, this was the very same question John had asked his mother when he was a kid back in about 1950 after examining his father's arrowhead collection.

"Not that I know of," she answered, "Did you take the trash out?"

That was about all that was said about the matter back then.

"Well, I don't know if we've got any Indian in our veins, but I know we do in our hearts. What brought that question on, Son?"

"Oh, a kid at school said that he was part Indian; so I told him I was too."

"Fellas, I just remembered! My dad had an arrowhead collection. It's up in the attic somewhere. 'Want to go find it?"

"Yeah, Dad!" said the excited youngsters almost simultaneously.

The assortment of arrowheads, spear tips, and stone tools was a big hit with the Starr boys on that long November evening.

While touching and feeling the ancient relics, John could almost feel himself being pulled back. It frightened him, and he avoided touching them after having that feeling.

It was almost midnight before the boys turned in. Angie had been in bed for hours. John was left alone with his thoughts and a case of insomnia. He went into the den to read a while, hoping it would bring on sleep. On the desk, lay a book-size package, wrapped in plain brown paper. Then he remembered, just before supper Angie had mentioned that a package had come for him.

He read the return address:

William Raintree
County Rd 21
West Blocton, Alabama

He untied the string and carefully unwrapped it. He felt the blood rush to his head and a weakening flush take control of his body when he saw the contents. Then, an ice-cold chill ran down his spine.

In front of him lay the chronicle of Padre Alvaro de la Torre.

Scarred and burnt, it was there, in front of him. He reached out and grasped both sides and held it up to the light.

His hands trembled as he turned the fragile pages. Then, there it was, at the top of a page, scribbled in his handwriting, jumping off the ancient parchment at him like an arrow. *This is crazy!* it read.

CHAPTER 25

# Quivers

As John struggled to gather his thoughts and make some kind of sense of things, he knew that one thing was certain. There would have to be a face-to-face parley with William Raintree if he ever expected to get to the bottom of it all.

Though the sense of urgency seemed great, he decided to carefully lay a plan of inquiry, and not go up there half cocked. *Do your homework, Starr,* he reasoned. *Get as many facts as possible. See if there is any logical explanation for all of this.*

There was no way he could translate the ancient Spanish text of the chronicle. It would take a scholar to do so. Then, it dawned on him.

George Debarden might not have been good for much in the eyes of the world, but he did know the Spanish language. It was his minor in college.

Though it was well after midnight, John called and set up a meeting for the next day.


It was five in the afternoon before George showed up at John's office…almost dark. John handed him the chronicle: "George, can you translate this thing?"

George studied it for a few minutes: "Sure I can, but I'll need some time. It's using some very old words and weird text patterns. Where did you get this, anyway?"

"I'll explain later…how long…a week, two weeks…a month?"

"Give me a week. It's a good time to work on something like this, being I'm in between projects and all."

John felt weak-kneed as George departed with the ancient artifact that had so suddenly and profoundly affected his life. He wondered what it held.

He recalled that the crow in his dream spoke of a second quiver…one that was in his possession. *Could such a thing be here or at home,* he pondered, *somewhere right under my nose?*

For the next several days John racked his brain trying to think of what he might be looking for, where it might be and how he could recognize it. He searched every corner and cranny he could think of…the attic, the garage, the office.

Finally, after looking in every place he could imagine, he resigned to himself that there was no second quiver, and probably no quivers, period. He gave up the search.

There had to be a logical explanation for all this, though. Maybe the old chronicle, once translated, would shed light on all the coincidences and ridiculous notions going on in his head. He retired to the den to do some reading.

While scanning through the bookshelf, he noticed an old book that he had kept around since his days at the University. For some reason he rescued it from a pile of other old books that were being discarded at the library. He had saved the obscure publication all these years without even opening it. Its title was "Circles in the Wind."

He pulled it from the shelf. The old book was fragile. Its pages had yellowed and frayed around the edges. Its title page was missing, leaving no clue as to who wrote it, who published it, or how old it was.

Then, there it was in the prologue:

*"I have watched history paint itself across the canvas of time, and quite frankly all I have seen is circles in the wind. Eston McCloud"*

"I can't believe it," he said aloud, remembering what Bob had told him about William Raintree's ancestor's ill-fated book. "Jesus…I'm holding the only surviving copy of this thing!"

Suddenly, as if jerked from his hands, the book fell to the floor. It lay there open. He picked it up and began reading from the pages it had opened to:

*"At the town of Cahawba, de Soto asked her, Na-ha-no-me, the wife of Tuscaloosa, where she got the gold disk that hung around her neck.*

*'From where the Father of Waters flow, far to the west,' she answered.*

*Na-ha-no-me dared not tell him that the gold from which the disk was made came from beneath their feet, for she knew his true purpose, and that he would ravage the town should he learn the truth. She, like the others, just wanted him and his Conquistadors to leave.*

> *Before hearing Na-ha-no-me's misdirection, de Soto had planned to pick up provisions and porters at Mabila, and then march directly to the Bay of Mobile where ships waited to carry the expedition back to Cuba, thus ending it. Now, all had changed. He would re-supply at Mabila, but from there head west to the Mississippi River and find the cities of gold that had eluded him the whole of the expedition.*
>
> *Tuscaloosa, however, had other plans for the great de Soto and his arrogant band of Spaniards who dared enter his territory and try to intimidate him. At Mabila, he and his warriors secretly planned to destroy them."*

"My God," said John, almost in a shout, "this is it…the second quiver!"

He began scanning the book…its stories, the poems, the maps. Words flew from the pages like arrows.

"What's happening to me?" he cried out, "I can't buy into this craziness."

The phone rang:

"What the hell's going on, John?" shrilled the over-excited voice at the other end of the line.

"What are you talking about, George?"

"Your name is all over the place in this diary or chronicle…or whatever it is that you gave me to translate…that's what!"

John felt the chill go up his spine again, and struggled to keep his cool.

"I'm trying to get to the bottom of it myself. Have you finished with it yet?"

"Just about. I'll work on it all night if I have to and get it to you tomorrow…OK?"

" If you finish it tonight, call me, no matter what time it is. I'll come get it."

"You sound desperate, John."

"I am desperate…to know the truth."

"Will you tell me what this is all about?"

"It's too nutty to talk about right now, but I'll tell you when I figure it out if you promise to keep a lid on it. Can I trust you, George?"

"Yes, of course you can, but it sure sounds like the makings of some bizarre drama to me."

"It's more than bizarre, George."

# CHAPTER 26

# The Lost Chronicle

NOVEMBER 13, 1977 was a mild late fall day in Mobile. It was early afternoon when George dropped off the translated chronicle. John immediately went to his favorite lounge chair out back by the pool and began reading:

*May 25, 1539 The coast of La Florida came into view around the noon hour. As the fleet sailed into a large but shallow harbor, savage presence was evidenced by rising smoke from several settlements.*

*May 30 Upon making landfall and raising the banners of España on the beach, a brief skirmish with a small band of savages ensued. Two natives were killed and two of our horses wounded. The Governor-General, Hernando de Soto decided to find a more suitable bivouac for the army. After sending scouts to survey the area he chose a village that had been hastily abandoned by its inhabitants. It lay on the shore less than a league and a half north of our landing site. We hacked our way through palms and vines to get to this place as the ships struggled to reposition in the shallow depths.*

*June 2 On the beach of this abandoned town, a high man-made mound exists upon which stands a large pine log structure with overlaid palms as its roof. The governor has taken it for his headquarters. His first order has been to construct an altar where mass can be held.*

*June 3 Through interpreters, we have learned that the name of this town is Ocita.*

Half-reading, half-scanning, John turned the pages…tempted to go straight to October 2, 1540, but resisted.

*July 15 We departed Ocita this morning, marching north. A garrison along with the anchored ships remains behind to establish a base camp on the mainland as well as maintain communication with Cuba.*

*After much preparation by the Governor our journey begins in grandeur. This splendid army of over six hundred is led by a vanguard of mostly officers and gentlemen on horseback. Their armor glistens in the sun. Behind them march the main army and clergy, followed by several hundred servants, porters and slaves. Many of the women serve as concubines to the gentlemen and soldiers.*

*It takes five men to carry the governor's tent while the rest transport every item from nails and gold smelts to glass beads and trinkets for trade and gifts. There are greyhounds with the fleetness of the wind, and a large herd of swine. Our lines sometimes stretch out over a league.*

*Spirits are high among the men, for there is anticipation of much gold on this continent. We in the clergy, having an ample supply of robes, holy relics and sacraments are anxious to begin our task of saving savage souls. Our destination is Apalachee, where there is rumored to be gold and maize. Praise be to God…we are on our way.*

*July 26 We are lost in a great swamp. Adding to our dilemma, this place is devoid of food.*

*July 28 After several days of searching for a way out, one of the squadrons managed to capture a group of five Indians. It was the governor's intention that they be used as guides to lead us out of the marshes, but instead they took us into even deeper bogs where we suffered an Indian attack. This angered the governor so that he ordered four of them to be thrown to the war dogs. They were torn to pieces within minutes as the fifth man was forced to watch. Out of fear for his life he then led us with safe passage out of the swamp. The governor then set up his magnificent Peruvian tent and dined.*

Shaking his head, John flipped forward a half a dozen or so pages.

*October 5, 1539 The Apalachee will not give in to the Governor's demand for porters and women. They also burn their fields of maze, depriving us of much needed food. They constantly make war on us.*

*October 7 Apalachee weapons are no match for Spanish steel, nor the horses and war dogs. The Governor ordered the hands of the more defiant captives chopped off so they can never hold weapons again. The noses of others have been sliced off. "They shall think of their deeds when they go to blow their nose and cannot find their nostrils," said the Governor.*

*October 8 Two hundred captives were staked to the ground and shot with their own arrows.*

*High ranking men such as Elvas and Ranjel disapproved of the executions, considering it excessive and a waste, especially since the army is in desperate need of porters and servants. The Governor has replied to the criticism by saying that it was the fault of the savages…that they forced him to kill and torture them because of their unwillingness to submit. He goes on to speak of the hardships he suffers in the struggle to conquer these new lands, and only wishes that the lords of the Spanish council were here to see how well His Majesty is served.*

*I, as well as most of my fellow clergymen are greatly disturbed by this whole affair, but know not what to do about it. Perhaps the king of Ocale was right when he said that we are no more than a band of vagabonds reeking havoc on this land and these people. We have not been given the opportunity to save souls and at this rate there will be none to save.*

As John turned the fragile pages, the memory burned in his mind: *So…things really were like they were in the dream…just as brutal…just as cruel.* It seemed that his friend, Alvaro…real or imagined, did give truthful testimony…just as he said he would. And, the words did fly like arrows from the page, just as the old crow said they would. To John, they stung like arrows, too.

His finger traced the expeditions route on the old map…from landfall at Tampa Bay, up through central Florida to the city of Anhacia, where today, Tallahassee, Florida's State Capital, lies. According to Alvaro, the expedition wintered there.

The diary went on to read that between October 1539 and March 1540, deSoto dispatched expeditionary squadrons to the north to see what lay ahead, and also squadrons to the west along the coast in search of a suitable harbor where ships could anchor and meet up with the expedition at its conclusion in October of 1540.

*February 15, 1540 Maldonado's squadron has returned from the coast with news of a very desirable harbor west of Apalachee. It is called The Bay of Mobile.*

*February 16 The Governor has announced his master plan, which is to march the army north and make a wide westerly sweep, then head south to the coast and a place where in the coming October, ships would be waiting to take us all back to Cuba.*

*February 17 There are rumors of a distant providence to the north where there is much gold, silver and precious pearls. It is said that this land is ruled by a beautiful young queen with great power. The place is called Cofitachequi.*

*The governor and men are most excited. All are anxious to be underway...to the north and its certain treasures.*

*May 4 Hopes of finding wealth in the providence of Cofitachequi have been shattered. What the Queen has presented as gold turns out to be copper. What has been presented as silver, is mica. There is no gold here, only an abundance of flawed pearls, made less than perfect because holes had been cut in them and from the use of fire to open the oyster shells.*

*May 7 Although there is no gold, much discussion takes place among the men about establishing a colony here, for it is pleasant and well situated.*

*May 9 The Governor has quelled all talk of establishing a settlement here, citing that we must move on if we are to make our rendezvous with the ships in Mobile bay by October. He seems obsessed in his quest to find gold, somewhere.*

John continued tracing the expedition's route...through Georgia, South Carolina where Cofitachequi was located, and into North Carolina. The army then turned west, crossed the Appalachian Mountains, and entered Tennessee, then south and into Alabama. The Spaniards passed through many towns...demanding food, porters, and women. If denied, they not only took what they wanted, but severely punished the population, causing misery and suffering.

*July 16 We have entered the land of the Coosa. The king, in all his splendor has come from his capital to welcome us. The handsome young emperor, wearing a crown made of feathers, sits high on his throne shouldered by at least sixty nobles. Many Indians are around him, singing and dancing as if to celebrate our arrival.*

*He has welcomed us in a most gracious manner and offered us land within his providence to colonize. The Governor refuses the offer saying he requires only food, porters and women.*

*July 17 The Governor has placed the King of Coosa under house arrest as a precautionary measure, and ordered that the Capital city to be taken over by the army. Most of the native population has fled into the woods because of his demand for slaves and women.*

*July 18 The deserters have been captured and put in chains.*

*August 20 We are well rested, and departing the Capital of Coosa. Our destination is Talisi, a city on the southwestern border of this kingdom. The Governor has decided to take the emperor and his sister with us to insure safe passage.*

*September 18 We have arrived at Talisi. This walled city lies beside a large river, and is surrounded by great fields of maize. The city is abandoned.*

*September 19 The governor has set up his Peruvian tent within the walls. He has ordered squadrons out to round up the Indians who have deserted their city.*

*September 21 With great fanfare an emissary arrives, led by the son of a great warrior-king called Tuscaloosa whom it is said rules all lands south and west of here. Muscoda, the son is to lead us to his capital, Atahachi.*

*September 26 We depart, heading in a westerly direction.*

*October 1 We arrive in a Town called Cahawba through which a small blue-green river flows. To our surprise, we are met by Tuscaloosa, himself. His height is head and shoulders above any of us and he is as fierce in appearance as any man I have ever seen. The Governor makes a point to feed him flattering words through our interpreters. Tuscaloosa returns the favor, yet in a stern manner. There is great tension in the air.*

*October 2 While walking in the woods outside the Town of Cahawba in search of acorns and grapes, I came upon an Englishman on the path. He was naked and confused, and kept speaking of a savage friend of his in need of rescue. Though we were barely able to communicate he seemed to be of civil and sincere nature; so I gave him garments of the clergy, shaved the crown of his head and disguised him as a monk in fear that the governor might otherwise treat him as a captive.*

*He said his name was John Starr.*

John felt as if every drop of blood had drained from his body. "My God!" he cried out, "but, how?"

His mind became scrambled like eggs in a skillet, but he kept reading.

*This strange man and I seemed to share a kinship of sorts in that he was a Christian, and was also disturbed at the harsh treatment suffered by the Savages. Though being of some foreign brotherhood called Methodist, I knew he was a Christian, as God would have us be.*

*October 3 el señor Starr seemed most anxious to remain with the expedition upon learning that our destination was the bay of Mobile.*

*October 4 We managed to keep his identity hidden until, during the severe punishment of a savage who had stolen a pig from our herd, el señor Starr cried out demanding an end to it. In altercation, the Governor cut his face with the tip of a sword. The savage being abused jumped up and struck the Governor's mouth drawing blood. After being restrained by several men and forced to watch the savage being punished by having his nose and hand cut off, el señor Starr broke loose and dashed toward the river.*

*Upon reaching its bank with soldiers in pursuit, he dove in and disappeared beneath the waters. We saw him no more.*

John put the chronicle down.

CHAPTER 27

# Eyes of the Spirits

JOHN TRIED DESPERATELY to reconcile the contradiction of realities that had been thrust upon him. He picked up the old scarred and burnt chronicle that lay in his lap and examined it, then continued reading George's translation.

*October 8, 1540 We have departed Cahawba, and are making our way towards Atahachi, the capitol city of Tuscaloosa's providence. From there we will go to Mabila and re-supply. Then, it will be off to the bay of Mobile where ships wait to take us back to Cuba, thus ending the expedition.*

*Because of Tuscaloosa's size, the Governor has had to select a packhorse large enough to accommodate him. They ride side by side, the Governor never allowing him out of his sight. The king wears the red hat and cape given to him by the Governor.*

*October 10 We have arrived at the Atahachi capital. After formal greetings from nobles and principal men of the city, feasting begins.*

*The Great Tuscaloosa sits on a balcony on the side of a mound. His servants and retainers are all around. From behind, a man holds over him a sunshade made of deerskin. He wears a turban crown and a brilliantly colored feather cape. His large size, and handsome, yet stern, features cause him to have a commanding presence over his subjects, as well as us. The governor sits at his side.*

*Again, like at Cahawba, members of the cavalry put on a dazzling demonstration of horsemanship with battle charges and tight turns. Though disguised as entertainment, it serves as a warning of Spanish might to the people of Atahachi. Though his subjects are awed, Tuscaloosa, as before, appears to be unimpressed. He even has a look of distain on his face.*

*There is much feasting and dancing throughout the night. The Governor flatters the king and assures that he wants only to cross his lands in peace. As a token of appreciation he gives him a jewel-encrusted dagger. For the second time, Tuscaloosa assures his services, but makes it clear that he will not tolerate things he had heard about us from those in other providences.*

*October 11 The Governor has made demands for food, porters and women from the city of Atahachi. Upon the conclusion of heated discussion, Tuscaloosa again tells the Governor that his demands will be met at Mabila.*

*October 17 We have marched six days and are now told that we are close to our destination.*

*Since first noticing it at Cahawba, all have been intrigued by the gold medallion that hangs from the neck of Na-ha-no-me, Tuscaloosa's wife. The governor keeps asking her where it came from to which she always gives the same reply: "It comes from the banks of a great river to the west called Mississippi, The Father of Waters."*

*October 18 This morning before daybreak, the Governor, with Tuscaloosa, one hundred horsemen, one hundred infantry and three priests, one of whom is myself, leave the main army encampment and head toward Mabila which is reported to be only a short distance away.*

*Even though it is difficult to do, I continue writing down events as they unfold, even as I walk. I feel a great sense of urgency.*

*It is still early morning as the walled city of Mabila comes into view. Its huge timber palisades covered with plaster and high towers at its corners give the town a fortress-like appearance.*

*Many Indians have come out to greet us, as if we were guests of honor, singing and playing music on flutes made of reed. Upon entering through the gates, and into the grand plaza the Governor is given blankets of marten skins as gifts.*

*The Governor and king have dismounted.*

*Led by Tuscaloosa, the Governor, and the rest of us follow to the other side of the plaza where many large whitewashed plaster houses stand.*

*Now, feasting begins and fermented beverages are served as beautiful women dance in a most seductive manner, moving their bodies in slow gyrating motions. The men are intoxicated by this display.*

*During the festivities, Tuscaloosa abruptly takes leave and retreats into one of the houses.*

*The Governor has called for him to come out, but he refuses to do so.*

*I must write hurriedly, for I have a most uneasy feeling about this place.*

The shaky handwriting in the journal abruptly ended, leaving no clue as to what happened next.

John leaned back in his lounge recliner and looked around. A wooden privacy fence, about eight feet high, made of rough sawn vertical boards ran the perimeter of the Starr's back yard. John imagined it looking somewhat like the city walls of Mabila might have.

As he held the chronicle, looking at the last words written in it, an all too familiar sound pierced the air. He looked up, and there it was, in the far corner, perched atop a corner post of the fence…the crow.

"Crow!" he shouted without even thinking, "take me there!"

The creature cocked its head and looked straight at him…straight through him. A draining flush went through John's body. He tried to raise his arms but couldn't. The next thing he knew he was spiraling through what seemed to be a dark tunnel. His arms flailed as he tried to find an orientation as to what was up and what was down, but there was no up or down.

Then, in an instant, he was viewing himself in the recliner from the corner post where the crow had perched itself. His body appeared to be asleep. The chronicle and translation lay in his lap.

Suddenly, he felt himself lift and become airborne just as he had in the dream within the dream while comatose. He heard wings flapping and felt a rush of wind. He was viewing the world from above, soaring over a vast forest canopy. All of his senses seemed heightened. He could even smell the long ago scent of unspoiled woodlands. Then, he was over large open fields of corn.

There was little doubt in his mind that he was back in the ancient world he had been trapped in three months before, viewing it through eyes other than his own.

Unexpectedly, while trying to understand what was happening, a memory flung out from the whirlwind in his mind. He recalled what the old crow communicated to him before: "I am the watcher… the eyes of the spirits." He began to calm.

In the distance a walled town came into view. As his feathered host approached, it became clear that the fortified city was from another era.

*Mabila*, flashed through his mind.

He felt the soft landing atop one of the city's high towers. From this vantage point he watched as the Spaniards and Atahachee townspeople nervously moved about in the plaza.

Suddenly, like a swarm of bees, hundreds of warriors poured from the houses. Deafening war cries filled the air as they attacked. de Soto and his outnumbered band of conquistadors were trapped on the far side of the plaza. Cut off from the horses that were bridled near the gate, they began hacking their way through the swarm with sword and shield.

Stunned, John watched as the ground became soaked in blood and war cries turned to screams and moans. Severed arms and heads fell to the ground followed by bodies. The crystal stream that flowed through the compound now flowed red. It seemed that the Atahachee's stone weapons were no match against the Spaniards razor sharp swords.

As horrible as it was to watch, he was in awe as the tenacious Spaniards did their dirty work. The scurrilous bunch of gamblers, whoremongers and dandies he remembered from before had transfigured themselves into a highly efficient killing machine, with de Soto being the most daring of them all.

After slashing their way through, he and the majority of his men finally reached the horses and made a hasty retreat to the fields outside the city.

A trumpet blared, after which the main part of the Spanish army began to appear, galloping across the field towards de Soto and his battered men.

The Indians regrouped and went on the offensive. Hundreds of warriors rushed outside through the city gates and attacked. Clouds of arrows descended on the Spaniards. Many were wounded, and at least twenty fell to the ground dead. For the most part, though, the Spaniard's armor warded off fatal injury. Many of those in the saddle looked like porcupines with arrows embedded in the quilted parts of their armor.

Spanish archers arrived at the scene and replied in kind, killing and wounding several hundred of the unprotected warriors. The Atahachi were driven back, retreating to within the city walls.

The Spaniards attacked the gate again and again and hacked away at it with axes and swords. They were relentless as stones and arrows rained down on them from the natives stationed in the towers above. Then, Spanish archers sent flaming arrows into the city, setting it on fire.

Finally, the conquistadors hacked their way through the gates, and all hell broke loose as the Spaniards poured into the breached fortress-town. This time, with the fury of the whole army they began the slaughter. Fire was everywhere. The whole city was ablaze.

John saw Alvaro out in the plaza…clutching the leather chronicle.

"Oh humanity, where art thou?" the priest cried out, as the carnage of battle raged around him.

For John, viewing it all from his vantage point high above on the tower, the cruelty and brutality, was almost beyond comprehension…more than he had seen in Viet Nam.

Just then, an arrow struck Alvaro in the breast.

He lingered on his feet for a moment. The diary slipped from his hand, and then he fell to the ground…face up in the blood-soaked soil. The splattered diary lay at his side as bits of flaming ash fell all around.

John winced and tried to turn away, but couldn't, nor could he even close his eyes. Without reprieve they remained fixed on the mayhem. He felt himself sicken at the site of hundreds, maybe a thousand, including women being lanced and dismembered.

The Spaniards, too, were taking a bloody beating. Hardly a man among them was not wounded.

deSoto raised himself in the saddle. He was about to throw his lance when an arrow pierced deep into his buttocks through an unprotected place in his armor. John saw him wince once, then while standing in his stirrups, continued fighting with wreckless abandon.

Bodies piled up in the plaza like firewood…at least a thousand, and the smell of burning flesh filled the air. Most all of the houses were on fire. Screams could be heard from those who had taken refuge inside and were now trapped as the blazes consumed them.

It was almost sunset. The warring armies had almost annihilated each other, and what was left of the city smoldered as the dead lay in heaps, and the moans of the dying and the smell of burnt flesh permeated the air. There was no sign of Tuscaloosa.

John watched as weary and wounded Spaniards, exhausted from the hysterical killing spree knelt down, almost collapsing, to drink from a stream that now flowed red.

He heard Angie's voice in the distance.

"John," she called out, "you have a phone call. It's a Mr. Raintree."

Suddenly, he was back…in his lounge recliner by the pool.

Part Four

# Off to Raintree's

John's Monte Carlo straddled the ruts on the old pig trail leading to William Raintree's cabin. He told Angie that he was going to Birmingham for a few days to visit his mother, now widowed for the second time. Joe had died the year before from a heart attack.

There it was…the mound Bob spoke of. In the field surrounding it were rows of brown corn stalks, remains of last year's crop.

He passed the old cabin on the right.

Then, a short distance ahead, Raintree's cabin came into view. Bob was right on target. It was like going back in time a hundred years, or more, except for the Studebaker pick up truck under the shed, and an older model Ford parked under the oak tree beside the cabin.

As he drove up, the dogs came up barking and snarling with the same furor as the war dogs in his de Soto experience. They even looked the same.

Raintree came out from around the front side of the cabin, which faced the river.

"Git back to the house, boys," he said in a calm tone, pointing his finger towards the cabin.

"Hello, Mr. Starr, I'm William Raintree. Thank you for comin'."

"I'm glad I could make it, Mr. Raintree."

John handed him the brown paper bag: "Here's the chronicle you sent me."

"Did it help?" asked Raintree.

"It just confirmed that something crazy's going on, that's all. Why did you send it to me, sir?"

"Let's go in the house, Mr. Starr."

John was not the only company Raintree had that day.

"This is my daughter, Anna and my granddaughter, Allison."

He felt a surprised rush as he gazed upon the hauntingly beautiful woman sitting on the couch. She brushed back her dark brown shoulder-length hair.

"Hello, Anna, I'm John Starr. We met a long time ago. You were just a little girl, then."

"Yes, I remember," she replied.

"Its been over twenty years since we rode together in the back of your Dad's pickup truck…sure you remember?"

"I remember."

"Hi, Allison, I'm John. You're as pretty as your mother was at your age."

The little girl, about eight, shyly smiled then turned to her mother.

"What do you say, Allison?" Anna prompted.

She turned back to John.

"Thank you," she said.

Anna looked up at him. The light from the fireplace and candles that scattered about began to reveal just how intriguing her face really was.

"I heard you're a good lawyer, Mr. Starr, I hope you can help Daddy."

"I hope so too, Anna…please call me John."

"Daddy, Allison and I need to go. You two have a lot to talk about, and I have to get ready for work tomorrow. It's nice to see you, John…again."

" Same here, Anna. I hope to see you again soon…sooner than twenty years, I hope."

"Me too. Help Daddy if you can."

She stood and reached for the small coat that lay on the back of the couch. Outlined by the snug fitting jeans, her slim well-proportioned form revealed itself.

Meticulously, she wrapped Allison, then slipped on an old Navy pea coat.

John had to see more. He got up and walked to the door with her and her father… then to the porch. The outside light caught her eyes. They were as blue as the November skies…and stood out in striking contrast to her smooth sunset complexion.

"I'll be back in a minute," said Raintree, "I'm gonna' walk them to the car."

John went back into the cabin and began to look around. Like Bob had said, the place was as neat as a pen. There, on the other side of the room was the bookcase filled with old books. On the desk next to it set the huge stone ax head that supposedly had belonged to Tuscaloosa. Bob had not mentioned it, but beside the ax head lay a dagger with a jewel-encrusted handle, apparently used as a letter opener.

He remembered reading in the chronicle that deSoto gave Tuscaloosa such a dagger as a peace offering just before the battle at Mabila. He picked it up, and with his index finger touched the blade's point.

*Could this be it?* he briefly pondered.

Just then Raintree returned.

"I never got to thank you," said John, "for what you did after the plane crash, Mr. Raintree…thank you. You know, Bob was like a brother to me."

"I know, and I'm sorry about the way things turned out…do you think you can help with the situation regardin' Salvo.?"

"I don't know. That's partly why I'm here. But, first, I have to know what the hell's going on with me."

"I know you do, and you have a right to know."

"How can you know?" asked John.

"Mr. Starr…John…there are things goin' on in this world that are beyond explanation. Be a little patient for now. You'll understand before this day is over. Come on with me. I'll show you the heart of this place."

They crossed the river in Raintree's flat- bottom boat, then walked the path along its bank. John followed Raintree up the path next to a stream, until a small hill came into view. Through brush and bramble, they made their way to the other side of it.

Raintree began removing limbs, leaves, and then timbers that concealed an opening in the hillside.

They descended down a rough homemade wooden ladder into the hole, Raintree first. John raised his lantern. It was just as Bob described it. The yellow vein streaked across the cavern wall, looking like a bolt of lightening. On the cavern floor, nuggets scattered in and about the stream. He imagined himself as Bob seeing this for the first time.

"Does your daughter know about this?"

"No."

"Why not?

"Anna has troubles, big troubles…marriage troubles."

I'm afraid to burden her with this secret. It would only make matters worse…maybe even dangerous. I couldn't take it if harm came to her or my granddaughter."

"Why do you say that? Is the gold cursed or something?"

"In a way it is. Anyone who has ever tried to take it has come to a bad end."

"But, you've taken some, and gave some to Bob."

"Yes, but not to become rich in a worldly way. What's been taken has only been used for the cause of preserving the land. We are only the keepers."

"We, what do you mean, 'We'?"

"Raintree walked to the other side of the cave, and lowered his lantern. There, laid out on a slab of rock, was the scorched skeleton of what was once a very large person. On the skull rested a rusty-red turban-like cap. A moldy and tattered feathered cape draped the huge frame.

"That's him…Tuscaloosa. After Mabila his burnt bones were brought here. This has been his resting place since then. It's all that's left of him except for the blood that flows through my veins…and yours…and once Bob's."

"What are you saying to me…that you and me, and Bob are descendants of Tuscaloosa?"

"Yes."

"How do you know these things? How do you even know these are Tuscaloosa's bones?"

"The same way you know what you know."

"The crow?" said John.

"Yes, the crow. He's come to me too, just like he did old Eston. "

"My God, Mr. Raintree," John blurted in a final attempt to deny, "Surely you don't believe in all this hocus pocus."

"Believe it or not, John Starr, you and me, and Bob Savage come from this man lyin' here. And, the truth is, you've been chosen…like I was."

"Chosen for what…by whom?"

"To be the keeper of this land after I'm gone, by the spirits of our ancestors. They are preparing you for it. This is their resting place…not to be disturbed by anyone. Bob was to be the one, but he let the gold taint his mind."

"Then, you know about the things that have been going on with me, don't you…the dream…deSoto, Tuscaloosa, Mabila."

"Yes."

"So, I'm in this thing…like it or not."

"Yes, John…like it or not. Like old Eston said, the world is made up of circles. A circle comes back around to meet itself. Things come back around to repeat themselves; Salvo is now what deSoto was then. You're the one to stop him."

William walked to the stream and picked up three large nuggets.

"Take these…to cover the cost of the greater cause. You know where to cash them in."


John departed Raintree's at about 4:30. In the short winter day, darkness was already approaching. His head swam in the confusion that was rapidly taking over his life.

Driving the old Bibb County road that he and Bob had walked carrying the canoe so many years before, he tried to gather his thoughts. The pendulum in his mind kept swinging back and forth.

*So, Bob and I are blood kin…the old bastard's crazy, and so am I…should go back to Mobile right now and forget this whole thing.*

Upon reaching the Helena road, he turned left towards Birmingham, and his mother's house.

Beside him, on the seat, lay Eston McCloud's book, 'Circles in the Wind.' "

He didn't remember bringing it from Mobile, or of it being beside him in the car…until now.


Florence, John's mother, was as doting as ever…in her own way: "John, you look so thin…and you've started smoking…I can smell it."

"Mom, when I was a kid I asked you if we had any Indian blood in us. You said you didn't know of any. Were you sure?"

"No, not sure. You know that your father was adopted; so we don't know anything about his real family tree. There's none on my side that I'm aware of, though. Why do you ask?"

"No particular reason…just curious."

It was approaching midnight. His mother had long since retired. His old room hadn't changed much. Even the posters of Natalie Wood and Jacques Cousteau still hung on the wall.

He went into the bathroom to brush his teeth and get ready to turn in for the night. The man in the mirror was Anglo, no doubt about that…medium complexion, hazel eyes, brown hair. But, there were some other things…high cheekbones, deep-set eyes with a hint of slant, and something about the brow.

"Goodnight Tonto," he said to the mirror with a crooked little smile.

He returned to his room. There on the bed Eston's book lay open. He had no recollection of even bringing it in from the car, much less placing it in this spot. He picked it up and looked at the open page. It appeared to be a poem. He began to read.

# Tuscaloosa's Vision

Young Tuscaloosa stood on a bluff,
Alone but for quiver and bow.
He wondered and pondered on many a thing,
As cooking fires lit in the valley below.
He shown like copper in the sunset glare,
Feathers of turkey donned raven hair.
Wondering and pondering on many a thing,
Just he, his thoughts, his quiver and bow.

A warrior came forth in his mind's eye,
Took shape from a cloud in the mid-summer sky,
He drifted in sunset…west from east,
Mounted upon an unknown beast,
A hawk soared high riding the wind,
High and free as in the dreams of men.
Then out of the cloud an eagle came,
And killed this hawk that was high on the wind.
"What means this sign?" he asked Great Spirit,
"Who is this eagle, who should fear it?

Darkness came, the Moon rose high,
The breath of spirits pushed clouds swiftly by,
Warriors of old glittered as stars, scattered the sky,
Full and silver, the Moon rose high.

He asked ancient warriors, " What means the sign?"
But heard only whispers in the rustling pines,
He asked again but got no reply,
Troubled Tuscaloosa got no reply.

Sleep fell upon the weary young brave,
A vision came forth from a misty haze.
A wise old crow, perched on a limb,
Cocked his head and spoke to him.
"Go to the place where your ancestors sleep,
Wake them, they know the answers you seek,
Go in winter, and do so in fast,
For only your hunger can bring this to pass.
Take holly leaves for the black drink tea,
Eat only acorns from a strong oak tree,
Fashion a shelter from branches and straw,
Let four moons pass till the springtime thaw.
Go forth Tuscaloosa, let the old ones guide,
Great Spirit will keep you: he will provide."

Summer passed and the days, they quickened,
Squirrels gathered nuts, and the rabbits' fur thickened.
The woodlands were painted, meadows turned gold,
Nights grew colder, and the Sun hung low.
Children asked mothers, " Who painted the leaves?
Tell me Mother; Why crimson the trees?"
Mother sang softly, sweetly and low,
"Tis the Changer of Seasons; He has made it so."

To the river called Warrior journeyed Tuscaloosa,
To the place it is said where his ancestors slept,
Where the builders of mounds once lived and prospered,
Where all the secrets and answers were kept.

Sleeping in the womb of this sacred Earth,
Patiently waiting 'neath thistle and turf,
Patiently waiting till wakened and beckoned,
Ancestors slept 'neath this sacred Earth.

Winter came with its blanket of death,
As did the signs foretell.
The land grew cold with biting winds,
The Changer of Seasons had cast his spell.
As hard days came, and long nights passed,
He summoned with chant and prayer,
"Spirits come forth," Tuscaloosa beckoned,
But none it seemed could be awakened,
He fell into deep despair.
In hunger his body and soul grew weak,
Had the spirits forsaken, would they never speak?
He fell into deep despair.

Then one crystal cloudless night,
Star warriors danced in a full moon's light,
The Moon became a fiery Sun,
Whatever was to be had now begun.
And there he was, in clear sight,
The eagle, his claws, and all his might.
On the back of a strange and unknown beast,
Rode the great warrior from beyond the east.
With shinning bonnet, pale face with hair,
He peered ahead in an ice-cold stare.
In glittering garment like tortoise shell,
He stared ahead, cold and pale.

Behind him marched his many braves,
Our people in bondage, our people his slaves.

With thundering sticks that threw killing stones,
Long knives at their side to pierce flesh and bone.
Pushing forward, more, ever more,
conquering all that lay before.
His quest was to find the yellow gold,
To hostage our people, to capture our souls.

The Sun became the Moon again,
Pale and blue as the mist came in.
And from the mist an image appeared,
Tuscaloosa called out as the ghost drew near,
"Is it you my father, is it you I see?"
"Yes Tuscaloosa, it is me."
"I have missed you Father. Where have you been?"
"With clouds and stars, in dreams and the wind."
"Who is the warrior, what is his claim?"
"Destroyer of nations…de Soto's his name.
Beware of this eagle for he will kill,
Any and all who challenge his will.
Beware Tuscaloosa, one day he will come,
You must face him…you are the one."

Then spirits rose up from the mystic mist,
And danced 'round foxfire in their midst.
They danced and sang to sacred drums,
And chanted, "Tuscaloosa, You are the one.
Beware Tuscaloosa, Soto will come.
You must face him…you are the one."
They danced and chanted till just before dawn,
Then in a heartbeat the spirits were gone.
Flying Bear spoke from a misty-blue hue,
"Now, hear me my Son; what I bid you to do.
Take aim with an arrow toward the morning Sun,

Let it fly free, its will be done.
Farewell Tuscaloosa, for now I go",
Then he faded away into dawn's dim glow.

The Sun broke brilliant in the morning sky,
Tuscaloosa took aim, let his arrow fly.
The shaft found its mark by its own will.
His brother, the deer lay quiet and still,
So, as the crow had prophesied,
The Old Ones gave answers,
And the Great Spirit, he did provide.

# Chapter 30

# Dreams of Anna

THE UNCANNY PARALLELS in the poem he had just read and what was happening in the present boggled John's mind. He struggled, trying to connect the dots. Eagles, hawks, ghosts of the fathers', Soto, Salvo, sacred land, gold…the crow, it seemed impossible to make sense out of anything. He had to read on:

Na-ha- no-me

Tuscaloosa left the Holy Grounds,
And on his journey home,
Came to the valley of the Cahawba,
Where friendly tribes were known.
There on the banks of the blue-green river,
Bathed the beautiful Na-ha-no-me.
Flower of the Moon her father called her,
For she lit the night-time sky.
She looked up, and she asked him,
"Who are you tall, weary one?
And he answered, "Tuscaloosa,
"I am on my journey home."
He was raptured by her beauty,
As she bathed in gentle waters,
As her hair fell to her shoulders,
Midst the blooming river lilies.
Then she took him to her village,

To her father's splendid place,
And the greeting there was friendly,
Welcomed by her father's grace,

Yet this brave did fall prisoner,
With no hope of escape,
His eyes and heart could only yield,
To the spell of Na-ha-no-me's face.
And he courted this young maiden,
Beside the river's shinning shoals,
On the trails, in the Moonlight,
In the woodland's flowered wold.
He asked her then to share his path,
And with the blessings of her father,
Took the lovely Na-ha-no-me,
Flower of the Moon for his wife.
Homeward bound down the river,
gliding over rushing waters,
Riding, guiding the bobbing canoe,
While within his lovely flower,
The seed of Tuscaloosa grew.

John's eyelids grew heavy. He laid the book on his nightstand, and felt himself drift towards sleep…then, deep into dreams.

In his dream, it must have been May; because the Cahaba Lilies were in full bloom. The snow-white orchid-like flowers clustered in the shallow water in and around the shoals. They were everywhere…in the middle of the river, along the shore…everywhere.

Mid-way across the stream, at a place where one of many river shoals began, John found himself sitting on a smooth flat boulder that lay among the thousands of loose water-worn stones and rock shelves that formed the shoals. The boulder, looking like a huge medieval tabletop, protruded about a foot above the water. His feet dangled in the currents as he took in the natural beauty around him. The sound of the rushing water as it cascaded over rock shelves and stones was pleasant to his ears…exciting, yet soothing. Scattered about within the shoal areas lay calm shallow ponds where lilies grew profusely. The shoals continued on for forty or so yards, after which the river flowed deep and calm again.

About a hundred yards upstream was another set of shoals. In between lay a calm river-lake. Trees draped over the water. Their new light-green leaves announced the arrival of spring. A doe and her fawn drank in the slow moving currents. The air was spring-fresh with a hint of distant honeysuckle.

Out of his peripheral vision he caught a glimpse of someone on the shore. He turned to see. She stood there, on the banks of the blue-green river. It was Anna.

She waved, then reached her hand out to him.

He slipped into the shallow water and made his way towards her, cautiously, so as not to slip on the mossy river stones.

When he reached her, she asked: "Where did you come from?"

"I don't know. I'm just here," he answered, "Let's go back to the rock."

He took her hand, and together, they waded to the boulder. There, they sat facing each other. Lilies were all around…a field of them surrounding the river-island.

"I wanted to see you again," he said.

"I wanted to see you, too."

He turned to the edge of the rock and picked the largest lily he saw and placed it in her hair, above her left ear.

She looked at him: "Do you want me?"

"Yes, I want you."

She smiled and lay back on the warm weatherworn boulder. Her dark brown hair spread on the rock, framing a mysterious and beautiful face. In the reflecting sky, her eyes became deep crystal pools of blue.

He leaned over her, and kissed her, gently at first. The sound of the shoals seemed to fade into the distance.

He unbuttoned her blouse. It seemed the natural thing to do. She didn't discourage his action as he laid it open, exposing her to the mid-day sun…and him. He removed her blouse; then pulled his T-shirt over his head and off.

"You OK?" he asked.

"Yes," she answered.

He unbuttoned the top button of her jeans and slid the zipper down. She arched her back as he tugged and slipped them off her. What he saw paled the lilies, the shoals and everything else in sight.

Hurriedly, he shed his own blue jeans, along with all inhibitions. He felt a watery build-up under his tongue as his shadow moved over her body. He engaged her lips, kissing her deeply, then, with his knees, nudged her into position. She laid herself open to him and writhed as he dispensed his wetness on her.

"Now," she said.

Briefly, he looked up and glimpsed the field of lilies, heard the rushing waters and caught a scent of honeysuckle. Then, it all went away. He saw nothing, heard nothing, smelled nothing, felt nothing…except her. To him, she was all that existed.

His knees burned, but it didn't matter. He was making love to sweet Anna.


The clock on the nightstand read 6:00AM when the alarm went off.

He reached down and felt his knees.

# Circle of Fire

IT SEEMED AS if every event in John's life, even his dreams drew him ever closer to Raintree. On his second cup of coffee, sitting at his mother's breakfast table, he decided to give in to the inevitable. He would take on Salvo. But, Angie couldn't know. He had to call her…come up with something as to why he was staying over.

"Hi, Angie, it's me."

"Where are you?" she asked.

"I'm at Mom's. I'll be up here for a couple of more days."

"John, are you getting involved with that Indian thing?"

"No…I'm going to help Joseph Bonaparte hammer out some Condominium covenants, that's all."

"Well, Rad's giving a surprise cocktail party tomorrow night to celebrate Terry Wayne's birthday. I'm going with or without you."

"Do what you've got to do, Angie. I'll be at Mom's…or Joseph's."

It was late afternoon when John arrived at Raintree's cabin. He brought his old sleeping bag and a change of clothes, planning to stay the evening.

Raintree's truck was not there, but Anna's car was. He felt an adrenalin rush.

The dogs greeted him barking, but with wagging tails.

He looked up from petting them.

There she was, in a simple flowery dress, as beautiful as in his dream…except for the bruise on her left cheek.

"How did you get the shiner…run into a door?"

"Something like that. Come on in."

Allison sat on the floor playing with her Barbie doll…coddling and combing its hair.

"Look Mommy, I put a new dress on her."

"Hi, Allison," said John.

"Hello," she responded, barely looking up.

"Allison, Honey, could you go outside and play a little while," said Anna, "I need to talk with Mr. John."

"OK," she said, as she picked up her doll along with its assortment of clothes, and headed toward the porch.

"Where is your Father?" asked John.

"He's gone to look for Dennis, my husband. He got drunk last night and did this to me."

"Has it ever happened before?" he asked, trying not to let his outrage show.

"Yes, but I never told anyone, especially not Daddy. This time, though, it got so bad I had to take Allison and leave. I didn't have any place to go, except here."

"What do you think your Daddy will do?"

"I don't know, but I'm worried sick. Dennis is deathly afraid of him. He's probably hiding out at his mother's, up in Jasper."

As darkness approached, she asked, "Can you stay for supper?"

"That would be nice. Can I help?" he asked watching her light the stove's firebox.

"No, just make yourself comfortable."

As John browsed through Raintree's books, a faintly familiar aroma began to fill the cabin. "What's cooking?" he asked.

"Fat back, beans and cornbread…I was raised on this stuff."

"Smells good."

"Better hold the complements till you've tasted it."

"I've decided to try to help your father get that Salvo bunch off his back," said John, "that's why I came out here this afternoon."

"I'm glad you came."

"I am too. I just hate the circumstances. When do you think he'll be back?"

"He won't…not tonight. Daddy can hardly see when it gets dark. He'll pull his truck over and sleep in it. He won't be back till in the morning…unless he's done something foolish. I just hope he didn't find Dennis. I really shouldn't have come here…Allison, come on in, now…supper's almost ready."

"It's been a long time since I've had something like this…it's very good," said John, reaching for a second helping, "Allison, you've hardly eaten," he commented.

"I'm not very hungry…besides I'm saving room for desert."

"Honey," said Anna, "I'm afraid we're not going to have desert tonight… except for maybe an apple."

"Oh…then I guess I'll have some more."

John chuckled, "I wish I had a little girl just like you."

Allison dropped her eyes and stared into her plate.

"Things will be all right, sweetheart…just wait and see," he said. "Well, I guess I better get going. It's after eight."

"No, please don't go. I don't want to stay here alone."

He felt a tingle in the upper part of his spine and shoulders. "What about your daddy? Wouldn't it upset him if I stayed?"

"No, he would want you to. Allison can sleep on the couch, and you can take daddy's bed."

"What about you?"

She went to her father's bed, which blocked the door to the other room.

"Help me push it away."

"I've wondered what was behind that door," he said.

"It was Mama and Daddy's room. He shut it off when she left. As far as I know he's not slept there since then."

She took a candle and entered. He followed her. Allison, already lying on the couch, was just about asleep.

In the shadowy candlelight, the room, about twelve-foot square, appeared to be in perfect order…not even a cobweb. The four-poster bed was neatly made. Obviously, Raintree had maintained it over the years.

"I'll be right out side the door, Anna…sweet dreams."

"No, stay here with me…please."

"Are you sure that's what you want."

"Yes."

"I'll be back in a couple of minutes," he said.

He went out on the porch. It was unusually mild and balmy, even for a Southern November night. A mist had risen from the river, blocking the moon, causing an eerie glow. The air was still. There was dead silence. His heart raced, hardly believing the situation. He looked around in an attempt to assure himself that Raintree wouldn't be back during the night.

He returned to the back room. Anna lay there, under the covers. Her hair spread over the pillow, much like in his dream the night before. The candle stood in its stand on the end table. Concerns of Raintree's return and everything else left his mind as he gazed at her in the flickering light.

"I had a dream about you last night," he said.

"I hope it was good."

"Yes…it was good."

He stood beside the bed in full view of her and began undressing, looking into her eyes all the while.

Standing before her naked in the chilly, dimly lit room, he felt the need of her approval.

She smiled and held out her hand. Without his eyes ever leaving hers, he slipped under the patchwork quilt and between the sheets. He held her close. Every part of her body felt familiar. He had held her before…but only in a dream. Now, she was real…no longer a conjured up fantasy.

"Please don't judge me," she said, just above a whisper, "I just need to be held."

He threw the covers back and slipped his hand beneath her thigh as she opened herself to him. Her hands clutched his upper back as they made love. Her breathing and soft moans aroused him even the more. It's what he wanted to hear. He wanted to please her.

Her fingernails dug into his back as she released a final sigh. It brought him to his peak.

He knew he had pleased her.

They lay there, coupled in each other's arms.

"Was it like your dream?" she asked.

"Yes," he replied, "even better."

As Anna quietly slept. John lay there, nestled against her skin, contemplating, anticipating the rising conflict. He had never been unfaithful to Angie…never even thought about it. Now, with little or no thought he had crossed the line. He was well aware that he could lose it all.

*God, why don't I regret this?*

The air in the room began to chill down. He pulled the covers higher.

During the night John was awakened by an old familiar sound in the distance. The choppy noise of blades cutting through the air grew louder. It could only be one thing.

He looked over at Anna. She was asleep.

It was overhead…hovering.

Suddenly a flash outside the window lit up the room. Then came another. Something hit the roof in the next room; sounding like it had crashed through. Allison's screams followed.

He jumped out of bed, stumbling as he struggled to get his jeans on while running to the adjoining room.

The place was on fire.

"Allison!" screamed Anna.

"Get out of the house, Anna!" he shouted.

He made it to the outside door. Allison was running towards the river. She was on fire…a streaking, screaming human torch.

Like in a nightmare, he couldn't seem to get enough traction, nor would his legs move fast enough to catch her. She disappeared into the misty river. Her screams stopped.

Half running, half stumbling John hit the cold dark water. He dove under once, then again and again, desperately reaching out in all directions, feeling his way along the bottom…but found nothing.

Anna stood on the bank, wrapped in the quilt he had just made love to her on, screaming Allison's name.

After numerous attempts to find her, John emerged from the river. The cabin was rapidly becoming engulfed in flames.

"The cars," he shouted," are the keys in your car?"

"Yes," she shouted back.

He ran past the burning cabin and first moved his car back to a safe distance, then Anna's. Then, made a mad rush to the cabin.

Feeling his body sear from the intense heat, he pulled at a burning piece of sap-laden wood. It made a natural torch.

He ran back to the bank with it, holding the handle end as it smoldered. He felt his hand blister as he thrust it into the ground.

Pushing Raintree's flat bottom boat down the bank, he shouted, "Help me get this thing in the water!"

They launched with Anna sitting at the bow holding the torch and John at the stern paddling, shivering uncontrollably in the pre-dawn chill. They zigzagged the river, searching every foot of its banks and shores.

After traveling about a hundred yards down stream, Anna suddenly screamed:

"Oh, no…Oh, my God, no!".

Allison was there, in front of them, held in the shadowy limbs of a tree that draped over the river.

As John untangled her fragile body, an old memory surfaced, one he had kept buried for many years. There was another little girl, in another time and place. She was on fire, too.

An ice cold chill ran up his spine as he looked closely. The blistered whelps on what he could see of her face and arms showed the severity of her burns. Only patches of hair remained on her scalp.

"She's gone, Anna, she's gone," he said, his voice breaking as he laid her down in the bottom of the boat.

Anna went to her knees, and put her hands to her face.

"Oh, no," she kept repeating, "Oh, no."

John struggled as he paddled their way back against the currents. Anna lay draped over her child.

The cabin fire raged on, giving a hellish orange-red light to the darkness. A sweating heat radiated…even a hundred feet from it, there on the riverbank.

On their knees, clutching one another, John held Anna, rocking her back and forth. Allison lay beside them.

"We'll make it through this," he whispered.

"No, I'll never make it through this."

She covered Allison with the quilt, leaving herself with nothing. She lay down beside her, putting her arms around her, as if protecting her from the cold. John folded the quilt over Anna, shielding her somewhat from the chilling air. After a time she quieted down. Anna was still, except for an occasional twitch.

As he sat and watched the fire, the old memory kept buried for so many years wanted out. He tried to bury it again, but it wouldn't go back to the graveyard of memories that lay deep within his mind. Shock, horror, rage…it all bludgeoned him again, just as it did in that distant time and place. The words, "Guíp Toi!… Guíp Toi!" kept repeating themselves in his mind.

He looked down at the outline of Allison's small form and her anguished mother there on the banks of the Cahaba. He let go and sobbed.

Finally, dawn broke. Smoldering embers were all that remained of the cabin. Anna quietly lay next to Allison.

John went to his car and retrieved a sweatshirt and pair of work boots from the trunk. He looked in Anna's car and found a pair of jeans and blouse.

He didn't want to wake her, but knew he had to.

William Raintree drove up just as the sun began to burn the mist away.

"My God! What's happened?"

Then, he saw Allison and went dead silent for several moments.

"What happened?" he asked again, in a calm and deliberate voice.

"I'm not sure," John responded, "A helicopter hovered above the house last night. There were flashes, and then everything was on fire. It must have been firebombs or flairs…I'll go get the sheriff."

"We'll be gettin' nobody," said Raintree.

"We have to, Sir."

"No, she'll be buried up by the mound…where the others are. Nobody's to know."

"We can't do that, Mr. Raintree."

"You best leave, now, Mr. Starr."

John and Raintree dug Allison's grave at the foot of the mound. They carefully wrapped her in the quilt that had covered John and her mother the night before. Then, slowly lowered her body into the ground.

A lump formed in John's throat. He felt without a doubt, that this little girl was now a part of him.

As the three stood over the open grave, Raintree sprinkled ashes, corn kernels and sand into it…then dropped in the coal black feather of a crow.

"Ashes to ashes, dust to dust," he said, then, "God…Great Spirit, take this child's soul…to be with you and her ancestors. Be gentle with her, like she was gentle in this life."

He then chanted for a half-minute or so in some tongue lost to the ages. He raised his arms and looked towards the sky: "Now," he said, "fly away little bird."

Anna stood in silence. Only the tears running down her cheeks and the look in her blue eyes gave notice of her anguish.

As John and Raintree covered the grave, Anna finally broke down.

Raintree looked up at his daughter, "Cry for yourself, Anna, not Allison. She's with God and her ancestors, now…in a happy place."

There was little time for grieving after the burial. The threesome set about straightening up Raintree's father's old abandoned cabin. It had lain empty since his death, still furnished with chairs, sofa, a table, cooking utensils and two beds.

"Anna needs some time alone," said Raintree, "I know her. Let's go into West Blocton for some supplies."

First thing, upon arrival in the little town out in the middle of nowhere, Raintree went to the pay phone located just outside the general store. He pulled a folded piece of paper with a number on it from his wallet. "Got any change?" he asked.

John gave him what he had, and Raintree began feeding it in.

He slowly dialed a number.

"Is Mr. Salvo there?"

"No…well, will you deliver a message to him? It's very important that he gets it as soon as possible. This is William Raintree. Tell him I'm ready to talk. He'll know what I mean. Where is you alls' office?"

"You say in The Woodward Building in downtown Birmingham, fifth floor. Tell him I'll be there at eight o'clock this evenin'."

"I strongly advise against this, William," said John.

"You go on back to Mobile. Anna will take me," said Raintree, standing in the shadow of the storefront.

"No, I'm staying. I don't have a choice, now."

"You may live to regret those words, Son."

C H A P T E R  3 2

# Salvo's Lair

THE OFFICE WAS spacious, but Spartan and dated…more like a field office than what would be expected on the fifth floor of Birmingham's Woodward building.

The wiry bantam-size man, somewhere in his mid-fifties, paced the floor. His weather worn face was a telltale sign that he had spent most of his life outdoors. His body language and dark piercing eyes left no doubt that he was a man accustomed to being in charge.

Don Salvo, in animated fashion, discussed the previous night's sortie with his son, Don Jr., commonly known as, Bubba. Broad and beefy, Bubba was the physical opposite of his father. He sat in the easy chair with his hands resting on his stomach. "Well, Son," said Salvo, "if that didn't get the old bastard's attention, I don't know what will."

"Yeah, Pa Pa, no doubt about that. Maybe we should have stuck to the flares, though, and not dropped that can full of gasoline. I saw it go right through the roof. We might have killed him."

"I hope we did barbeque the old son-of –a-bitch. Nobody would miss him anyway."

"What about his daughter?"

"Bubba, all we'd have to do is wave a few thousand bucks under her nose, and she'd be out of our hair before the ink dried on the deed. That would be a pile of money for a grocery check-out clerk."

"What if she didn't go for it?"

"Then, we'd deal with her like we did her old man."

"Yeah, Pa Pa, shit happens, don't it?"

"Changing the subject," said Salvo Sr., "Rad Debarden, down in Mobile is already set up to launder the gold down in South America. He says the government in Chile wants as much as they can get, and don't care where it comes from. All we've got to do is crate it up, load it on the barges mixed in with the coal, and he takes it from there. He's just waiting on us. In fact, the SOB is worryin' the piss out of me… calls every other day, wantin' to know when we can start shipping.

Salvo walked over to the window. From there, on the fifth floor of the Woodard Building, a panoramic view of Birmingham's sky line was afforded along with that of Vulcan, the great iron statue, watching over the city from atop Red Mountain.

"There's a damn crow perched out on the ledge," said Salvo.

He hit the window: "Get your black-ass out of here," he yelled.

"Don't worry Pa, Pa," said Bubba, "it ain't gonna' talk to nobody."

Salvo hit the window again, hard. The crow pecked on the glass three times, as if in an act of defiance, and then flew away.

There was a knock at the door.

"Yeah, what do you want?" Salvo Sr. bellowed.

"There's a message for you, Mr. Salvo," said the timid voice on the other side. "A Mr. Raintree called and said that it was important that you got it."

"Come on in."

The intimidated looking secretary handed him a note and made for a quick exit.

"Well, I don't guess we killed him, but it looks like we did get Mr. Raintree's attention, Bubba. He says he'll be here at eight o'clock tonight…to talk."

"That's a good sign."

"Maybe, but you better round up Jake and Edgar just in case there's any trouble.

Tell them to be here by 7:30."

# Chapter 33

# All Hell Breaks Loose

As John poked through the ashes of the cabin, every rational bone in his body told him to notify the authorities or leave this place. But, he could not bring himself to do either.

He walked to the riverbank absorbed in thought.

There was no hard evidence of what started the fire. Could it have actually been caused by a spark from the stove or flue, and the helicopter part was just another one of his crazy dreams? Was Salvo involved?

*No, it was no dream,* he concluded, *Of course Salvo was involved.*

Then, there was Allison…and Anna. They deserved justice…maybe even beyond what the laws of man would allow.

*I have no choice…I've got to go with Raintree.*

He watched a leaf caught in the currents of the Cahaba.


"We'll take my vehicle, William."

"No, I want to take the truck."

John was past the point of trying to argue with William Raintree. At least the old man seemed to be calm and collected. Still, he did not know what to expect.

At six o'clock, they left, and headed towards Birmingham.

It was eight o'clock sharp when Raintree knocked on Salvo's fifth floor office. John stood behind him.

The door opened. Standing there was a tall, dark man with a pitted face.

Without a word, Raintree walked past him and straight toward Salvo, picking up his pace as he passed Bubba and another man. John had just crossed the threshold when, as if out of thin air, a dagger appeared in Raintree's hand.

He plunged it into Salvo's chest. It made a loud crunching sound as blood spewed. Salvo stood there a moment with an ungodly look on his face, then collapsed to the floor, landing flat on his back. Raintree moved like a cat as he turned and sliced Bubba's porky neck, then stabbed the man standing next to him. He seemed to do it all in one movement. The tall dark man standing by the door pulled a pistol and fired twice before John knocked the gun out of his hand. The gunman then ran from the room. Clicks echoed in the outside hall.

Salvo lay on his back in a pool of blood with his mouth open. His eyes, in a blank stare, fixed on the ceiling. Bubba, holding his neck gurgled and writhed on the floor, while the man next to him lay doubled over and moaning. Raintree, turned and calmly walked out the door holding his side. John followed.

"How bad are you hit?" asked John as they went down in the elevator.

"It's my side."

"We're going to a hospital, William."

"No, Its just a flesh wound, I'll be all right."

They reached the ground floor and got into the old Studebaker parked there on Twentieth Street. Blood oozed through Raintree's fingers where he held his side.

"William, we've got to get you to a hospital!

"Drive, boy, or I'll put this thing through my own heart!"

John looked over. He had the bloodstained jewel-handled dagger pressed to his chest.

"Why did you do it," he asked.

"Cause he did it."

"How do you know?"

"A big black bird told me…remember? Now, drive."

"The crow!" said John

Raintree did not reply.

It was approaching midnight when they drove up to the candle-lit cabin. Anna rushed out.

"Help me get him in, Anna. He's been shot."

Throughout the night, Raintree drifted in and out of consciousness.

During one of his conscious moments, he motioned for John to come near him.

"I'll be gone before mornin'," he whispered.

"You don't know that, William."

"Yes, I do. Swear to me two things, John Starr."

"Swear to, what?"

"Swear that you will never tell, and…," he coughed.

"What else?"

"That you'll take care of Anna."

"Yes, William…I swear."

"When I'm done, take me to the cave and lay me next to him. And, while you're there take enough gold to do her for the rest of her life. Take your share, too. You'll need it to get yourself out of this mess."

"Are you sure that's what you want?"

"That's what I want…and what the spirits want. There's some dynamite in the barn. After you've finished, blow it, and never go back."

Just before dawn, William Raintree opened his eyes, looked at John and spoke: "You're the keeper, now…like it or not." Then, he drew his last breath.

John felt his whole body fill with a flush, as if something had transferred itself from the old man to him. Now, it was too late to change anything. He knew that.

At first light, John and Anna drug Raintree's body on a hastily fashioned litter, across the river and to the cave opening. With a rope they lowered him down into it.

Without further preparation they laid him down next to the supposed remains of Tuscaloosa, then gathered enough nuggets to fill the burlap croaker sack found in the cabin.

Anna took on the calmness of her father as they struggled to get the gold out of the cave and drag it to a safe distance.

Then they went back to the opening. John lit the fuse on the three sticks of dynamite bound together and dropped it in the hole.

"God rest your soul, William," he said just before turning away.

He grasped Anna's hand, and they ran as hard as they could.

In ten seconds it all blew to hell. The entry was sealed...probably forever.

John briefly reflected. Now, his fate was sealed as surly as the cave opening...probably forever.

# CHAPTER 34

# Click, Click

IT WAS MID-MORNING by the time John and Anna returned to the cabin after taking Raintree to his final resting place and blowing the cave's entry. Exhausted, they sat down at the rustic hand-hewn dinner table.

"Anna," said John, "the only thing that makes any sense is to go to the police."

"And tell everything?"

"No, not everything. I'll have to think this thing through.

"What about Allison? I couldn't handle it if they disturbed her, now."

He touched her cheek, wiping away a tear. "I know," he said, "We'll have to come up with something that will keep them from poking around here too much."

John stepped outside into the brisk November air. As he stared at the mound across the way, standing in desolate silence behind the cornfield, every believable scenario that could substitute the truth raced through his mind.

*If, somehow, Allison and Raintree were together,* he considered, *not in the hereafter, but alive, in the here and now.* He mulled the thought until, slowly, a plan began to evolve.

After a half hour or so he went back into the cabin.

"Anna, where do you live in Birmingham?"

"Midfield."

"That's just outside of the city limits. We had to pass through there to get back here. Do you think your husband was home last night?"

"I doubt it. Like I said before, he always goes to his mother's up in Jasper when there's trouble. He usually stays a week or so."

"What does he do for a living?"

"He's a welder, when he works."

"Do you have any neighbors that keep tabs on what goes on at your place?"

"No, not that I know of."

"Then, here's our story. We've got to keep it simple and close enough to the truth so as not to trip ourselves up. You and Allison weren't here the night the cabin burned down…OK? I was here, though. As your father's attorney, we were discussing a counter claim regarding Salvo's attempt to swindle him out of the property. It was late, and he invited me to spend the night. The helicopter came just like it really did, and whoever was in it set the fire. Your father insisted on meeting with Salvo the next day…yesterday…just to talk. I advised him against it, but he said he was going with or without me. I went against my better judgment. I drove the truck. After the incident, he threatened to kill himself with the dagger he used on Salvo if I didn't do exactly what he told me to. He was wounded but said it was only superficial. As we drove through Midfield he made me pull over. Then, he jumped out of the truck and disappeared into the dark. He must have come to your house and taken Allison while you were asleep. Tell them he was obsessively protective of her, or something like that, and that he had a key to the house. I'll tell them I wasn't thinking clearly when I decided to come back here to get my car before going to the police. This will be our story, Anna. Stick with it, no matter what."

"Do you think they will believe it?" she asked.

"I don't know, but anything else I can come up with would open up an even bigger can of worms. There're a lot of, 'what ifs.' What if someone saw or talked to your father in Midfield the afternoon or evening of the fire? What if your husband came back before he usually does? It's risky and has holes, but if we don't go with it, you know what will happen… they'll be out here digging this whole place up. Anyway, it's no less believable than the truth. You need to go on back home, now, and report Alison as being missing. I'll go turn myself in to the Birmingham authorities."

"I've lost everything," she sobbed, "and, now, you will too."

"We've got to hold up, Anna. This is going to be high profile because of Salvo's prominence. You'll definitely be drug into it…just stick to the story. It will have to be up to them as to whether they believe it or not."

"Will I see you soon?"

"I don't know. They're probably going to charge me with something. Hide the gold in a safe place. Take a few nuggets to a man in downtown Birmingham by the name of Harry Cohen…Cohen Jewelry. He'll convert it to cash…just be careful."

"About you and me, John, before the fire…"

"We'll talk about that later. Know this, though. I'll be thinking of you every minute we're going through this thing."

"I'll be thinking of you, too."

"We've got to get going, now. Just stick to the story…no matter what."

In a lingering, parting kiss, they held each other, trying to delay the moment they had to part and take their separate journeys into an unknown future.

John had just put the half-filled croaker sack in the trunk of Anna's car, when he heard an approaching vehicle. The car, with Bibb County Sheriff's Dept. written on its side, rolled in kicking up dust in its wake. It came to an abrupt stop blocking his and Anna's cars. Two uniformed men emerged. The dogs barked and snarled, primed for attack, until Anna calmed them down.

"We're lookin' for William Raintree," said the barrel-chested sheriff, "and a man with a scar on his cheek, who looks like he might just be you, mister. What's your name?"

"I'm John Starr, Sheriff."

"And, who are you, Ma'am?"

"I'm Anna McBride, Mr. Raintree's daughter."

"Where is Mr. Raintree?" he asked, looking toward the cabin while placing his hand on the scabbard of his side arm.

"We don't know," said John, "We're looking for him, too."

"You watch these two, Percy," he said to the lanky deputy, "I'm gonna' go take a look inside." He proceeded toward the cabin with his pistol drawn. "Whoever's in there come on out," he shouted.

After getting no reply, he went inside, and returned within in a couple of minutes.

"Mind if we take a look in that car trunk missy?"

"No, I guess not," she coolly answered. The keys were still in it.

"Take a look Percy."

The croaker sack lay in full view. It seemed like time had stopped as the deputy held the trunk lid open and stared inside.

John felt his heart beating like a base drum.

The deputy slammed the trunk lid shut and removed the keys.

"Nothin' here," he said.

"What about your trunk, Mr. Starr?"

"Yes, Sir," John said handing over the keys.

"Nothin' here except for an old sleepin' bag," said the deputy as he patted it down.

"Are you sure you don't know the whereabouts of Raintree, Mr. Starr?"

"No, sir, but there's a long story regarding that."

"Yeah, I'll bet there is. You know why we're here don't you, Mr. Starr?"

"Yes, Sir, I do. I was on my way to the Birmingham police when you all came up."

"That won't be necessary. Just turn around slowly and put your hands behind your back." Then he pulled a piece paper from his pocket and began to recite: "You have the right to remain silent. Anything you say can and will be used against you in a court of law. You have the right to have an attorney present now and during any future questioning. If you cannot afford an attorney, one will be appointed to you free of charge if you wish."

John felt the cuffs being placed uncomfortably tight around his wrist…then, 'click,' 'click.'

# Careful What You Say

THE INTERROGATION ROOM at Birmingham city jail was windowless and small…
two chairs, a table and a telephone.

"Want a cigarette?" asked Detective Larry Kincaid, a tall, lean clean-cut
looking man in his mid-thirties…about John's age.

"Yes," John answered, "thanks."

"Do you know the whereabouts of William Raintree?"

"No."

"I understand you're an attorney. Is that correct?"

"Yes."

"On the night of the Salvo killing, were you present at the scene?"

"Yes."

"What happened?"

"Raintree walked into Salvo's office ahead of me. He didn't say anything, just
walked across the room where Salvo was standing, pulled a dagger and plunged
it into his chest. Then, he turned and slashed the throat of a younger heavyset
man and stabbed another man standing beside him in the stomach.

A third man pulled a pistol and started firing. Raintree was hit in the side.

I knocked the gun out of his hand, and he ran out of the room.

Right after all of that, Raintree walked out. I followed. It all happened in
matter of seconds."

"Describe the dagger, Mr. Starr."

"Well, it looked to be very old…had a jeweled handle. I saw it before, lying
on a desk in Mr. Raintree's cabin. Looked like he had been using it as a letter
opener.

"Why didn't you immediately go to the police after the incident?"

"Raintree held the dagger to his own chest and threatened to kill himself if I didn't drive him back to his place in Bibb County. We were in his old Studebaker truck. I tried to talk him into letting me take him to a hospital from where I would have called the police, but he wouldn't hear of it. He said his wound was superficial. When we were passing through Midfield he told me to pull over, which I did. Then, he jumped out of the truck and took off on foot."

"Why didn't you go to the police then?"

"I've asked myself that question a dozen times. I don't know…shock I suppose. All I could think about was getting to my car."

"What's your connection with Mr. Raintree? Why were you at the scene in the first place?"

"I was preparing to represent him in a land dispute with Salvo. Salvo claimed that Raintree's father had signed over mineral rights on their 320 acre homestead in Bibb County. Raintree claimed that it wasn't so. The land had been in his family for generations, and according to him they had always held full title to it. He said that Salvo's henchmen had been harassing him regarding the matter. The night before the killing, I was at Raintree's house located on the property. Actually, it was a cabin with no power or plumbing. We were discussing his legal options. It was late and he invited me to stay the night. Sometimes after midnight I was awakened by the sound of a helicopter hovering over the cabin. There were flashes, and something crashed through the roof. Then the place burst into flames. It burned to the ground. We barely got out in time."

"That's some story," Kincaid commented, "Why didn't you all call the sheriff then?"

"Raintree was backwoods in his thinking. He was fiercely independent and wanted to resolve the matter without involving the law, the government or any other authority. He refused to call anyone except Salvo, saying that all he wanted to do was go and talk to him.

As his council I strongly advised him against it…but instead call the sheriff. He said he was going with or without me. I went against my better judgment."

"Did you have any idea that he would kill Salvo?"

"No, beforehand, he seemed calm and rational; so I never expected any of this to happen."

"If he's the kind of man who likes to take care of things on his own, I wonder why he hired you."

"He probably wouldn't have if he felt like he had another option. They were already in the process of legally taking over his land."

"Do you think Salvo had a legitimate claim."

"No, I think he was trying to swindle Raintree using forged documents."

"You used the word 'was' referring to Raintree a minute ago, like he wasn't with us anymore.

"Well he isn't, is he?"

"Why would you, a lawyer from Mobile take a case up here?"

"It was a referral."

"A referral from who?"

"Bob Savage, a friend. He's now deceased."

"How did he die?"

"He was with me in my airplane back in August. We were looking over Mr. Raintree's property from the air when a freak storm caused us to crash. I survived…Bob didn't."

"So, you representing Mr. Raintree has a personal dimension to it."

"Well, I wouldn't say that, but Bob Savage was my best friend."

"About, Mrs. McBride, Raintree's daughter, do you know her?"

"We briefly met the day before the fire when I was out at Mr. Raintree's place for the first time."

"Are you aware that her nine-year-old daughter is missing?"

"Yes, I was about to leave this morning to come and report to the police when she drove up looking for Mr. Raintree. She thought her alcoholic husband who had left the night before after beating her had come back home during the night and taken the child while she was asleep. She came seeking help from her father."

John felt the sweat in his palms, hoping Anna's version of this part of the story matched his.

"I'll be frank with you," said Kincaid, "something smells fishy about this whole thing. You may have a problem, Mr. Starr. Do you want to call yourself an attorney?"

"Yes, do you have a phone book?"

"I'll get one."

Kincaid left the room, closing the door behind him.

As he looked at the camera mounted near the ceiling at the opposite corner of the room, he recapped what had been asked and told during the questioning thus far.

*Was that little slip of the tongue significant? Kincaid's listening for them... careful what you say.*

At least ten minutes passed before Kincaid returned with the phonebook.

"I'm afraid I'm going to have to charge you, Mr. Starr."

"With what?"

"As an accessory to murder...for now. Better call that attorney."

"This is John Starr, is Joseph Bonaparte available?"

"Hey, John, what's up?"

"I've got a problem, Joseph. Can you come down to the Birmingham city jail...ASAP?"

# CHAPTER 36

# Dark side of the Starr

JOSEPH BONAPART'S OFFICE was typically lawyer-like, comfortable…well appointed but not pretentious. John noticed among several framed photographs on the wall, one of him with his arm around Joseph who at the time was about fifteen. Coincidentally, the office was in the Woodward building…tenth floor.

"The cops have been crawling all over this place today," said Joseph, settling back in his chair. "How in God's name did you get involved in this thing, John?"

"That's what I've been asking myself, Joseph. Thank you for arranging bail…$50,000, right?"

"Yes. Does the family know what's going on?"

"No, not yet. I'll be going back this afternoon, to face the music."

"What about Jack Wainwright, your partner?"

"No, he doesn't know either."

"Don't you think he should be in on this?"

"Not yet. I want you and me to sort things out before getting anybody else involved."

"OK, if that's the way you want it…start from the top…tell me everything."

He hit the RECORD/START button on the tape recorder.

"Turn it off, Joseph. Just take notes."

As John made his way through the bizarre story, Joseph listened patiently, sometimes taking notes, sometimes looking at his friend and client, sometimes looking at the floor. At the end he commented: "I've never heard anything even close to this…gold, Spanish conquistadors, talking crows and crazy dreams, all leading to the death of three people. That's weird stuff, Man."

"I know it sounds crazy, but it's true."

"Why would you put yourself out on a limb by concocting a lie regarding what happened? You know the law…the consequences."

"It's not a total lie… not the relevant facts."

"You are not thinking clearly, John. You're in one of those deals where you're going to have to prove your innocence. Exhumed bodies are about the only evidence that can accomplish that."

"I can't allow their graves to be disturbed, besides, you know what would happen if word got out that gold is on the property."

"Is it worth it not to tell; because the truth is about the only thing that will save your ass…is it the woman?"

"Yes…partially."

"Well, Raintree's daughter would be wealthy, and there sure as hell could be a case made that Salvo and his accomplices killed the little girl."

"Like I told you, Raintree told me some of my ancestors are buried out there."

"How did he know that?"

"He said the crow told him."

"Come on, John, there ain't no crow. That's something you dreamed. This is reality, man. You know that…don't flip out on me."

John got up out of the chair, walked to the window and blankly stared out at Birmingham's skyline.

"John," said Joseph, breaking the silence, "Remember when you first came to Mobile after you and Angie married, and during those Debarden parties you would come back to the kitchen where Mama and I were?"

"Yes, I remember."

"You were like a fish out of water, being thrown in that high society whirl."

"Yeah, no doubt about that."

"Remember when we'd sit out back, sometimes for hours on that old brick wall next to the oak tree and talk about every thing from yours and your buddy, Bob Savage's adventures to the birds and bees while the party went on inside?"

"Yes, we had a lot of good talks. You were a good kid, Joseph."

"You know, not many men, especially white men, would have paid any attention to, much less spent time with a wide-eyed fifteen-year-old colored kid like me….but you did. You were my mentor, my father and older brother all in one package. You're the reason I became a lawyer, but you know that."

John continued staring out the window.

"What about Viet Nam, John? As much as we talked, you always avoided it. What happened over there? Tell me about it."

John turned…"Do you have a cigarette?"

"No, but I'll send out for some."

"No…no need to…it was '63, a time before America became involved in actual combat there. I was accompanying a South Vietnamese patrol as a US observer. The little village was somewhere in the countryside. There were rumors of Viet Cong activity in the area. Colonel Tu, the squadron commander, gave orders to burn the village down. I tried to talk him out of it, but it didn't do any good.

As the troops carried out his orders, a little girl emerged from one of the burning huts. She was on fire…screaming. She ran towards us…where Tu and I stood. There was unspeakable terror in her eyes. She screamed with her arms stretched… reaching out towards us, crying for help. I never will forget those words, 'Guíp Toi…Guíp Toi!', (Help me…help me!")

Tu pulled his pistol and shot her dead, right there on the spot. She fell only a few feet from us. It was horrible. The shock and madness hit me all at once. I felt like I was on the dark side of some star."

Tears began to well in John's eyes.

"It's OK, John, go on."

"The same feelings came over me as I knelt over Allison's body there on the banks of the Cahaba…her burnt little body."

"What happened next…in Nam?"

"I motioned for Tu to follow me behind one of the burning huts as if there were something he needed to see. When we were out of sight, I pulled out my service revolver and shot him point blank in the head, blowing the opposite side of it off. The impact knocked him off his feet as brains and skull fragments flew through the air. I blew his brains out, Joseph. It was quick and cold…just like he had been with the little girl. Then, I yelled, 'Sniper!' which brought on a barrage of gunfire from the troops…spraying the surrounding forest. Then, they turned on the people. Within minutes everyone in the hamlet lay dead."

"So," said Joseph, "you've been carrying this around inside you all these years?"

"Yes, I've never told anybody…not even Bob. I've tried to keep it buried… but sometimes it won't stay."

John turned back towards the window and focused on the great iron statue, Vulcan that stood atop Red Mountain.

"I had never killed anything before in my life…not even a bird with my BB gun when I was a kid, but that morning, in the blink of an eye, I became one of them, Joseph…I am one of them, and to this day I'm glad I killed Tu. And, I wanted that son-of-a-bitch, Salvo, dead, too. Don't think I didn't know something was going to happen when I went with Raintree that night. If he hadn't done it, I probably would have. It might as well have been me who plunged that dagger in his heart."

"But, you didn't…did you?".

"No…no, I didn't."

"You know you've been twisted, John."

"I know."

"Well, I can't even imagine what you've been through, but that was then and now is now. Bury it again and let's put on our lawyer caps. We've got a trial to prepare for."

# CHAPTER 37

# The Long Road Home

TWO HUNDRED AND sixty miles separated Birmingham and Mobile…about a four-and-a- half hour drive. John's troubled mind recapped events as he traveled the long road home.

*Can they really make an accessory charge stick*, he wondered. *Will Anna's story match mine as to why she was at Raintree's when the sheriff came. Did Joseph get to her before they did? Where is she? What's she doing?*

As he passed through Montgomery with a hundred and sixty miles to go, his thoughts turned to the dread of what he had to face. He had not called Angie in three days.

*Maybe the Mobile Press Register has already picked up the story…plastered my name all over the front page.*

*Maybe they're all at the house, the whole family…ready to pounce as soon as I come in.*

*God, I hate to go home…wonder what Anna's doing…right now…this minute.*

The grueling hours passed without mental reprieve. Then, the Mobile City Limits sign came into view. The twenty-minute drive across town seemed an eternity as he prepared himself for whatever was to come. Now, It was time to face the music.

He drove into the driveway…and into the garage, parking next to Angie's station wagon. He looked at his watch…10:00 PM. A dog's bark in the neighborhood broke the silence.

Except for the usual stairwell light being on, the house was dark. The quiet stillness gave no comfort. It was not a comforting place…it never really was.

He slowly climbed the stairs and entered the bedroom. Angie lay asleep.

He went into the bathroom, relieved himself and brushed his teeth.

As he stripped to his briefs, ready to crawl in bed, Angie turned over.

"Well, did you finally decide to come home?"

"Angie, we need to talk."

"It'll have to wait till morning."

She rolled back over. There was silence.

As usual John rose at 6:30. The gnaw that accompanied his restless half -conscious sleep continued. Angie was in deep slumber. He would have to wait.

He showered, shaved and dressed. As he entered the den downstairs to gather his thoughts and wait for Angie and the boys to rise, the phone rang.

"What in God's name is goin' on, John Starr?" said the unmistakable voice of his mother-in-law, "Rad just called and said you were involved in a killing up in Birmingham. He was terribly upset."

"A client went berserk, Fannie. I was there when it happened…I was at the wrong place at the wrong time. I'm working on getting it straightened out."

"Let me speak to Angie, please."

Just then, he heard her coming down the stairs.

"She's still asleep. I'll have her call, OK?"

He hurriedly hung up the phone.

"Well," Angie said entering the den, "you must have had a good time with Joseph up in Birmingham. I haven't heard a word from you in three days."

"Angie, hear me out before saying anything, else."

"Well, the stage is yours, Mr."

"I witnessed a murder and have been drawn into it as a suspect."

"What! Don't they know you won't even kick over an ant hill?"

"That's not the point. I've been charged as an accessory. I'm out on bail."

"It's that Indian thing, isn't it? You've gone and gotten yourself mixed up with that nutty old man."

"Yes, I guess I did."

"You lied to me, John Starr. You said you were up there working on some papers or something with Joseph Bonaparte."

"Angie, I can't tell you anything anymore without you putting me down. That's why I lied."

"Well, you see where it's gotten you, Mr. Attorney."

She turned and walked out of the room.

In less than a minute he heard her talking on the phone with Fannie.

In less than another minute, she shouted, "Mama says you've ruined the family name, and you're a bastard."

John arrived at his office about 9:00 AM. Martha, the secretary had a sheepish look on her face as he passed her giving his usual greeting. He went directly into Jack's office where he sat leaning back in his chair with his feet propped up on his desk, reading the newspaper.

" Morning, Jack."

"You know, you're front page news," he replied, "Why didn't you call me?"

"There wasn't time. I had to call Joseph Bonaparte."

"How deep are you in this thing, John?"

"Deep…looks like the D.A. is hell bent on making a case against me, especially since Raintree and the little girl are missing."

"What do you want me to do?"

"Nothing for now, Jack. Joseph's got a handle on it, but I'm sure I'll need your help as we get into it…and thank you."

Within minutes phone calls started coming in…from news paper reporters, TV anchors, and even a radio talk show host, who, of all things asked, "Why was a knife used instead of a gun?" John hung up on him.

Rad Debarden's call came about ten o'clock.

"John," he said, 'I'm sorry to hear about your troubles."

"Thanks for your concern, Rad. It's all a big mistake. I think I can work through it."

"Can you come to my office this afternoon, say about three?"

"I don't think so, I've got a lot of things to take care of."

"John, I think it would be in your best interest to come."

Rad Debarden's office was dimly lit, in keeping with the dark stone of a man that sat behind the desk. "Hello, John, I appreciate you coming," he said.

"It sounds important. What's going on?"

"Yes, it is important. I remember you asking me about Salvo at the party last Friday evening. I told you that I knew him through a business relationship. We transfer coal from his barges to ocean carriers."

"Yes, I remember, too."

"You may or may not know it, but he and I were also involved as partners in several other enterprises."

"No, I didn't know that."

"I understand that you took on William Raintree as a client. Is that true?"

John felt a sudden chill. *How did he know that?*

"Yes, I was about to take him on as a client when what happened, happened."

"I'm assuming it was over a dispute regarding mineral rights of the Raintree property."

"Yes."

"Do you know the significance of those mineral rights?"

*Play it cool, Starr.* "No, other than Mr. Raintree said that Salvo didn't own them."

"I think you do know the significance of those mineral rights, John."

He felt the second chill. *The bastard's in on it.*

"Let me get to the point," said Debarden, "if you can find it in yourself to cooperate, Don Salvo Jr. and the other witnesses will testify in your behalf. Most likely all charges will be dropped before it gets anywhere near a courtroom. You can be free of this thing, completely exonerated and become a wealthy man in the process. Give it serious thought, John. We want you to be on our team."

"I'll give it serious thought, Rad."

"By the way, I understand Joseph is representing you. You may want to share this conversation with him."


By five that afternoon the piper was in the wind, headed north toward Birmingham.

Joseph met John at the airport.

After picking up a couple of burgers at a drive through, they went to the office for what would undoubtedly be a long night.

"So," said Joseph, "Rad Debarden wants you to help Bubba and his bunch screw Raintree's daughter out of the land. In return you get off the hook…and get rich."

"That's it in a nut shell."

"Small world," Joseph muttered, "the man who hardly gave me a 'hello' when I was growing up, yet paid for my education is in this thing up to his eyebrows. He's already got more money than he can ever spend. Why the hell would he involve himself in something like this?"

"Greed, Joseph…greed, my man."

"I wonder exactly what part he plays in all of this?"

"I'm pretty sure I've got that figured out…Salvo loads the gold on barges, hidden in the coal. The barges go down the Warrior River and Tombigbee to Mobile.

Rad takes it from there…transfers it to outgoing ships and launders it off shore.

"I think you've got it pegged, John."

"That's about all it could be."

"I think he thinks he's got us both by the nuts," said Joseph," if we don't play along or if we get him involved in any way, it could mean a conflict of interest for me, not to mention Mama's situation with the Debarden clan."

"Don't think he didn't know that when he called me to come to his office. He calculated the risk or would have never stuck his neck out. He always plays it safe. I know him that well."

"Well, we both know the easy way out, John, but I know you, and I know that ain't the way it's gonna' go down."

"No. I've already thought about it and decided not to respond. We'll keep him guessing for now. When he figures out that I'm not going to take the deal, he'll back off and distance himself. In the meantime, we'll let him sweat a little. The last thing Rad Debarden wants is to be pulled in as a hostile witness."

"Well, to tell you the truth, I don't think there's much he can do to hurt you, seeing that Bubba and his thugs have already told the police who did the killing. They'd have a hard time changing their story at this point."

"The main thing is to keep it quiet about the gold, Joseph, which means Raintree and his granddaughter have to remain at large. Just stick to the script."

"As your attorney, I advise against it, but as your friend, I'm with you."

"Thank you, Joseph."

"So much for ethics…by the way, Mama and I have never told anyone, but there's strong family rumor that she's Rad's half-sister."

"Well, hello Uncle Rad. You know what, Joseph? Nothing surprises me anymore…or disappoints me."

# CHAPTER 38

# Humpty Dumpty

THE TRIAL WAS set for June 10, 1978…seven months away. Contrary to how he thought it would be, John was received with a degree of celebrity among Mobiles' gentry…or perhaps he was just a curiosity. Either way, it was a notoriety he much preferred not to have.

Angie had very little to say, but immediately moved into the spare bedroom. There didn't seem to be any point in trying to talk to her; so for the most part he remained silent.

On increasing occasions John came in from work to find Mrs. Johnson, the baby sitter, there. Angie had left the house in early afternoon and was not returning until after dark. She would head straight to her bedroom without uttering a word. John lay in what was once their bed wondering, worrying…speculating the worst. He recalled the helpless feeling Bob described as his marriage to Lori unraveled…like a snowball rolling down hill, getting bigger and picking up speed, unstoppable as it headed straight to hell. An overwhelming emptiness came over him. Seeking some kind of comfort…any kind of comfort, his mind wandered to Anna. *How is she… what is she doing?*

Christmas of '77 approached, marking the beginning of Mobile's party season. Knowing Angie didn't want him to go anyway, John skipped the first gala that took place December twenty first, using the excuse of having a severe headache. He stayed home with the boys, Johnny and Cart. They popped corn, played Monopoly and listened to old records while whiling away the evening.

"This is one your Mom and I danced to many years ago, way before you guys were born."

He put 'Blue Christmas' on the turntable.

As he listened and the boys mimicked Elvis's moves, the lump in his throat made it hard to swallow.

It was indeed a blue Christmas. Angie left out on the afternoon of Christmas Eve and didn't come in until after eleven.

"Where have you been, Angie?"

"I was with Mama, wrapping the new golf clubs she got for Daddy. Do you have a problem with that?"

"Yes, I do. In the first place you should have been here with the boys and me. In the second place, who do you think you are, waltzing out of here any old time you want to without telling anybody where you're going and then coming back whenever you feel like it?"

"Who do I think I am…who do you think you are, Mister?"

"I'm your husband, damn it. I have a right…"

"Rights," she interrupted, "after ruining this family's name?"

She turned and stomped up the stairs.

After setting out the boys' booty from Santa, he headed for the liquor cabinet.

Carter and Fannie came over about ten the next morning, bringing gifts and wanting to see what Santa had brought the boys.

Carter was his usual friendly laid back self, but had a concerned look on his face. Fannie was cool but civil. Angie came down in her robe, still sleepy eyed but seemingly in a pleasant mood.

After opening presents and small talk, Carter asked John to step out back with him.

"I'm here, John, if you ever need to talk."

*Ironic*, thought John. The very things he needed to discuss with Carter, he couldn't. He needed to talk to him about the bastard he played golf with every Saturday, and called a friend…expose him for what he was, but couldn't. He needed to talk about his daughter, whose contempt and disrespect was out of control, but couldn't.

"You know, Angie's mother and I are greatly concerned about you all," he continued. "I know it's a strain under the circumstances, but we're still a family.

We're all we have. I told Fannie this. She's having a hard time too, but agrees. It will take a little time for her, but you know Fannie, she'll come around.

"I hope so. Carter…I'm really sorry to have gotten you all involved in this mess, but believe me, I didn't intend for it to happen."

"I know you didn't, Son. Maybe it would help if you came to the New Year's Eve party at the Debardens."

Carter looked him square in the eyes.

"John, you really do need to accompany Angie to this thing."

John's sixth sense told him that his father-in-law was trying to say more than he was saying.

"OK, Carter, But only if she wants me to go with her."

"She'll go with you. I'll see to that if necessary…and, for what its worth, I don't like going to those things any more than you do…never did. But, it's just the way things work around here."

"Yeah, by the way, was Angie over at you all's last night?"

"No, why do you ask?"

"No reason, she must have been doing some last minute shopping."


It was a big night for the Whaleboners. After all it was New Years Eve 1830 when the first mystic society was born.

John and Angie walked in, greeted by Bea as usual. The dance band was playing an upbeat tune, and the guests seemed to be especially lively. It looked like everyone was on their way towards having a good time, Mobile style. Predictably, Angie shot off on her own as usual, presumably, to find her mother.

He felt all eyes on him as he made his way through the crowd…on his way to the bar. George was his first encounter on the journey.

"John, I'm sorry to hear about your troubles. I know what it's like to have troubles, and to be in the spotlight."

"Thanks for the concern, George. I think things will turn out all right."

"Tell me, confidentially, is there any connections between what's going on and that old Spanish chronicle I translated for you?"

"I don't know. You haven't told anyone, have you?"

"Oh, no, not even Ted. But I do want you to tell me all about it once you get things sorted out."

"I will. You just might be the only one who won't think I'm nuts…George, you look awfully thin and tired. Are you all right?"

"I have been feeling washed out lately. Don't feel like doing a damn thing. So is Ted. I think we're both anemic."

About that time, Howard Bartholomew came strolling up.

"Hello, John, my boy. Sounds like you got yourself into a bit of a scrape up there in Birmingham."

"Yes, but I think everything will be OK."

"I heard Beatrice's boy is representing you."

"Yes, Joseph Boneparte."

"John, you should know better than that. He's an amateur. Besides, what chance do you think a Negro boy is gonna' have against those great white sharks. They'll eat him alive…and you too. Why don't you let my firm get the job done for you?"

"I'll give that thought…please excuse me, Howard. I need to go find my better half."

Slowly, but surely he was making his way towards the other end of the ball room, when: "How are things, John?"

"Couldn't be better, Rad, how are things with you?"

"Doing well, thank you."

There was a long moment of silence as the two faced off.

John fought to keep his cool as Rad's deep-set steel-gray eyes peered into his. Then, without a word, he turned and walked away.

"Nice party," said John in a loud voice as Rad disappeared into the crowd.


He made it to the bar and ordered a bourbon and coke. The Jack Daniels went down warm and smooth. He turned and scanned the ballroom.

It looked like everyone was well into the process of letting their hair down. Most had made several visits to Bea's rum punch fountain.

Even Sophie was laughing and cutting up like a young girl. An older man Terry Wayne had brought in from up north to head up his sales department was her escort. He wasn't much to look at…short, stocky with a face like a bulldog, but apparently he was giving her the kind of much needed attention she had been denied all her life.

Then, along came Horace…glassy eyed and swaying…accompanied by Colleen.

"Hey, Big Bad John. About the ruckus up in Birmingham…tell old Horace, just between you and me…did you help kill that sum-bitch?"

"No, that 'sum-bitch' got killed by a damned old Indian. I just watched him do it."

"Well, I'll be a sum-bitch."

John looked at his watch. It was a minute till midnight.

"I'll talk to you later, Horace. Need to find Angie."

"Give her a kiss for me, Killer."

Traditionally, when the bell tolled, spouses and significant ones kissed to welcome in the New Year. John did not want to let the opportunity to do a little mending slip by, but Angie was nowhere in sight. Anxiously, he walked towards the ballroom's adjoining veranda. What he saw when he got there and peered outside through the panes of the huge double French door stopped him in his tracks.

They were outside on the veranda. Angie was in his arms…Terry Wayne's arms. The kiss displayed all the passion he once knew from her.

As the band played Auld Lang Syne and the rum flowed, John Starr felt his essence drain from him. He turned and walked away, back towards the bar.

"Jack Daniels, on the rocks," he commanded to the bartender. He gulped it down. "Another," he said. Three in a row did not quell the volcano inside. He clinched the glass sitting on the bar and squeezed as his mind went into a tailspin.

*I should kill him right now…her too.*

He turned his head and looked around the ballroom, at the merry makers.

*Damn you all.*

He felt a sharp pain in the palm of his hand as the glass broke.

"What have you done, man," said the bartender as he reached for a bar rag to wrap the bleeding wound, "you may have to have stitches on this."

"No, it'll be OK. Sorry for making a mess."

He turned and walked towards the kitchen.

"Lordy, Mr. John, what have you gone and done to yourself?"

"I'll be OK, Bea. I just nicked it on a broken glass."

"Here, let me take a look." She took his hand and unwrapped the still-bleeding gash.

"This ain't no nick. You need stitches."

"I'll see to it tomorrow. Right now I need a cup of coffee."

"I sure hope you go see about that," she said while pouring him a cup of chicory laced coffee. He took a sip.

"It's all going to hell in a hand basket, Bea…the marriage, my life, everything.

"Now, settle down Mr. John, tell Bea all about it."

Just then, Angie walked into the kitchen.

"What on earth has happened, John?"

"I cut myself on a glass…it's time for us to go, Angie."

"Yes, I think you're right."

There would be none of the usual long goodbyes this evening as the Starrs departed.


Angie took the wheel.

"Does it hurt very bad?"

"No."

Then, came the silence. He was determined to keep his mouth shut, but as they passed through the streets of downtown Mobile crowded with merry-makers, it came out:

"Humpty Dumpty set on the wall.

Humpty Dumpty had a great fall, and

All the kings horses and all the king's men,

Couldn't put poor Humpty together again…I saw you out on the veranda with him, Angie."

"Well, it's not what you think, at least not on my part. He grabbed me, not me him. I guess he had too much to drink…just like you."

"Fuck you, Angie." He slammed his hand down on the dashboard.

"Speaking of which, Mr. Attorney," she said in an untypical raised voice, "I saw a picture of Mr. Raintree's daughter in the paper. I suppose that's what you've been doing with her up there in Birmingham."

No more words passed between them on the long drive home.

Six-thirty in the A.M. came and passed. It was the first time in years his internal alarm clock failed to go off. It was after nine before he drug himself out of bed. His hand throbbed.

He went into the bathroom. Shep followed. The sting from pulling the rag soaked with dry blood from the wound fully awakened him.

"It needs stitches," he muttered.

As he looked at the man in the mirror, haggard and bewildered, this morning looking older than his years, he spoke: "Are we going to make it through this thing, Shep?"

The old dog's sad loyal eyes looked up at him. John reached down and petted his head.

"Dad, can we go up today," asked John Jr. as soon as he reached the bottom step.

"Yeah, Dad," Cart piped in, "Can we go flyin'?"

"Sorry fellas, not today," he said, glancing towards the den. Angie was there, watching TV. "I cut my hand on a glass last night…got to go get it stitched up."

"Can we go with you, Dad?" asked Cart.

"Best not, son. I've got to go to the office afterwards."

He left without saying anything to Angie.

After six stitches at the local Doc-in-a-box, John went to his office. Then, upon getting the number he was after from the long-distance operator, he picked up the phone and dialed.

"Hello, Anna, it's John."

"John, are you all right?"

"I want to see you."

"You know we're not supposed to even talk, much less see each other."

"Anna, I need to see you. Can you pick me up at the Bessemer airport at three?"

"I'll be there."

# Chapter 39

# A Day with Anna

As he taxied towards the runway, his thoughts turned to the boys' asking him to take them up this day.

"I really am sorry, fellas," he said under his breath, "We'll have our day to fly…I promise."

A minute later he was rolling down the runway, picking up speed, leaving it all behind, at least for a little while.

As the engine screamed taking the piper up into the cold crystal sky, his head began to clear. He felt himself coming back together again.

After two hours in the air, the Bessemer airport came into view. It was a small private facility fifteen or so miles west of Birmingham. As John made his approach he saw her standing by her car, looking up, shielding her eyes from the afternoon sun. He felt the same rush as when he first saw her.

It was a perfect landing on an imperfect day. He taxied right up to where she was, anxiously unharnessing himself and grabbing at the door.

As they embraced on the tarmac, and kissed in the light of day, the dark world he left behind began to fade.

"What happened to your hand?"

"I cut it on a broken glass yesterday."

"How have things been?" asked John as they drove towards the Bessemer Highway.

"Not too good. Dennis is blaming everything on me, Allison's disappearance, his drinking, the problems in our marriage…everything.

"Has he been physically abusive?"

"No, I think he's afraid Daddy's stalking him. He came home briefly, then took off again. I don't know where he is…at his mother's, I guess."

"Did you hide the gold in a safe place?"

"I hope so. I took three nuggets out of the sack like you said then buried it under the crawl space of the cabin."

"Did you have any trouble cashing in the nuggets?"

"No, Mr. Cohen was very nice…very concerned about Daddy and the situation."

"I've missed you terribly, Anna, and need you now more than you'll ever know."

"I've missed you too, John."

"We've got a lot of catching up to do," he said, "pull in there."

The old motel was in a state of decline, but it would do: "I'll check us in…be right back."

In the darkened room they disrobed. He gazed upon her, determined to rid himself of the ghosts that haunted.

She pulled the covers back and slipped between them. He followed her.

It felt good holding her, touching her. He ran his hands over her body, his fingertips exploring, rediscovering.

He was ready; she was ready. He came up over her and commenced to make love to her.

Suddenly, it hit him…the image Wayne and Angie on the veranda…then, an image of Angie with Wayne, like he was with Anna. His thrusts became fury, causing the bed to shake violently.

"Why are you being so rough with me?" she cried out, pushing him away. "Have I done something?"

"No, of course not. You've done nothing. I don't know what came over me. I'm sorry….I'm sorry."

He lay back down beside her and stared at the ceiling. Pangs of his own sins began to creep into his mind.

"You've been under a lot of stress," she said, snuggling up to him, gently stroking. But, her touch failed to arouse him.

"I don't know what's wrong," he said, "I want you so bad."

"Maybe I can fix it," she whispered, edging downward, kissing his chest and stomach along the way.

As they made love, the troubles in John's mind finally began to melt away. He began to feel that he was with who he was suppose to be, and that this was the way it was supposed to be.

"Penny for your thoughts," she said.

"I love you," he answered, wondering if he really meant it.

"I love you, too."

He pulled her to him. They made love again.

# CHAPTER 40

# The Trial: Day One

JUNE 10, 1978...the trial date finally arrived.

From the defendant's table John scanned the courtroom. Across the bar in the gallery, a small group, obviously Salvo's family, sat huddled to one side on the first and second rows. Though the voices were muddled, he felt the anger coming from that direction.

He surmised that the heavyset woman blowing her nose and patting her eyes with tissue was Salvo's wife.

A few reporters and curiosity seekers sat scattered about the gallery. Except for Jack, no one from Mobile was there, which was just as well. John preferred it that way.

Joseph sat beside him, shuffling papers. "Looks like this thing's not going to be as high profile as I thought," he remarked, "I'm glad of that."

"Me too," said John, as he looked over at the stone cold face of Eddie Farber, the D.A., "I think he knows he has a weak case," whispered Joseph.

"All rise," intoned the Bailiff.

Judge Scott Mahan was a young bearded man, with a swagger in his walk.

"He looks like a kid," said John.

"Don't let that throw you. He's as sharp as they come."

After announcement of the case number, the jury was invited in.

One by one they took their seat in the jury box. There were nine men...six white and three black. There were three women, all white, plus two female alternates, one of which was obviously of Asian descent.

An old man, juror number six, immediately caught John's eye. There was something about him. Who is it, was the question that bounced about in his mind as he tried to match the face with those he knew or had ever known. It was like seeing a familiar telephone number, but not being able to place the person it belonged to.

"I know that old guy from somewhere," whispered John.

"Who do you think he is?" asked Joseph.

"I don't know. I can't remember."

"Why didn't you say something about it during jury selection?"

"It didn't register then."

"Well, I hope you haven't pissed him off somewhere along the way."

"No, it's something else."

John looked at him again.

As their eyes fixed on one another, the old man gave a crooked little smile and winked.

"My God, it's him."

"Keep it down, John. Who is it?"

"Bob Savage, with thirty years on him."

"For God's sake, don't go there, man. Settle down."

In his opening statement, Farber left no doubt that he intended to nail John, prove him guilty of aiding and abetting in the murder. Joseph drove home the point that John was merely a witness…a man in the wrong place at the wrong time.

"Call your first witness, Mr. Farber," said Judge Mahan.

Edgar Jones, the man who fired the shots that evening took the stand and told his version of the story after being asked to do so by Farber.

"Everything happened so fast," he began. "The old man just walked in and stabbed Mr. Salvo, first thing, without saying a word. Then he turned and slashed Bubba's throat. After that he stabbed Jake in the belly. He moved like a panther, or something…it happened so fast. I figured he was comin' after me next; so I pulled my gun and fired. That's when that man," he pointed to John, "knocked it out of my hand. I took off running. I don't know what happened after that. All I know is that I had to get out of there or I'd have been a dead man."

"For the record, Mr. Jones," said Farber, "That man…the one you just pointed at. The one you are referring to: His name is John Starr."

It came time for Joseph's cross-examination.

"Up until the time Mr. Starr knocked the gun out of your hand, Mr. Jones, where was he?"

"He was standin' in the doorway."

"So, he had nothing to do with Mr. Raintree's activity?"

"No, I don't guess so…not until he attacked me."

"Exactly when did Mr. Starr knock the gun out of your hand, Mr. Jones? I'm assuming it was after the two shots were fired."

"Yes, Sir."

"So, you're saying that Mr. Starr didn't get involved until Mr. Salvo was stabbed, Mr. Salvo Jr.'s throat was slashed and Mr. Howard was stabbed, all of which was done by Mr. Raintree; right?"

"Yes, Sir."

"How many rounds did your gun hold?"

"Six."

"Six minus two equals four, Mr. Jones. Do you think that perhaps Mr. Starr knocked the gun out of your hand because he thought you would shoot him, too?"

"Objection," shouted Farber, "he's leading the witness."

"Sustained."

"What kind of gun do you have, Mr. Jones?"

"A .38 Special."

"Do you have a pistol permit?"

"No, Sir."

"Have you ever been convicted of a felony."

"Yes, but that was over twenty years ago. I was just a kid."

"What were you convicted of, Mr. Jones?"

"Armed robbery. A friend of mine and I robbed a filling station."

"How old are you, now, Mr. Jones?"

"Forty-five."

"Old enough to know better than to carry a pistol without a permit, right?"

"Objection, Your Honor. This is argumentive."

"Sustained."

"Mr. Jones, are you aware that a felon in possession of a pistol constitutes a felony?"

"No."

"I have no further questions, Your Honor."

Bubba Salvo took the stand. Other than a neck brace and raspy voice, he seemed to have made a full recovery from his injury.

Farber proceeded with his examination.

Bubba's account of what happened, at least up until the time he got his throat slashed, was reasonably close to that of Jones's.

Then, it came Joseph's time to cross-examine. "Mr. Salvo," he began…"may I call you Bubba?"

"OK," came the reply.

"Bubba, does Salvo Mining Company own a helicopter?"

"Yes."

"On the night of November 20th, 1977, did anyone in your organization use it to fire bomb Mr. Raintree's cabin located on the Cahaba River?"

"Objection, Your Honor, that has nothing to do with this case," yelled Farber, "Besides, I have a report from the Bibb County sheriff's department that determined the fire was caused by a faulty flue, not a firebomb."

Joseph jumped in before Mahan had a chance to respond: "May we have a side-bar, Your Honor?"

"Approach the bench, Mr. Bonaparte…Mr, Farber," said Mahan with a displeased look on his face.

"The fire has everything to do with this case, Your Honor," said Joseph, "It establishes a motive for murder for one party, and one party only. Whether so or not, Mr. Raintree believed that Don Salvo was behind the burning down of his house. Mr. Starr had no motive to kill anyone or be involved in any way. He was a lawyer just like you and me…trying to do his job when he got caught up in something beyond his control. He was at the wrong place at the wrong time, that's all.

"Alright," said Mahan, "I've heard enough. Now, stand back, please."

Joseph and Farber returned to their respective places in the courtroom.

"Objection overruled," said Mahan.

I ask you again, Bubba," said Joseph, "on the night of November 20<sup>th</sup>, 1977, did anyone in your organization use a helicopter to fire bomb Mr. Raintree's cabin located on the Cahaba River?"

"No, Sir, answered Bubba."

"May we have a side bar, Your Honor?" said Joseph.

"Jury members, take a fifteen minute break," said Mahan. "Approach the Bench, Gentlemen."

"What's on your mind this time, Mr. Bonaparte?" said Mahan as the last juror left the courtroom.

"Your Honor, I don't know why my client is here," said Joseph, "It's obvious that Mr. Starr had nothing to do with this. You can end it, right now, if you will. I hereby move for Judgment of Acquittal."

"I'm surprised you would even ask for that at this point in the proceedings, Mr. Bonaparte. The answer is, no…motion denied. Finish your cross-examination, or if you have finished, you need to Rest your Case-In-Chief." Now, stand-back. Bailiff, bring the jurors back in."

John couldn't resist. As the jurors came back in he looked over at the old man. Their eyes fixed. He heard an inner voice say: *I'll do every thing I can to get your ass out of this sling, John Boy.*

The old man smiled and gave a nod: *Watch out for that woman, though, the voice continued, the Asian one. She's trouble.*

John looked over at her. She was glaring a hole through him.

One by one the witnesses took the stand. Jake Howard, the man who was stabbed seemed to have made a full recovery. He was examined by Farber and cross-examined by Joseph, as were the Bibb County sheriff and his deputy. None gave testimony that significantly added to or disputed what had already been given. Then, came Anna's time.

"Raise your right hand, please," said the bailiff, "Do you swear to tell the truth, the whole truth, and nothing but the truth, so help you God?"

"I do," said Anna.

"State your name, please," said Farber.

"Anna McBride."

"Where were you living November 20th, 1977."

"1300 Midfield Ave."

"On the night your daughter was abducted, was she with you…at that address?"

"Yes."

"Was your husband there?"

"No, he was in Jasper, at his mother's house."

"Was anyone else there?"

"No…no one except my daughter, Allison."

"Where in the house was your daughter that night…the night of the disappearance?"

"She was in her bedroom."

"When did you realize she was missing?"

"The next morning."

"Did you call the police?"

"No."

"Why not?"

"I thought my husband had come back and taken her. We were having marital problems."

"It's strange that you didn't hear anything, Mrs. McBride."

"Objection, Your Honor. That is argumentative."

"Overruled."

"Yes, it is, but I'm a heavy sleeper."

"Did you make any attempt to learn the whereabouts of your daughter…call your husband's mother, do anything."

"Not immediately. I was afraid of my husband. He has a violent temper, especially when he drinks, which is most of the time. I went down to my daddy's place the next morning for his help, but he wasn't there." She began to tear up. "The home place was burned down."

"Was anyone there on the property, Mrs. McBride?"

"Yes, Mr. Starr was."

"Did he say why he was there?"

"Yes, he told me what happened. He said he came back to get his car and was fixing to go to the police. That's when the sheriff and his deputy came up."

"Did you know Mr. Starr prior to that time?

"I met him once, about two weeks earlier, at daddy's house."

"Have you had any contact with him since that time?"

"No."

"Do you know the consequences of lying to this court, Mrs. McBride?"

"Objection, that was uncalled for, Your Honor," protested Joseph.

"Sustained," said Mahan, "watch it Mr. Farber."

"I have no further questions, Your Honor."

"It was Joseph's turn to cross-examine. He asked her only one question:

"Does your father, Mr. Raintree, have a key to your house?"

"Yes," she answered.

"I have no further questions, Your Honor."

Anna was escorted from the courtroom without ever having looked in John's direction. She had been cool and collected on the stand. She lied well, thought John. Though it was absolutely necessary that she did so, he felt a tinge of disquiet.

"Court is adjourned until nine A.M. tomorrow," proclaimed Mahan.

As they drove toward Joseph's home, John said: "I appreciate your inviting me stay with you and your family. I hope it won't be too much of an imposition."

"John, you're family. Delores and I wouldn't have it any other way. If it weren't for you I wouldn't even be here practicing law."

"You're the one who worked your butt off and made it happen, Joseph. All I did was try to give a little encouragement along the way."

"John, do you remember how sometimes you had to jerk me up and talk Dutch Uncle?"

"Yeah."

"Now, I guess its my turn to do the same to you."

"Yeah?"

"That old man in the jury box was not Bob. Bob's dead. Forget the old man. Don't even look his way anymore, OK?"

"OK, Joseph. You're right, of course. It seems ridiculous now, but at the time it all seemed so real. I don't know what comes over me. Ever since the plane crash…."

"John, I'm convinced you're suffering from the leftovers of what you experienced in Nam. Maybe the crash triggered something, I don't know, but you're going to have to fight it until this thing is over. Then, get some help, OK?"

"OK, you're right on all accounts…and I will get help…if this thing ever gets over with."

"Now, that being clear," said Joseph, "we need to put our lawyer hats back on and talk strategy. Farber's no fool. He knows that there's more to this thing than he's been able to drag out of you, and maybe Anna. I think the judge knows it too."

"Yes, but we've got to stick to the script, Joseph."

"I know, but when you start twisting the truth, all sorts of things can happen. Remember, we're dealing with experts at getting to the truth. I guess it was stupid on my part when I tried to get Mahan to throw it out, but I was worried about Anna taking the stand."

"Well, she was as cool as a cucumber."

"Yes, she was. I just hope they don't know about you all's little liaisons during the past six months."

"If they did, wouldn't Farber have nailed her during examination?"

"I don't know, but I do think Farber's got something up his sleeve. I can smell it, and he's going to spring it on us…probably towards the end of the trial. I want to put you on the stand, John. Are you up to it?"

"Yes."

"Faulty flue," said Joseph, shaking his head. "It's pretty obvious that the sheriff down in Bibb County sat on his fat ass and let 'Einstein,' his deputy, do all the on- site investigation. He probably thought what was left of the gas can was a milk bucket. I guess that's good in a way, though. It means nobody's poked around too much down there."

John looked out the window as they drove through the neighborhoods with their well groomed lawns leading to Joseph's home. He looked at the trees with their bright green early summer leaves. Children played in front yards and rode bikes on the sidewalks. Dogs with wagging tails trotted alongside them. Life does go on, he thought.

Joseph's wife, Delores, was an attractive, upbeat young woman. The total support she gave her husband was obvious. Their daughter, Tanya, about Allison's age, was a pretty girl with a creamy cinnamon complexion and inquisitive chestnut-colored eyes.

"You guys wash up for supper," said Delores, "we're having southern fried chicken with rice and gravy. Joseph says it's a favorite of yours, John."

*God, it's good to be around normal, happy people for a change*, he thought.

# CHAPTER 41

# The Trial: Taking the Stand

"MR. STARR, WHY did you knock the gun out of Mr. Jones's hand?"

"I was afraid he was going to shoot me."

It was the second day of the trial, and John was on the stand being grilled by Farber.

"Did you leave the scene with Mr. Raintree after he killed Mr. Salvo and stabbed Mr. Howard and Mr. Salvo Jr.?"

"Yes."

"Did Mr. Raintree threaten or coerce you in any way to leave with him?

"No."

"Now, here's the sixty-four dollar question, Mr. Starr. Why didn't you go to the police instead of leaving the scene with Mr. Raintree?"

"I've asked myself that question a dozen times. I don't know…shock I suppose.

"Where did you and Mr. Raintree go after leaving the scene?"

"To his truck."

"Then what?"

"When I came to my senses and realized that he had been shot, I told him I was going to drive him to a hospital and call the police. He held the dagger to his chest and threatened to kill himself if I didn't drive towards Midfield. When we got there he told me to pull over. He got out and disappeared into the night."

"So," said Farber, "he was wounded by at least one of the shots fired by Mr. Jones?"

"Yes."

"How badly was he wounded?"

"I don't know. He said it was only a flesh wound."

"There was blood in the truck," said Farber, "but none found in or around Mrs. McBride's home. I wonder how that could be, Mr. Starr?"

"I have no idea."

"Why didn't you go directly to the police after letting Mr. Raintree out of the truck?"

"I felt an overwhelming need to get to my car, which was at Mr. Raintree's place down in Bibb County. I was planning to go to the police, but at the time getting to my vehicle was all I could think of."

John couldn't help himself. He glanced over at the old man in the jury box. He had a sullen look.

"Come on, Mr. Starr!" yelled Farber," There's more to this, and you know it, I know it, and everyone in this courtroom knows it. Why don't you just come clean and let's get this thing over with?"

The gavel came down hard.

"I will not tolerate this kind of outburst in my courtroom, Mr. Farber. Do you understand?"

"Yes, Your Honor."

"Do you understand, Mr. Farber?"

"Yes, Sir."

"Then, proceed."

"Since the fire on the night of November twentieth that destroyed Mr. Raintree's cabin has been deemed pertinent, I would like to ask where you were at that time."

"I was there, spending the night."

"How long had you been there?"

"I got there about 1:00 that afternoon."

"Were you with Mr. Raintree at his place from that time on?"

"Yes."

"Was your assessment as to what caused the fire the same as Mr. Raintree's?"

"All I knew was that a helicopter hovered over the cabin and something crashed through the roof and set the place on fire."

"Did it anger you that someone might have done something like that?"

"I was dismayed and confused."

"But, were you angry?"

"No, Mr. Farber. I just said what I was."

"Why did you accompany Mr. Raintree to his meeting with Mr. Salvo."

"Mr. Raintree wanted me to go…as his counsel."

"Now, as I understand it, you were with Mr. Raintree from the time of the fire, during the killing and up until he got out of the truck in Midfield. Is that correct?"

"That's correct."

"This means you had plenty of time to discuss what would go down at the meeting with Salvo, right?"

"Objection…that's argumentive."

"Objection overruled."

"We were together, but there was no talk of causing Mr. Salvo harm."

"Then, what was to be the purpose of the meeting?"

"Mr. Raintree said he wanted to question Mr. Salvo as to his possible involvement with the fire."

"Did it not occur to you to contact the authorities regarding this matter instead of going off half-cocked like you-all did."

"I strongly advised Mr. Raintree to turn it over to the sheriff, but he is a stubborn, independent man.

"I have no further questions, Your Honor."

Just then, a gasp came from the jury box. The old man was holding his throat with both hands as if being strangled by some invisible cord. His face contorted as he struggled to breathe. Suddenly, he lurched forward and slumped over the juror that sat in front of him.

*Bob, what's happening*, John shouted in silence, straining his mind to connect.

*It's her*, he heard come back to him. Then, there was silence.

All eyes were focused on the commotion, except for one pair. John glanced towards the Asian woman…the alternate. She was looking straight at him, her eyes burning. There was a crooked smile on her face.

"Get that man some help, quick!" shouted Mahan, "Court is adjourned until nine o'clock tomorrow morning."

"I wonder what in God's name came over the old man," commented Joseph as they drove home.

John decided to say the least possible regarding the incident.

"I can't imagine. He looked in awfully bad shape, though." He then quickly changed the subject: "I don't feel like I did well on the stand. How bad was it?"

"You came off like you should have. Lawyer or not, you're as vulnerable as any other human being given the circumstances. That's what I wanted the jury to see."

"I hope they bought it," said John.

"Well, we might know by this time tomorrow evening. Since Farber doesn't have any more witnesses to call things should wrap up fairly quickly. Unless he pulls a rabbit out of his hat I just don't think he has the goods to convince Judge or jury that you were in any way involved with the killing.

# CHAPTER 42

# The Trial: Judgment Day

NINE O'CLOCK DIDN'T come any too early for John. He had spent most of the night lying in bed replaying events. What he considered a lack-luster performance while on the stand gnawed at him. He wondered about Anna. For whatever reason, it bothered him that she was able to spin the tale so flawlessly on the stand. He thought about the old man, trying to convince himself that he wasn't an incarnation of Bob. What was the connection with the Asian woman? His mind drifted to Angie. No need to call home, she had made her feelings clear, just as the rest of the family had. Was she with him…Terry Wayne? In his heart and mind, he knew the answer. He thought of his boys.

It was the third day of the trial…judgment day.

John followed Joseph into the courtroom. He anticipated the queasy feeling, but not to be as strong as it was.

He didn't look up as the jury came in.

"Uh, oh," said Joseph.

John looked up towards the jury box. The old man wasn't there. In his place sat the Asian woman.

He looked at her; she looked at him.

She smirked.

"My God, Almighty," he blurted, "It's you!"

Mahan, grabbed his gavel and came down so hard the cracking sound of its wooden handle echoed through the courtroom.

"I want to see you, you and you in my chambers immediately," he shouted pointing to Farber, Joseph, and John. Jury dismissed…please be back in fifteen minutes."

"You all are making a circus out of my courtroom," barked Mahan behind the closed doors of his chambers, "and I don't like it worth a damn. I want it stopped immediately or I'll hold you all in contempt. Farber, you and Bonaparte both know that I don't make idle threats, and Starr, the next time I hear an outburst like that from you, I'm gonna' have your ass hauled off to the crazy house… understand?"

An almost simultaneous, "Yes sir," came from the trio.

"What happened to the juror that's missing…the old man?" asked Joseph.

"He died last night in the hospital," answered Mahan, "I was told that something caused his throat to swell, blocking his air passage. Strangulation was the cause of death…bad way to go. Ms. Tu, the alternate is taking his place."

John felt a great flush as blood rushed to his head. His hands broke into a cold, clammy sweat.

"Scotty…Your Honor," said Farber, "may I say something just between the three of us…off the record?"

"Go ahead."

"Mr. Starr, personally I don't think you had any more to do with that killing than I did, but I have a job to do. You're covering up something. We all know it. It makes no sense that Raintree, wounded, on foot, abducted his granddaughter and simply disappeared, without a trace. You can get your butt off the hot seat if you come clean now, but once you're caught up in the system it will be too late for Joseph or anyone else to help you. As a lawyer you should know this."

"I've told you all I can, Mr. Farber."

On the heels of that, Farber, in a casual voice said, "Your Honor, we do have one more witness."

"What?" said Joseph, "we haven't been informed of any more witnesses."

"It just came up, his name is Roy Akins. He lives next door to Anna McBride."

"You've been holding him in the wings, haven't you Eddie?" said Joseph.

"No, it just came up."

"Shut up, the both of you," said Mahan, "Now, let's go back out there and get on with this thing."

"What was that outburst of yours that got us into trouble with Mahan all about?" asked Joseph as they made their way back to the courtroom.

"Nothing, it just came out."

"How do you feel?"

"Like a piece of raw meat in a lion's den."

"Hang on, John. We're both gonna' need our cool. I knew Farber had something up his sleeve. I guess this was it. We'll have to wing it from here on out."

John stared at the Asian woman as they passed the jury box.

*Tu, I knew it was you*, he said silently. *You bastard, you've come back as a woman.*

She stared back with a contemptuous smile.

"Mr. Akins", asked Farber after establishing that he lived next door to Anna and her family, "on the afternoon of November 20th, 1977, what did you see going on at the McBride house?"

"An old man with a pony tail was beatin' on the door."

"About what time was that?"

"Well, it was just before dark…about five I guess."

"Did you see any vehicle he may have been driving?"

"Yes, Sir."

"What kind of vehicle?"

"An old red pickup truck."

"What happened then?"

"After he saw there wasn't anybody home, he got in the truck and drove off."

"That's strange. Mr. Starr testified that he spent all afternoon in Bibb County with a gentleman whose appearance and vehicle perfectly match what you just described.

I have no further questions."

As Joseph got up to cross examine, he whispered to John:

"Look at that red puffy face. I'm going for a 'Hail Mary.' "

"Mr. Akins, are you sure about the date that you saw what you just described."

"Sure as I'm sittin' here."

"Do you drink?"

"I take a snort now and then."

"How many DUI's have you had in the last year, Mr. Akins," asked Joseph.

"Two…I think."

"I have no further questions, Your Honor."

Finally, the State rested.

With the jury excused from the courtroom, Joseph, again, asked for Judgment of Acquittal, claiming that Farber failed to make his case.

"Based on the facts of this case," said Mahan, "there is enough evidence to continue." His answer was, "No."

Once all the procedural wrangling had run its course, Joseph had no choice but to rest his case.

In his closing argument, Farber presented John as a self-appointed vigilante who accompanied Raintree to Salvo's office with the intent to aid and abet in the murder. He harped on the fact that John did not go to the police when he had every opportunity to do so… and that both his and Anna's testimony conflicted with that of his witness, Akins. He accused them both of hiding critical facts.

Joseph stressed John's lack of motive, and emphasized that his actions weren't uncommon for any individual under that degree of stress…that it was simply a matter of being at the wrong place at the wrong time. "Do any of us know how we would react under such circumstances?" he said. "John Starr may be guilty of using poor and clouded judgment, but certainly not aiding and abetting in a murder. As far as Mr. Akins' testimony, it's clear that the man has a drinking problem, and his recollection of fact cannot be relied on."

John, Joseph and Jack Wainwright were waiting at Joseph's office when the call came that the jury had reached a verdict. It had only been three hours since they left the courthouse.

"Well, they're ready for us," said Joseph.

"Damn, that was quick," Jack commented.

"Maybe it's a good sign," said Joseph, "Let's go."

As John stood waiting to hear the verdict, his legs unsteady and shaking, it occurred to him that twelve people had already decided his fate. One of the twelve was a mortal enemy who surely did everything and anything to influence the others. In a few seconds he would know his fate.

The foreman stood and read: "We the jury"…now, less than two seconds to know…"find the defendant"…less than a second…"guilty of aiding and abetting in the murder of Donald Salvo…" no seconds to go…nothing left to know. He felt the numb…then, the flush…then, his heart drop to the floor.

Joseph turned to him: "We'll appeal…all the way to the Supreme Court if we have to."

John glanced over at the woman as they handcuffed him. She had a broad smile on her face.

Two guards, one on either side of him, grasped his arms and led him from the courtroom.

# Hard Time: Orientation

Gilmore penitentiary was located in south Alabama…about fifty miles from Mobile. John arrived there August 20, 1978. It was within a week from being a year since Bob's phone call. This would be home for a while, or at least until Joseph could pull off an appeal.

After being mustered in, he was taken to his cell.

"What are you in for?" were the first words out of his cellmate's mouth.

"Something I didn't do," he replied.

"Me too, I just got caught at it. I'm T. J. Vickers. Who are you?"

"John Starr."

"Pleased to meet you."

"Likewise. How long have you been here?"

"Three years…three to go. How long are you in for?"

"Ten years, if my appeal is denied. How is it at this place?"

"It ain't so bad. I've been in and out of jails all my life. There's a lot worse places than this.

"Sounds like you like being here."

"Sure, like they say, three hots and a cot, and all the sex you want."

T. J. Vickers, a skinny fellow of average height with sandy brown hair was somewhere in his thirties and had an obvious gift of gab. He seemed harmless enough, and John knew he had to get along with him since they would be living together in close quarters.

"What are you in here for, T. J.?" he asked.

"Burglary. A buddy of mine and I got drunk and needed some more beer. We thought it was a good idea to break into a barbeque joint that was closed for the night. I climbed on the roof and crawled through the heating ducts to get in. I got out OK with the beer, but that slab of ribs left on the grill smelled so good I had to go back for it. That's when I got stuck in the damn ductwork. The fire department had to chop me out. So, here I am…a three-time loser. What are you here for."

"Aiding and abetting in a murder."

"You ain't gonna' kill me, are you?"

"No, I'm not planning to,"

Nine o'clock came, and it was lights out. John climbed to the top bunk that had been consigned to him. Knowing morning would come all too soon, and a work detail awaited, he tried to empty his mind enough to go to sleep. As he lay there, dealing with the nauseating smell of some ammonia cleaning agent that mingled with the odors of sweat, urine and cigarette smoke, an inmate in a nearby cell blurted out:

"Let me outta' here you sons-of-bitches! It's after me!"

Obviously, the man was having a nightmare.

Another inmate piped in, "I want out, too!"

Then came a shout from yet another direction:

"Shut up you Mothers, I'm tryin' to sleep!"

Suddenly, the whole cellblock filled with screaming, cursing and venting.

The guards rushed in: "Knock it off, or there'll be no breakfast for you people."

The threat seemed to work. Things began quieting down.

John lay there on his back, looking at shadows on the ceiling. A shiver went through him. *I don't think I'm going to make it.*

After a while, only the sound of snoring echoed through the cellblock. In spite of this he began to drift a little towards sleep. He was almost there when the springs in the lower bunk began to squeak. Then, the whole bed unit began to shake. It went on for about forty-five seconds, after which a groaning sigh came from below.

He heard a cigarette being lit. Smoke rose permeating the air.

After a few minutes, the squeaking began again, and the bed started to shake.

"I hope you don't set this damn bed on fire, fella'," he said.

Not a word came from below, but the squeaking stopped.

*God, get me out of this place*, he prayed.

Finally, he managed to slip into a half sleep. Then, in what seemed like minutes, an irritating high-pitched voice yelped, giving reminisce of fingernails on a chalk board.

"Rise and shine, boys."

It was guard Number 201, nicknamed Squeaky, giving the wakeup call. It was 5:30.

"Better eat up," said T. J., "They only give us a half hour to eat, shit and shave before muster."

"That's generous of them," muttered John, his eyes feeling so heavy he could barely hold them open.


The prison community grew its own vegetables; so after being handed a hoe, it was off to the fields. John had been assigned to the gardening detail. He was dog-tired, and the day had just begun.

As the sun bore down while weeding row after row, his prison garb soon became soaked. He took off his shirt and wrapped it around his head. Sweat fell from his body like a summer shower. It quickly absorbed into the thirsty ground.

"You'd better swallow a salt tablet or two, Starr," yelled the guard, "and slow down a bit. You've got a long time to hoe those rows."

After a while, John and his hoe settled into a rhythm…not too fast…not too slow. It became hypnotic.

*Must have been the way slaves in the old plantation days dealt with it*, he contemplated. *Poor devils*, at least he had the hope of appeal.


By day's end with his body spent and mind numbed, there was no doubt that sleep would come this evening, even through the stench, the noise and whatever T.J. had planned for himself. After turning in his hoe, all he wanted was to lie down. Even the pangs of hunger seemed less important.

Supper did come, though and afterward mail call. There was a letter for him...from Fannie. *Odd*, he thought. She had hardly spoken to him since the troubles began.

Upon being returned to his cell, he opened it and began to read.

*Dearest John,*

*You bastard, you. You have disgraced this family, deserted your wife and children, and ruined your own life while chasing some...*

He crumpled it up, threw it to the other side of the cell, and climbed to his bunk.

T. J. picked the wadded paper up and began reading it.

"Man, she's pissed...your wife?"

"No, mother-in-law... T. J. I don't want to deal with it tonight. Give me a little quiet, will you?"

"OK, my man, you got it."

It wasn't long before John drifted into deep sleep...and dreams.

He and Angie were at the Debarden's gazebo next to the bay. It was a warm starry night like at the housewarming party the year before.

They were alone, as they were then...dancing to songs of the crickets and tree frogs. This time, as they kissed she melted into him. He felt her hand slip down and gently rub.

"I love you, John Starr," she said.

He became aroused as they danced and she gingerly massaged.

Suddenly, there was a disruptive squeeze.

His eyes flew open.

T. J. stood there with his hand on John's crotch.

"What the hell are you doing, man?"

"I'm just tryin' to give you a little comfort."

"Get your freakin' hand off me."

"I was jus tryin'..."

Before T. J. got the words out, John's fist connected with his mouth.

He stumbled backwards and sprawled across the commode.

"Don't kill me," he screamed.

"I should tear your head off, you damn pervert."

The commotion brought on the guards.

"Looks like you're getting started out on the wrong foot, Starr," said warden, Jessie Coleman, as John stood before him the next morning.

"Sir, he tried to molest me. It was self defense."

"This is prison, boy, not Disneyland."

"But…"

"No buts…I don't allow fighting in my institution under any circumstances. You're going to spend the next five days in Solitary to figure some way to deal with this sort of thing besides hauling off and pollocking whoever.

And, don't think Vickers is getting off Scot-free. Before I'm through with him, he won't even want to touch his own dick."

The eight-by-eight foot cell of solitary was nothing more than bare walls with a light bulb hanging from the ceiling and a small window toward the top of one wall.

Somewhere between despair and relief from the smell and ever-present noise in the cellblock, John lay in his bunk and stared at the ceiling. His thoughts drifted to things that continually weighed and nagged…things he could only wonder about:

Cool, beautiful, mysterious Anna…where was she…what was she doing… when would he hear from her…see her? Even after all that had happened he was still under her spell. Was he in love with her…or obsessed?

Then, there was the gnaw of Angie, once his fantasy in the flesh…love of his life…mother of his children. What went wrong? What could he, should he have done different? Did he still love her? Was she with that bastard, Terry Wayne?

Why should any of it matter now? He was powerless to do anything about anything…but it did matter. With feelings of helplessness and hopelessness came overwhelming despair. He wondered whether to curse or cry.

Trying to empty his mind, he focused on the dim light emitting from the bulb hanging from the ceiling. He stared at it, concentrated on it until it became the only thing in the room…the only thing in the world. He felt his eyelids grow heavy and mind drift in no particular direction.

Then, the light began to brighten. It became so intense he wanted to turn his head away from it…but couldn't.

A shadow appeared in the middle of the white hot light, creating a halo around it. From the shadow emerged the image of a man.

"Well," said a voice coming from the apparition, "since you didn't try to conjure me up, I thought I would conjure you up. You don't look like a happy camper, John Boy."

"Bobby, is that you?"

"Yeah, it's me, alive and well….well, anyway, I'm well."

"Where the hell have you been?"

"That's exactly where I've been."

"Hell…that's not good…what's it like?"

"It ain't like you think it is, Johnny. I'll tell you about it sometimes…but not now."

"Why'd you go to hell?"

"Oh, just some 'after school' stuff for interfering too much. Don't worry, though, I'm on my way back to those castles in the sky."

"Can I come with you, Bobby?" I don't think I can make it in this place. It's all over for me, anyway."

"No, it's not your time, yet. You have a destiny, John, and it's not to rot away in here."

"Well, For God's sake what is it?"

"You'll know when the time comes."

"How do I get out of here?"

"You'll know that, too, when the time comes."

"When the time comes…I'm going nuts in this place. Hell couldn't be much worse than this."

"Now you're getting the drift, John Boy. You'll get out of here, just keep the faith and be patient for a while."

"How can I get in touch with you…you know, like we are now."

"Well, I can't come just anytime. Never know when the portal will be open. 'You Know Who,' controls that."

"You mean…"

"Yeah, the big enchilada, but I'll tell you a little trick that will help you cope in the meanwhile."

"OK, shoot."

"Watch that word, 'shoot,' John Boy…remember?

"Yeah, I remember."

"Skip a few meals, and try to get alone. Then, focus on an object like you did the light bulb. Usually, especially for you, something interesting will happen… like I just might show up. I've been assigned to be your guardian, you know."

"You mean, like Guardian Angel."

"Yeah, kinda' that."

"Then, why did you leave me when I needed you most…at the trial?"

"Well, your buddy, Tu, blindsided me. When you got intimidated by him and your will to keep me around slipped, he kicked my butt."

"I didn't let that bastard intimidate me."

"No, not the conscious you, but the inner you, your spirit did."

"So, I'm the cause of you re-dying."

"No big deal, Johnny. I just hate it that I couldn't help get you out of this mess."

"Guardian Angel," he said with burgeoning self-anger, "give me a break. I can't count on you. You're just a figment of my screwed-up mind."

"Believe what you will, John."

Just then, a mouse scampered across the floor. John turned away for a moment. When he looked back, the apparition was gone. The brilliant light was gone…only the dim light bulb hanging from the ceiling, and stark gray walls.

"Bob! Where are you?"

There was only silence.

# Chapter 44

# Hard Time: Letters

AFTER SERVING HIS time in solitary, John was taken back to his cell…to the noise, the smells and T.J.'s incessant chatter.

"John, about that night…I'm not really a queer, you know. I just thought… "

"Forget it, T. J. What's been going on?"

"Squeaky said you had a lady visitor last week, a real looker, he said."

"Who was it?"

"I don't know. You'll have to ask him."

John lay in his bunk and wondered which one it was. Which one had come to see him? For the answer, he would have to wait until morning when Squeaky came with his wakeup call. Which one did he want it to be? He knew it would be a long night.

The resonance of inmates snoring, bickering, and the occasional beating on the bars with cups and whatever else made sleep impossible, especially after getting accustomed to the quiet of solitary. He wanted to go back. At least there he could escape into himself.

In an hour or so after 'lights out' when things finally quieted he managed to drift into an uneasy sleep.

As dawn made its way, and the fields lay in waiting, he dreamt that he was in his Piper, flying over an open ocean. Land was nowhere in site. There was an uneasy sense of urgency about the whole thing.

"Time to rise and shine," harked the high-pitched voice.

John, shaking off his drowsiness, jumped from his bunk and grabbed the bars.

"Who came to see me last week, Squeaky?"

"I don't know, but she was somethin' to look at."

"What did she look like?"

"Long dark brown hair, real blue eyes."

*Anna, it was Anna.*

A peephole of light had entered his world of despair. She cared enough to come this far to see him. It changed everything. Today, he could face the draining heat of the fields. If phone privileges were allowed, he would call her tonight.

As he and his hoe settled into their rhythm a phrase in his head kept repeating itself:

*Hurry day, I've got a date… Hurry sundown, Anna waits.*

His hands trembled as the quarters clanked though the wall phone's mechanism. He counted the rings…finally the connection.

"The number you have dialed is no longer in service."

More quarters…dial "0."

"This is your operator…what party are you trying to reach, please?"

"Anna…or, Dennis McBride in Birmingham…on Midfield Avenue."

"I'm sorry, sir, that number is unlisted by request of the customer."

"Thank you, Operator, good bye."

*Think…call Joseph. He'll track her down.*

With the last of his change he dialed, got through and delivered his plea.

"Don't worry, John," said Joseph in a reassuring voice. "I'll find her, and write giving you the skinny. By the way, immediately after the trial I filed a 'Motion for a New Trial'. Judge Mahan has sole authority to grant it. We should be hearing something soon."

"Thank you, Joseph. My time is up. I have to get off the phone. Thank you again, and take care.

He hung up; seeking what comfort he could in Joseph's words:

*He'll get to the bottom of this…I'll see her soon. She came once…she'll come again.*

A letter from Anna arrived the next day.

*Dear John,*

*I came down there last week, but they wouldn't let me see you. They said you were in solitary confinement. I hope it isn't too serious.*

*I wanted to say what I have to face-to-face, but this will have to do.*

*Dennis is devastated over not knowing the whereabouts of Allison. I am overwhelmed with guilt for not being able to tell him. Despite the things he's done, he is her father, and I feel like I owe him something.*

*He has begged me to take him back saying he will die if I don't. I have agreed to do so on the condition that he stop drinking.*

*John, I am so sorry that you were drug into the mess involving my family. I will never forget you. I will love you forever.*

*Anna*

John slowly folded the letter, placed it back in the envelope, and stuck it under his pillow.

"What's wrong, you look pale as a sheep."

"T.J., I need to get back to solitary. Pucker up, I'm fixing to bust you in the mouth."

"Don't do that, man! Just act like you hit me. That'll be just as good."

"I need some quiet time, OK."

"Sure, John. I'll be so quiet you won't even know I'm here."

Shortly after receiving Anna's letter, one came from Joseph.

*Dear John,*

*Mahan turned down our Motion for a New Trial, even after admitting that in his opinion there was too little evidence for a conviction in the first place. He gave no explanation except to say that he had no choice, and recommended that we take it to the 'Court of Criminal Appeals,' which is at the State level.*

*John, someone got to him. Never would I have dreamed that Mahan could be bought. I guess it just goes to show that everyone has his price. There are rumors that he's having an affair with his secretary. He has a wife and three kids. Maybe it's blackmail. At this point it really doesn't matter. Today, I'm filing with the 'Court of Criminal Appeals.'*

*Don't get discouraged.*


*Joseph*


Weeks slowly turned into months. John's first year at Gilmore came…and passed. There had been two visits by Joseph and one by Jack. Jack did write often keeping him abreast of the happenings in Mobile. The gossip train there was running wide open, as usual.

The most surprising among newsworthy events was that Horace had been dethroned as president and CEO of Gulf States Savings and Loan Association. Because of recent national scandal, the Federal Government had come down hard on all S&Ls, enforcing a law that limits the terms of executive officers. Colleen left shortly afterwards.

George Debarden had come down with a strange illness, the origin of which was Africa. There, it was called Slims Disease because of the rapid weight loss it caused. Here, the medical community had coined it AIDS.

There had not been a word from Angie since he arrived at Gilmore. John had written several times without response. He tried to call, but both the home phone and that of the LaBeau's had been blocked from receiving calls from the only number he was allowed to call out on.

While waiting for 'lights out' one especially long lonely evening, John reread the short note received from Carter early on during his incarceration.


*Dear John,*

*I regret the situation, but life must go on. I feel, now, that it is my duty to do all I can to see that my daughter and grandchildren live with some sense of normalcy.*

*I can't help you, but do wish you the best.*


*Carter*

Then, there was the letter from his boys:

*Dear Dad,*

*Cart and me are writing this letter together. We miss you and hope you're doing OK.*

*Mom and Grand Ma Ma are mad at you, but we are not mad at you. We know you didn't mean to do anything wrong. Please come home soon.*

*Love,*
*Johnny and Cart*

*P.S.*
*Cart wants to know if there are any real murderers there.*

On December 20, 1979, John got the letter he most feared. He had been at Gilmore one year and four months.

*John,*

*I want a divorce. Please don't fight me on this. We both know it's for the best.*

*Angie*

*12/21/79*
*Dear Jack,*

*Angie wants a divorce. I know that I shouldn't be surprised or shocked, but its like I've been hit by a bolt of lightening. I don't know what to say or do. I've never felt so helpless. Forgive my muddled display of self-pity, but words cannot express my despair at this moment.*

*I do think its best to get it over with quickly; so I'm prepared to give her whatever she wants. I've already lost everything that's important to me, anyway.*

*I'll be depending on you to handle things.*

*John*

Strange irony he thought as he sealed the envelope…the anguish he now felt as he faced the reality of losing the woman he was so willing to give up for another.

*12/28/79*

*John,*

*Carter has died of a massive heart attack. Fannie and Angie are taking it quite hard. Fannie is angry with God, and refused to have a funeral. Angie is in a deep state of depression. I heard that after having him cremated they took the urn containing his ashes to a bar. They got smashed and then took the urn out on Terry Wayne's yacht and spread Carter's ashes in Mobile bay.*

*I will keep you abreast of further details.*

*Jack*

Two months passed without hearing anything more regarding Angie's intention of filing for divorce.

*2/22/80*

*Dear John,*

*Our appeal has been denied. Apparently we've underestimated Rad Debarden's sphere of influence.*

*We aren't beaten yet, John. I meant it when I said we would take it to the State Supreme Court.*

*Hang tough, my brother.*

*Joseph.*

*3/16/80*

*Dear Dad,*

*Sheppy died. Mom said it was old age, but Cart & I know he had a broken heart over you not being here.*

*I hope you are doing OK*

*Love,*

*Johnny*

# Hard Time: Midnight Flight

HAVING NO APPETITE for life in general, John spent most of his cell time lying in his bunk trying to block out T.J.'s gibbering, and escape into his inner-self. He stared in silence at the small wire mesh and glass window high on the wall. All that could be seen from his vantage point was a little piece of sky. At night, on occasion, the moon made an appearance.

"Why do you keep lookin' up there," T.J. asked.

"I don't know…I guess it's the closest thing to freedom I've got."

Around midnight on April 23, 1980 John was in the middle of what had become a reoccurring dream. He was in his Piper flying over open water. No land was in site. His heading was south…always due south. He was abruptly awakened by the sounds of moaning from below.

"What's wrong, T.J.?"

"Call the guard," he said, "I think I'm havin' a heart attack."


As they wheeled T.J. out on a stretcher, distant thunder announced the approach of a storm.

John was totally alone for the first time in over two years…since solitary. He lay in his bunk, wondering and concerned about T.J. as the storm moved in.

The small window near the ceiling lit with almost constant lightning flashes, followed by great bursts of thunder.

He couldn't take his eyes off it. Something strange was going on. He could feel it. The smell of ozone filled the air.

Suddenly, the window expanded to the size of a storefront and centered itself on the wall. The glass and wire mesh were gone, and the wind swirled as the rains came down in sheets. He drew back and crouched against the wall as the winds and rain whipped through the cell.

*Why don't the guards come? How can they not hear this?* streaked through his mind.

Then, there on the window's ledge, midst a backdrop of lightening bolts and deafening thunder clashes, perched the crow, his head cocked, staring at him.

"What do you want from me?" he shouted.

"What have you got?" the crow replied.

"Nothing, every thing's been taken away from me. I've got nothing."

"Then, I want nothing."

The big bird sheened blue in the lightning flashes.


In his next moment of awareness, John was in flight, and as he had experienced years before, was seeing the world through the eyes of his host. The lights of Gilmore were beneath him as he rose to meet the violent storm. Soon, the lights were below and behind, dimming in the distance.

He could feel powerful wings flapping, but not the physical strain of it. The driving rain felt like dampened droplets on a raincoat. He felt no wetness or cold. The best he could tell, the heading was north.

As the journey progressed all sense of time became lost. Somewhere along the way the weather began to clear. He could see lights from the structures and roadways below.

After a while, the eastern skies began to lighten. Then, a spectacular dawn broke, beaming rays above the horizon. Familiar landmarks came into view in the light of day. To the North, Vulcan, the great iron statue stood on its pedestal atop Red Mountain, overlooking Birmingham. Left of it, in the distance, smoke spewed from the Fairfield steel mills.

It was to be a clear day...blue skies spackled with highflying cumulus clouds. He began to settle down and feel the freedom of flight. It had been a long time since he had had this feeling.

His host turned westward, away from the rising sun.

As they sailed over the rooftops, cars and people in the suburbs, he wondered where the journey would end. Three hundred feet below was Bluff Park, his home turf. There… there was his house, the one he grew up in. He was flying right over it. His mother, Florence was in the back yard, cutting roses from the old rose bush. He called out, but the only thing that came forth was the 'caw, caw' of the crow. She looked up, shading her eyes from the morning sun. Then, in flight he left it all behind, heading in a southwesterly direction, continuing until reaching a vast forest.

While soaring down the river valley he began to recognize other landmarks. It was the Cahaba below him.

The Helena Bridge passed below, then the railroad bridge and Booths forge. William Raintree's place came into view.

He felt the gentle landing on a high branch of an oak tree that stood at the now-covered cave site where the gold, William Raintree and supposedly the bones of Tuscaloosa lay buried.

"Why are we here?" he asked in silence.

"You will know," came the reply.

He dosed as the hours stretched to mid-day.

"Why are we here?" he asked again.

"You will know," came the reply again.

Just then, he heard the rustling sound of bushes and crunching leaves from approaching footsteps. A large man appeared beneath them. John recognized him.

*"Bubba Salvo…what is he doing here?"*

The crow remained silent.

As Salvo poked around the sealed cave entry, John watched through the eyes of the crow.

There was a large rock just above where the entry once was.

Bubba got down on his knees and with bare hands started scratching around in the loose dirt and rocks. In less than half-a-minute there was a rustle in the near-by thistle. Then, a large snake appeared.

The moccasin struck from the rock above…sinking its fangs deep into Bubba's neck.

He reeled backwards, pulling at the snake as he fell. On the ground, he trembled and went into convulsions…it, hanging on all the while. He grasped his throat and gagged.

Then it was over. He lay on his back with eyes wide open in a cold still stare. The snake then let go and slithered away into the brush.

John's eyes popped wide open. He was laying flat on his back in a hard bed. The smell of medicinal alcohol was in the air. He turned his head to the right. In a bed next to him was T.J.

"Where are we?"

"In the infirmary," T.J. answered.

John paused a moment. "Are you OK?" he asked.

"Yeah, they thought I had a heart attack last night, but it was just gas. The Doc. laughed and said I had a fart attack. I guess he thought it was funny…I didn't."

"Why am I here?"

"Squeaky couldn't wake you up this morning. He thought you had a stroke or somethin'."

A copy of the Birmingham Post-Herald made its way to cell 8A. On its second page a small headliner read: "Donald Salvo Jr. Missing."

Next to it an even smaller article read, "Radell Debarden, prominent Mobile business leader and society king pin, has suffered a stroke leaving him paralyzed and unable to speak."

"You have a visitor, Starr," said Squeaky.

# Chapter 46

# Hard Time: Time to Go

"Anna, I never thought I'd see you again. How are you?"

"It didn't work, John. I tried, but it didn't work. How are you?"

"I'm making it. That's about it. Tell me about you…your situation."

"Things got back to the way they were…even worse. Dennis's drinking and abuse made it impossible to pick up the pieces. I should have known it would be this way."

"What are you going to do?"

"I'm going where I belong…back to the home place."

"You mean to your daddy's place?"

"Yes."

"Anna, there's nothing there…and so isolated. It's no place for a woman to be alone."

"I'll be waiting there for you, John…if you want to come."

"My appeal has been denied. It'll be another three years before I'm even eligible for parole."

"I'll be waiting for you, whether you come or not."

He put his hand up to the glass separating them. She placed her hand to his. In that moment he became more a prisoner of her eyes than of Gilmore.

"Will you write me?" he asked.

"Yes."

He leaned close to the glass and spoke in almost a whisper:

"If you do go back, don't go near the cave site for a while. Wait a couple of months. The animals should have done their work by then. You'll find human bones. Bury them."

"Who do they belong to?"

"Bubba Salvo."

"How do you know this, John?"

"Anna, have you ever, in any way, had an encounter with a crow?"

"Just in a crazy dream. It told me to go back to the home place."

"It wasn't just a dream, Sweetheart. The thing is real. It took me there. I saw Bubba die. A snake bit him in the neck."

"John, are you sure you're all right?"

A month after Anna's visit, John received a letter from Jack. In it he said that Gulf States Savings and Loan had fallen victim to the recession, and of all things, Horace was now living with Fannie. Also, Angie's attorney, Howard Bartholomew relayed to him that Angie had decided to put the divorce proceedings on hold for a while. She was still trying to come to terms with the loss of her father, and it was too much to deal with at this time.

"Too much to deal with," muttered John under his breath, "while I rot in this place."

"You always get a frown on your face after gettin' a letter," remarked T.J. "What's wrong this time?"

"She's left me dangling in mid-air…as usual."

"Who?"

"Angie! It's about Angie. It's always been about Angie. She never has given a damn about how I've felt…about anything."

"At least you get a letter from somebody besides your mother. All mine ever says is for me to brush my teeth and wash my privates."

"Shut up, T.J."

John and T.J. graduated from working the gardens to road detail. Now, he spent his days picking up trash along the highways and byways of South Alabama.

This job was a great improvement over working the gardens. He was outside the prison confines and able to get a sense of civilization again. Passing cars and trucks kept the air stirred, staving off the heat a bit.

The guards were lax, sometimes napping in the truck while inmates strung out a quarter mile or more.

On the morning of June 5th 1980, while readying himself for work, John looked up to see Squeaky outside his cell:

"The warden wants to see you in his office, he said."
"Now what have I done?"
"I don't know. He just said he wants to see you."

"Starr," said Warden Coleman, "you need to call Mr. Wainwright at his office in Mobile. Here, use this phone."
John dialed the old familiar number.
The secretary's voice was unfamiliar. *Must be new*, he thought.
"Jack, its John. What's going on?"
"John," said the voice at the other end of the receiver…almost cracking, "Angie is missing at sea. She was with him on his yacht…Terry Wayne's yacht. The Coast Guard thinks they got caught in a squall, and the boat went down. It's been three days of searching, now. There's no sign of the Fiddle-De-Dee. No debris or anything else has washed ashore. They did say that there had been reports of drug runners commandeering boats in the gulf recently. I don't know what else to tell you, John. What do you want me to do?"
"Nothing, Jack…nothing."
"Why don't you take the day off, Son," said Coleman.
"No, I want to go to work. I need to go to work."

John went through the motions…picking up discarded fast food sacks, beer cans and soft drink bottles that lay on the side of the road.
"You look like a zombie, man," said T.J. working about ten feet away, "you OK?"
"Yeah, I'm fine."
"I think I'm gonna' go to the truck and get me some water and a salt tablet. You wanna' come?"
"No, I'm fine."

The woods were close to the road in the area where he was working. There was no one around. The guard was napping in the truck a hundred yards away.

It was now or never.

He quietly slipped into the woods.

# CHAPTER 47

# The Escape

THROUGH BRIARS AND bramble, John ran as hard as he could. He backtracked parallel to the road towards the farmhouse he had seen on the way to work. There had been a pick up truck sitting in the front yard. Maybe it was still there. Maybe it was unlocked…if not, maybe he could hot-wire it.

As he approached, three dogs came out from under the house…barking and snarling.

God was good to him this day. Not only had the truck been left unlocked, the key was in it. As John opened the door a shirtless, hairy, bald headed man came out on the front porch.

"Hey, what the hell are you doin', fella'?" he shouted.

John jumped in and cranked the engine as the man ran back into the house. He was back almost immediately, with a shotgun, aimed and ready to fire.

Wheels spun and turf flew as the truck sped, slipping and sliding towards the highway.

"Come back here you son-of –a-bitch," yelled the man, as he fired.

John felt the shattered pieces of glass from the rear window hit the back of his head and neck. He put the peddle to the floor as the tires screeched, burning rubber out on Highway 31, heading southwest.

As he passed back by the work site, none of the inmates noticed, except for T.J. who grinned and gave a thumbs up. The profile of a straw hat in the cab of the work truck was about all John could see of the napping guard.

Mobile was only fifty miles away, but could he make it without being spotted? Should he go for it in daylight or hide out till dark then take the back roads? Waiting till dark seemed to make most sense. There was a problem, though. The gas gauge showed only a quarter tank of gas. He didn't have a penny on him, was in prison garb, and surely by now the owner had reported the theft of his truck.

He drove up a pitted little dead end road off the highway, turned the engine off and took the bright orange shirt off.

Finally, the last glimmer of daylight faded away. In the dark of a moonless night he pulled out on old US 31 and headed towards Mobile. Traffic was sparse but utmost caution prevailed. He winced at every headlight that came up behind him and every vehicle stopped at a side road waiting for him to pass. If the pick up could only remain un-noticed for the next hour or so he would be home. Each mile traveled became a triumph.

After driving forty miles, his luck was still holding. The gas gauge was showing almost empty, but he began to feel that he would make it.

His senses heightened as the familiar coastal smells began filling the air.

Then, Mobile bay came into view and the city lights danced in the reflection of its dark waters. He was home free.

He pulled into the driveway. Other than the headlights' reflection on the garage door, the house was dark and abandoned looking. A feeling of emptiness came over him.

He got out of the truck and made his way in the darkness to a shrub next to the front door. On the ground, under a rock next to it, he had always kept a key hidden.

After fumbling around and dropping the key twice, he got the door open and turned on a few lights. He wandered through the rooms…the study, the kitchen. It hit him…he was no longer a part of this place. All that it had been was now lost to him. It was of the past…too cold, too lonely, even for ghosts. He felt his heart sink.

Time, however, would not allow the luxury of much grief and despair. It was after 10:00 PM, and he had to see his boys before commencing the task that lay ahead.

He went to the garage just off the kitchen to pull the truck inside, making it safe from discovery. Instead of the family station wagon being there in Angie's parking place, there was a new Lincoln Continental. "That son-of-a-bitch," he muttered, "he gave her a freakin' car."

After pulling the pick up inside and closing the garage door, he went up-stairs to shower, change clothes and scrounge up some cash.

In his drawer were boxer shorts. He never wore boxer shorts. In the closet among his things were someone else's shirts, pants and sport coats.

Again, there was no time to address the anger and rage that seethed inside. There was only the mission. Nothing could come between him and what he had to do.

He went back to the garage with the keys he found on the kitchen counter top, got into the Lincoln and was off.


Within twenty minutes, John was standing on his mother-in-law's front porch. He rang the chimes and rapped on the door till his knuckles felt numb.

Finally, lights came on inside and door opened just beyond a crack. "What are you doing here, John Starr?" Fannie blurted.

"I came to see my boys, Fannie."

"They're asleep. Do you know that it's after midnight?"

"Wake them up."

"I'm going to call the police."

"Not right now, you're not...go get them," he said, pushing the door open and walking in, "Don't worry, I'll be leaving after I see them."

At that moment, Horace, in his robe, walked in. He had lost weight since John last saw him, and looked gaunt.

"John," he said, "How'd you get out?"

"I've got to see the boys, Horace. Tell her to go get them. I don't have time to fool around...tell her to get them!"

Horace turned to her, "Go get them, Fannie."

She left the room and a few minutes later returned with John Jr. and Cart rubbing their eyes and yawning.

"Dad," Johnny cried out, "you're back."

"Just for a while, Son, but I had to see you two before I have to go again."

"Suddenly, Cart, now wide-eyed, ran to his father."

John, stooped down, and the boy clung to his neck.

"We want you and Mom back, and all of us to be together again, Dad."

"I want that, too, Cart…more than anything else in the world."
John stood, Cart hanging on:

"Horace, get with Jack Wainwright regarding an insurance policy on me and some other financial matters. There's enough that you'll all be OK."

"What are you up to, John Starr?" Fannie asked, "Where are you going?"
"I'm going after Angie…I'm going to find her and bring her home."
"You're crazy…you know that?"
"I've got to go, now. Take care of our boys till I get back."
Fannie's eyes began to well.
He looked at her: "I'm sorry for the way things have turned out," he said.
"I'm sorry, too, John. Believe it or not, I've always cared for you, just like I have this Pig's Ear standin' next to me."
"Looks like you still have a few rows to hoe with this woman, Horace," he said trying to lighten the dark moment.
"I guess It'll always be that way, John. I know I can't talk you out of this; so I'll just say, good luck."
"Dad, when will you be back?" asked Johnny as tears streamed down his face.
"I don't know, Son. In the meanwhile, you boys take care of Grand Ma Ma and Uncle Horace…OK?"

John was off, heading towards the little private airport located on the edge of town…where his piper waited.

# The Final Flight

JOHN FINALLY ARRIVED at the gate of the small deserted airport. An eight-foot chain link fence stood between him and the hangers. He turned on the interior light of the Lincoln and looked down at his watch… 3:33 AM. His eyelids were heavy. If only he could catch a little sleep, but there was no time for that. He had to push on. She was out there, somewhere…waiting for him to come…to rescue her. He felt it in his gut…Someplace was calling from across the gulf…maybe Yucatan.

In the light from the car's headlamps he scaled the gate, then made his way to the hanger that housed his Piper.

He turned on the hanger lights.

There it was, in a row among the others, still in its old parking place.

He walked up to it, and touched the aluminum skin.

"Miss me?" he said.

He began inspecting it…every inch of it. Obviously Joe, the mechanic, had taken special care of John's flying machine. She seemed ready to take to the skies. Even the fuel tank was full and topped off, as if Joe knew he were coming.

The only problem was a matter of the key, but one swift kick to the office door solved that.

He slipped the key into the ignition switch. After a few turns the engine came alive, abruptly breaking the silence…echoing throughout the building. A small flock of startled sparrows made a hasty exit from the hanger. Soon, John followed, taxiing towards the runway.

The little craft's landing lights flooded the darkness. The wind seemed just right.

As he made his way down the tarmac, to the end of the runway, he felt him-self come alive…awake, alert…the same rush as in the old days.

He turned the plane into the wind and pushed full throttle. He was off… into the darkness.

The sensation of lift and becoming airborne, gave temporary reprieve from his obsessed thoughts of the mission that lay ahead.

The plane gained altitude, then leveled out at five thousand feet. It wasn't long before Mobile's city lights disappeared behind him. Ahead, the glow from ships at sea dotted the gulf waters…some blinking, some glowing steady.

Flying only by compass, he headed due south, into the darkness.

He looked at his watch…4:15…less than an hour before daybreak.

The Piper hummed along as the eastern sky began to lighten. The minutes passed, and as John settled in for a long journey, he began questioning his hasty calculations before take off, wondering if there was actually enough fuel to make it across the Gulf. He tried to re-figure, but his mind was scrambled eggs. After a minute or so he decided that God and the tail winds would have to make the call.

Then, from an orange pre-dawn sky the sun broke through…a spectacular Sunrise. Now, everything was in clear view. He looked around…front, sides and rear…360 degrees. No land was in sight…just sky and the Gulf of Mexico. He held his course…due south.

The re-occurring dream at Gilmore had become reality, but now its purpose was revealed.

Before taking off he had intentionally left the radio off. For no reason it came on. First there was static, then, a voice came through:

"John, can you hear me?"

"Yes. Is this who I think it is?"

"Yeah, it's me."

"Why don't you show yourself?"

"I've already gone down in one of these things once…been there, done that, don't think I want to do it again."

"You've really gotten to be a pussy, Bob."

"You do know you're going down if you don't abandon this ridiculous notion of yours."

"I've got to find her."

"You're a fugitive, John. What would you do if you should happen to find her?"

"We'd start over again, maybe in Mexico…get it right this time."

"Ever heard of destiny, John Boy?"

"Of course I have."

"Well, Angie has already met hers, and not you or me or anybody else is going to change it.

"What are you talking about? She's out there. Pirates or drug runners are holding her. I can feel it in my gut."

"Your gut's wrong, Buddy. That wasn't her destiny."

"Then, what was…where is she?"

"That's not for me to say. But, I can tell you this…it's not yours to run out of gas and ditch in the middle of the gulf."

"What's happened to Angie, Bob? You know I've got to know."

"What do you think about her being with Terry Wayne?"

"I'll tear his freakin' head off. That's what I think about Terry Wayne, now where is Angie?"

"She and Wayne have met their fate. You're chasing ghosts, John. Let it go and do what you're supposed to do…go to your destiny."

"What the hell is my destiny?"

"You already know…deep down."

The radio went silent. There was only the hum of the engine.

"Screw you, you dead bastard. You're just in my head anyway…like all that other shit. Don't ever bother me again. Do you read?"


There was no reply.

John looked around. There was nothing but sea and sky with a few high-flying clouds.

"You're right, Bob," he shouted, "She's gone…she's gone! God, let me let go. Wash me clean from this madness!"

He banked the plane and made a wide arch until the compass showed due north.

In less than an hour he passed over Dauphin Island. Soon, the city of Mobile was behind him. Then, it was over the Delta with its checkered fields as he continued north.

The foothills and forest lay ahead.

He looked down at the fuel gauge. It read almost empty as Raintree's place came into view. He circled the cornfield and mound, positioning for a decent landing. As he made the approach, he saw her come from the old cabin by the field. She stood there, her hand shadowing her eyes from the sun as the wheels touched down.

The little plane bounced across the ruts trying to stay airborne, as if it knew this was its final flight. Then, it gave up and came to rest.

Anna ran towards it as John un-strapped, her long brown hair flowing in the breeze.

"I knew you would come," she said embracing him.

"Everything's going to be all right, now," he said, holding her to him, "no more ghost. We're going to be together from now on."

"I know," she said. The kiss lingered.

John rose at dawn the next morning, while Anna slept. He went across the way to the field where the plane rested. While walking around the little craft that had brought him so far, he reached down and picked up a dry corn stalk.

He ran his hands over the plane's skin…caressing it.

"I'm sorry," he said, tipping the kerosene can to soak the stalk from one end to the other.

As if performing a sacred sacrificial ritual, he slowly turned the fuel tank cap, all the while trying to reconcile that there was no choice…that there could be no turning back.

He gently lowered the stalk down the throat leading to the fuel tank until its end rested on the bottom. About a foot of it protruded out of the top…like a candle wick. Then, he drenched the plane with the rest of the kerosene.

As he lit the corn stalk wick, sadness reeked through every part of his mind and body.

He stepped back. There was a sudden "woof". In the next moment the plane was engulfed in flames.

As he watched his beloved flying machine burn, he silently acknowledged that this was the last bridge to burn between past and present.

Within a half hour, there was nothing but charred smoldering ruins of what once had been his passport to freedom. He walked away without looking back, entering the cabin where sweet Anna slept.

As she lay there softly breathing, her head resting on the pillow, slightly turned, he felt the beauty of her face.

*This is it*, he thought, his life from now on. He would spend the rest of his days here, hidden from the outside world. But, after all he was a loner, always looking for a way to escape people and their pretenses. Maybe this place held the key to his completeness and peace. Maybe the seeker, the lonely, restless, hungry, searching soul had finally found its home. And, really, what more could he want than lovely Anna? Maybe this was the way it was supposed to be.

There were the boys, though. He would have to find a way to let them know he was alive and well. Could they keep the secret?

He stroked her perfect eyebrow, then leaned down and kissed her cheek: "Good morning sunshine."

"John," she said stretching and yawning, "have you been up long?"

"Not too long."

"You have a look on your face…a penny for your thoughts."

"I was thinking that it's just you and me from now on. Are you sure you're all right with that?"

"Yes, of course I am. I was told it would be this way, but I didn't believe it at the time."

"Who told you such a thing?"

"You know."

"No, I don't know. Who told you?"

She smiled and put a finger to his lips.

"Well," she said, "a big black bird told me."

By mid-afternoon what was left of the plane had cooled enough to touch. John noticed that the dogs were no longer around. Maude, Raintree's mule, which seemed to be the only creature to survive this place unscathed watched with disinterest as the ax came down, chopping and dismembering what was left of the plane into manageable pieces. The task took a couple of hours.

He walked to the shed where the old Studebaker truck was parked, wondering if it would crank. Miraculously, it did. He drove it to the cornfield and filled its bed with pieces of the wreckage. Then, he drove it the length of two football fields down the trail leading to the site where Raintree's cabin once stood by the Cahaba. He backed up to its bank, and flung the remains, piece by piece, into the blue-green waters. He hauled load after load until all the remains rested on the bottom.

It was late afternoon when the task was completed. A gentle breeze rustled the trees as the lazy little river flowed. He set on the bank and observed all that was around him.

So, this is it, he reflected…destiny…what it was about all along. His whole life, everything…Bob, Nam, Angie, Mobile, his plunge into the ancient past, Raintree…all was with purpose…to prepare him for this…to be keeper of this land. And now, after all the ordeals, triumphs and tragedies, it was his turn.

He watched a leaf ride the currents. There was a sense of peace and calm all around.

Anna came and sat beside him there on the banks of the Cahaba. She put her hand in his and nestled close.

"Where are the dogs?" he asked.

"I don't know. They disappeared after we buried Daddy."

"Did you bury Bubba's bones?"

"No, I haven't been up there, yet."

"I'll take care of it this afternoon. What about a vehicle? He had to get here someway."

"The keys were in it. I parked it in the woods behind the mound."

"I'll dump it in the river."

"John," she said, "even after all the bad things that have happened here, I still love this spot. It brings me peace."

He turned to her and kissed her: "We'll rebuild the cabin," he said.

# Thanksgiving 1985

JOHN HELD HIS aim steady, then let the taut string slip from his fingers. The arrow took flight and found its mark. The doe leaped then dropped to the ground.

He walked to his kill and stroked its side.

"Thank you," he said.

He hoisted the deer over his shoulders and began walking. As he carried his gift from nature along the path leading home, he thought about how much had changed since June 6th 1981, the day he landed his plane here. His mind traveled back, recalling that shortly after his arrival he went to West Blocton disguised as a drifter. There, he made three phone calls. One was to Jack, apprising him of the situation and instructing him to get word to his boys that he was alive and well. He wanted two messages relayed to his sons…one that he loved and deeply cared for them. The other was a promise that someday they would be together again…one he hoped he could keep. Jack was to do this without Fannie knowing. John learned later that Jacked talked Fannie into allowing him to take the boys fishing. That's when he told them that their father was alive, and of the promise. Jack swore them to secrecy. So far, to John's and Jack's knowledge, they had kept it.

Another call was to Joseph, and the other was to his mother. He would never forget her wail upon hearing his voice.

Even though he was sure that the outside world had long since presumed him dead, it was a world he no longer had the freedom to live in. This place, however, offered another kind of freedom. Here, in nature's realm, he was free to roam the woodlands, feel its heartbeat, and be a part of it. He could flow with the river and smell Mother Earth's freshly turned soil. Here, he was free to love Anna. He was accountable only to the land. He was now its keeper.

Over the years, through Harry Cohen, John arranged to have gold exchanged for cash and sent to Mobile. Jack told Fannie that it was from a trust fund set up by John before he went to jail. She never questioned the story.

"I feel sure she knows you're out there somewhere," said Jack during one of their rare phone conversations, "I think she knows it's best not to ask questions…for the sake of the boys."

John's mind snapped back to the present when the cabin came into view. He and Anna had just completed it. They built it on the same site where Raintree's once stood next to the Cahaba. It was the same except for a couple of added luxuries. Now there was running water along with a bathroom, and though it was out of the question to obtain service from any utility company, John wired the cabin for electricity. A generator supplied power when needed. Though rarely used, it was good to have.

Anna busily trekked between the cabin, the garden and barn, gathering the makings for a special meal. It was two days before Thanksgiving, and there would be guests. Jack Wainwright was bringing the boys, Johnny and Cart. It would be the first time John had seen them since that night at Fannie's some three and a half years before.

He could hardly wait to see his sons. It had been much too long, but until now the time never seemed right. Now that the recast of his life was complete, he was ready for them to see him as he was.

Thanksgiving Day…it had come at last. As the venison slowly simmered in the old iron pot that hung on the swinging hook in the fireplace, he nervously asked: "What time is it, Anna, shouldn't they be here by now?"

"Be patient, John. It's just a little after ten. They'll be here soon."

A horn honked.

"It's them," he said making a dash towards the door. Then, he stopped just before opening it: "I need you with me."

She dried her hands, and together they went out to greet their guests.

He could hardly believe it. Johnny was almost as tall as he was. The seventeen year old standing before him that he had last seen three and a half years before was lean, handsome and well on his way to becoming a man. Cart, now fourteen was no longer the scrappy-headed kid he remembered. His reddish hair was neatly combed, and he was just as handsome as his older brother.

John stood facing his children, the only passion left of his past. Anna stood behind him. Jack stood behind the boys. There was a moment when there seemed nothing to say. Then, Johnny came out with it: "I like your beard, Dad…a little gray around the edges, but it looks good on you."

"That looks like more than peach fuzz on your face, fella," John retorted, then stepped forward and wrapped his arms around them both. Beforehand, he had sworn not to allow himself to get too emotional.

"God, I've missed you guys," he blurted, his voice breaking.

Tears streamed down his face…then theirs, then Anna's, and then Jack's.

Anna laid out the Thanksgiving feast on the plank table John had made especially for the occasion. There was venison, wild turkey with dressing and giblet gravy, corn pudding, squash, and buttermilk biscuits.

"Where did you get all this good stuff?" asked Cart.

"We grew most of it," John answered, "The woodlands provided the rest."

"Dad," said Johnny, "you never hunted before. I remember you never even swatted a fly."

"Well, Son, I never had to before."

"What kind of gun do you have?" asked Cart.

"I hunt with a bow and arrow like the Indians did. The noise from a gun seems to disturb the harmony of things."

"You know, Dad, you've gotten a little weird," said Johnny.

Anna broke out in laughter: "A little weird?" she said.

"Speaking of weird," said John with a crooked smile, "How many women do you all know that can dress a deer, harness a mule and plow a field. She's the one who taught me how to do all that stuff."

"Well," she said, "I guess we both have to be a little weird to be living out here in the middle of the woods in the first place."

"Sweetheart, we're not exactly prisoners of this place. We do sneak out every once in a while, you know."

"Where do you all go, Dad?" asked Johnny.

"Well, the first time was when Anna and I went out and bought a truck… in her name, of course. I was a little nervous, but it got easier after that. Now, we go out together to get whatever we need. We've even been to the movies and walked in the malls. This old beard serves as a pretty good disguise…besides, I don't think anyone's particularly looking for me now."

"I notice you have a pretty elaborate setup here," said Jack, "even got running water and power."

"Yeah, the generator has really come in handy. We use it to pump water from the well into fifty-gallon drums for running water. I have one drum set up so that I can build a fire under it to heat up the water…need that hot shower every day. We use electricity pretty sparingly, though. For the most part we live like country folks did a hundred years ago."

"Why don't you come down to Mobile, Dad?" asked Cart.

"I'm afraid that would be pulling the devil's tail, Son. Somebody down there would probably recognize me, even with the beard. How is your Grand Ma Ma?"

"Oh, she's as feisty as ever. Maybe we could bring her up here sometimes."

"Maybe so, Son, but in the meantime let's keep all this a secret, OK?"

"I wonder how she would do up here." said Johnny, "I can see it now…her getting up in the morning and putting on her make up and high heels, then, going out to feed the chickens and milk the cow."

"How about Uncle Horace…how's he doing?"

"Not too good. He's got the gout."

"How do you get money, Dad?" asked Cart. "Grand Ma Ma says you set up a trust or something for Johnny and me."

"Oh, I had some put away before everything happened."

"I'll bet Dad makes moonshine," said Johnny with a wink.

"No, I leave that up to old Percy Skinner. He lives out even further than we do. I run into him in the woods every once in a while…talk about a recluse. Are you planning to retire anytime soon, Jack? You're pretty close to sixty five, aren't you?"

"I'll be sixty five next month but won't be retiring until they nail me in a box," he replied while sopping up gravy with a biscuit, "having too much fun going after the bigots and jousting with the likes of old Bartholomew. By the way, did you know that George Debarden died?"

"No," said John, "sad…very sad. As far as I'm concerned he was a decent human being…more so than a lot I've run across in my day. Say, would you all like to go for a walk? I'll show you around…are you up for it Jack?"

"No, you need some catch-up time with the boys; besides, I'm too full. I'll help Anna clean up around here."

"I'll do the cleaning up," said Anna, "I want you to sit in that chair over by the fireplace and tell me all about this man, John Starr in his younger years."

John showed his boys the mound, the old village site, and walked them along the riverbank. He spoke of many things regarding the land, but not of its secrets.

"Dad, were those graves I saw over by the mound?" asked Johnny.

"Yes, Son, they were graves."

"Whose?"

"Oh, some little girl and her grandfather that were here a long time ago," John replied.

A few minutes later, as they walked along the path by the river, Cart commented: "I like Anna. She's really nice…and pretty, too."

"I'm glad you like her, Cart. I like her, too."

"Are you all married?" asked Johnny.

"No, Son, we're not married…at least not by a preacher."

John detected relief on the boy's face.

"You know, Dad, they never found Mom."

"Yes, I know, Son.…let's head back to the cabin, I think some apple pie's waiting on us."

"Did your ears burn?" asked Anna, as they walked in the door.

"Yes they did. What did you tell this woman about me, Jack Wainwright?"

"Just the sordid stuff," he laughed.

As Anna served apple pie, the unexpected sound of an approaching vehicle interrupted.

"Did anyone know you all were coming here," asked John nervously.

"No," said Jack, "I told Fannie I was going to take the boys to a ball game in Birmingham."

"Quick," said John," help me move the table."

After sliding the table over, he pulled back a throw rug revealing a trap door in the floor. He opened it and began his descent.

"Now, put everything back like it was."

There was a loud knock at the door.

Anna approached the door as Jack and the boys pushed the table back in place.

"Who is it," She asked.

"Sheriff Sims and deputy Scruggs," came the reply.

She opened the door, "What can I do for you, Sheriff?"

"Mind if we come in?"

"Yes, I do, but come on in anyway."

The barrel-chested sheriff and his lanky deputy stepped over the threshold. They were the same two who had arrested John some eight years earlier.

Sims stood there, one hand on his hip, the other resting on his holster, "Who are you folks,"

He asked.

"I'm Jack Wainwright, Ms. McBride's attorney. These young men in my care for the day. And, we're all trying to have a peaceful Thanksgiving. Now, what are you doing here?"

"There's reports of marijuana bein' grown in the area. Somebody said they saw a car come in here from the main road. We came to check it out. Mind if we look around outside, Ms. McBride."

"Look all you want...all I grow is vegetables."

Jack's agitation was obvious from the redness in his face, "Let me advise you Sheriff...is it Sims?"

"Yeah, Sims."

"The next time you come barging in like this you best have a search warrant."

"Well, ya'll won't have to worry about that much longer. I'm retirin' next month. Then, as far as I'm concerned the whole county can go to hell. In the meanwhile I'm gonna' my job the best I can. Let's go Scruggs...have a nice Thanksgiving."

Sheriff Sims and his deputy went straight to their car and left.

Jack and the boys slid the table aside, removed the rug and opened the hatch.

"That was a little too close for comfort," said John as he emerged...see why we still have to be cautious?"

"That was a good reminder," remarked Anna.

As sunset approached, Jack stood: "We better head back boys. We've got a long drive."

"I wish you all could stay," said Anna.

"I do, too," Jack replied, "but we don't want to push our luck with Grand Ma Ma."

John felt a swell of melancholy. He felt, at least for the moment, his family being rebuilt on the ashes of the past. The day ended too soon.

# Chapter 50

# Seasons of the Vale

Anna loved to decorate at Christmas time. She sent John out to find an appropriate tree and gather pine branches for the making of wreaths. She also insisted that he string colored lights on the outside of the cabin.

In the evenings after supper he cranked up the generator. They bundled up and walked to the riverbank from where they viewed the cabin, all lit up with its star on the roof. He tried to sing to her, "I'm Dreaming of a White Christmas," but forgot the words.

Except for the dead of winter, there was always something to do around the place… crops to plant, care for and harvest, not to mention the constant need to repair or improve. Winter was a time for reading, indoor projects and for John, long walks.

Sometimes the woodlands looked like a great crystal palace. Ice-encrusted branches of the tall hardwoods, pines, mountain laurel and holly glistened in frozen silence. All was still and deathly quiet until off in the distance an ice-laden limb gave way under the weight, breaking silence with an eerie crackling sound. Then a thud echoed through the hollows. A rabbit scampered across the frozen forest floor.

Most of the birds had migrated further south, leaving only an occasional cardinal or robin pecking away at a frozen cluster of holly berries. The Crows never left though. From their perches on the tree-lined ridges they cawed, communicating back and forth with scouts that were flying about in search of food sources. Deer gnawed on the bark of trees and shrubs.

Among all the seasons of the woodland vale, winter was the harshest and sometimes most surreal.

Spring was John's favorite time of year. Each May, he and Anna canoed down to the shoals where the Cahaba lilies were in full bloom. With her in the bow facing him, he liked to nestle the boat in a field of lilies and just look at her, burning into his memory once again her beauty midst the blooms. He would pick an especially pretty one and place it in her hair, just above her left ear.

They played like children in the shoals. He imagined it was like this with Tuscaloosa and Na-ha-no-me in ancient times.

Once, they made love on a huge flat boulder in the middle of the river, surrounded by lilies...just like in his dream many years before.

In summer, they made a game of sneaking into the outside world. During this time they would go up to Birmingham and convert some gold to cash at Harry Cohen's, then eat at a fancy restaurant and pay a visit to the Bonapartes.

Like a kid in a toyshop John browsed the tool section at Sears and Roebuck, examining every new gadget, all the while attempting to rationalize why he should purchase it. Anna patiently waited as he partook in this ritual.

Their last stop on the way home would always be at his mother's. She was fond of Anna and was always delighted with the visits.

"John, you look thin. Do you two have enough to eat?" were always the first words out of her mouth.

Florence passed away in April of '94. John took it hard. Even though her life had known its share of heartbreak and disappointments, she never complained. He thought of the sacrifices she had made for him...providing the best she could for him in his youth and putting her life on hold while he was growing up. He regretted not being there to comfort her at the end.

Uncle Ralph, John's mother's brother was among those few aware of John's situation. He had to be the one to make arrangements for her burial.

Risking discovery, John and Anna anonymously stood in back at the graveside service, while Ralph, his wife, children and grandchildren sat under the tent where family members were traditionally seated. Most in attendance were members of Florence's church. John and Anna just hoped that they blended in unnoticed.

The seasons came and passed, and the years rolled by. Johnny grew up and became a lawyer, like his dad had been. He married a girl from Mobile and in 1997 she gave John a grandson, Shaun. Two years later a granddaughter, Angela came along.

Cart was in medical school…on his way to becoming a physician like his grandfather, Carter. He was one of Mobile's most eligible bachelors.

John was proud of his sons, and delighted by his grandchildren.

Thanksgiving did become a time of reunion. Both he and Anna looked forward to the event. These were good times.

Sometimes John sat on the cabin's front porch alone and watched the river that held so many secrets quietly flow. The land around him seemed at peace.

He never saw or heard from Bob again. Maybe his work was done…or maybe God had washed away the madness. At times, though, he could have sworn that he felt the presence of his old comrade in a breeze. John dared not try to conjure him up.

Now and then he saw the crow, but it never spoke or took him on a wild ride. Sometimes he even tried to call out to it, but only got an eerie 'caw' in return. It was just a crow.

For the most part John was content and at peace with himself as he looked out at his surroundings. The oak sapling he had planted next to the cabin twenty years before was now a tree.

It had been good with Anna. He never thought he could love as much as he did her.

Sometimes he thought of Angie…and felt great sadness inside.

C H A P T E R  51

# Start, Stop

SHOCK WRACKED JOSEPH Bonaparte when awakened by the early morning phone call on July 4th, 2006.

"Joseph, It's Anna. John's gone. He died in his sleep during the night."

"What?"

"He went peacefully," she said, her voice quavering, "It was about two this morning."

"I'm on my way," said Joseph.

"What's wrong?" asked his wife, Delores, as she rolled over in the bed.

"John Starr has passed away. You go on to the picnic, Honey," he said slipping into his bedroom shoes, "I've got to go…you know that."

"Of course."

As coffee brewed, he showered, shaved, then put on blue jeans and an old pair of hiking boots. He went into the study, which served as a home office to gather his thoughts before heading out to Bibb County. He opened the lower right hand drawer of his desk where some old photos lay stacked in one of the back corners. He pulled them out and shuffled through until coming to the one of him and John. While sipping coffee he leaned back in his chair and rested his feet on the desk. His mother, Bea, had taken the picture during one of John's visits to the old Debarden house in Mobile, back in the early years.

He and John were sitting on the brick wall next to an oak tree. John's arm was around him, resting on his shoulder. The fifteen-year-old kid in the photograph was grinning like a possum. John was smiling too. He was about twenty-six at the time.

Joseph recalled the feeling back then. It was like having a wise and protective older brother.

He ran his hand over the glossy surface, then returned it to the other photos and put the stack back into the drawer. He picked up his hand-held voice recorder and slipped it into his shirt pocket.

*Better get going,* he thought, turning up the coffee cup, taking the last swallow.

He went to the garage and put a shovel in the back of his Jeep Cherokee. Then, he was off, heading west.

About a half-hour into the hour-long drive, he reached in his pocket, pulled out the recorder and hit the record button, then START: "It is July 4th, 2006," he said into the microphone. "I've just received word that my friend, John Starr has passed away. Sixty-five is too young to die I think, but…" He tapped the Pause button. Gathering his thoughts, he tried to craft in his mind the words he was about to record. After a few minutes he hit the pause button and began recording again.

"It's with great reluctance that I relay the bazaar story of John Starr. Supposedly, I am a rational man, not taken in by hocus pocus, mystical happenings and things of that sort, but something did happen in John's life that is beyond any explanation I am able to attach. Could there actually be wormholes to the past that one occasionally falls into? Are there spirits around us that draw us to our destiny?

I'm sure that most would say the strange things he experienced were in his head, and the rest coincidence…"

He hit STOP: *Can't do this,* he thought, too *much risk, even now. His secrets will have to die with him. Gold, talking crows, trips back in time, ghost and spirits…who would believe it anyway? All of it was leftovers from Nam…leave it alone, Bonaparte.*

He slipped the recorder back into his shirt pocket.

It was about eight-thirty when Joseph arrived at the cabin, there on the banks of the Cahaba.

Anna met him at the door. He held her. "Are you all right."

"Yes, Joseph. I'll be fine."

John looked very much at peace, more asleep than void of life. He was older, of course, his beard had turned completely gray, but it was still John.

He watched as Anna, eternally beautiful, touched his face and ran her fingers through his steel gray hair. He noticed a thin line running down the left side of his beard that traced the scar laying beneath.

He turned to Anna, and looked into her blue, blue eyes.

"Are you sure you're going to be all right?"

"Yes, I'll be all right," she replied, "Don't you be too sad, Joseph. I felt him touch me as he left. He was in a breeze, and caressed me just like he had all those years. He'll find his way back...some way...in some form...maybe in dreams, I don't know, but he'll be back. You know how protective he is."

"So, you're going to stay on here?"

"Yes, this is where I belong...where the memories are...God, those memories."

A smile came across her face. "I can't leave them."

"But, Anna, it's so isolated here."

"Not anymore. See this, I called you on my cell phone."

"You two had a good life, didn't you?"

"Yes, Joseph, a good life...all twenty-five years of it was good."

Looking down on John, Joseph couldn't help but wonder if he was ever able to truly break free of the hauntings in his mind. Only Anna would know, but he dared not ask.

"Joseph," said Anna, "John and I made the decision that this land is to become a wild-life preserve after we are both gone. We want it safe from intruders forever. He planned to get with you to legally set it up. Can you handle it?"

"Yes, I'll do whatever's necessary."

Johnny and Cart arrived at mid-day. They brought Jack Wainwright. Now in his mid-eighties, he needed assistance walking.

As the sons viewed their father, Johnny commented: "I used to wonder about it, but now I'm sure that this is where he belonged. Remember what a kick he would get out of telling us tales about the Indians and Conquistadors that once roamed this land when we came up here at Thanksgiving?"

"Yes," said Cart, "and I remember how he lit up while telling your Shaun and Angela those tall tales about him and his buddy, Bob Savage's adventures … telling them over again just like he did with us when we were little kids. I think both he and Bob were a part of this place."

"Are you going to be alright, Anna?" asked Johnny.

"Yes, I'll be fine, Honey," she replied.

The afternoon skies were clear. With shovels in hand, Joseph, Johnny and Cart walked across the cornfield, to the foot of the mound. Next to the spots where William and Allison were buried, marked only by fieldstones, they began to dig John's grave. The ground seemed to pull at the shovels, as if the earth beckoned to receive him. Joseph and the young men dug it deep. When they were done, they went back to the cabin…and John.

Joseph and Anna wrapped him in a red blanket, then the men carried him out on a make-shift litter and laid him in the bed of the old Studebaker truck. Anna wanted it this way.

"John had worked hard to keep it running," she said.

As it sputtered to the gravesite where Jack and Anna waited, Joseph thought of the irony. This was probably the old pickup's last task.

As they lowered John into the ground, Anna finally broke. Large drops of rain began falling from a passing cloud. It was as if her tears brought on the summer shower. Soon it was over, as were Anna's tears.

Jack was elected, unanimously, to say a few parting words. "Lord," he said, "We pray that you take this uncommon soul to a place of eternal peace. God's speed, John Starr…Amen."

Joseph was surprised when Anna dropped a wild rose and the glossy black feather of a crow into the grave. There was a reason, he thought.

Joseph and the young men covered the grave, after which all but Joseph quietly walked away.

He got in the old truck and drove it back to what was to be its final resting place, the shed attached to the barn.

After parking it, he stepped around to the back of the barn to relieve himself.

Standing under a large oak tree Joseph took a deep breath, then, slowly exhaled, trying to maintain his cool. But, he lost it and began to sob.

Suddenly, he heard something above…wings flapping. He looked up, and there, perched on a limb was a large crow.

It looked down at him and cocked its head. Then, he heard in a clear coherent parrot-like voice: "Hello, Joseph. Don't worry, all is well."

Joseph stumbled backwards and fell to the ground as the big bird flew away.

His hand trembled as he reached to pick up the recorder that had fallen out of his shirt pocket. It was running.

He hit STOP, then REWIND. After a couple of seconds he hit STOP again, then PLAY.

"Hello, Joseph," came out loud and clear from the tiny speaker, "Don't worry, all is well."

He hit STOP.

www.ingramcontent.com/pod-product-compliance
Lightning Source LLC
Chambersburg PA
CBHW071457110726
47908CB00003B/641